A Reluctant Debut

A Novel of Regency Romance

Teresa Sweeney

Courting Romance Publishing
California

A Reluctant Debut is a work of fiction. Names, characters, places, and incidents are the products of the author's imagination or are used fictitiously. Any resemblance to actual events, locales, or persons, living or dead, is entirely coincidental.

Published in the United States by Courting Romance Publishing

ISBN 978-1-940319-08-7

First Edition

Cover Model: Christina Brusaca

By Teresa Sweeney

Always Rebecca

The Brentwood Tales
A Love Match, Indeed!
An Uncommon Affair
Only a Captain Will Do

The Reluctant Series
The Reluctant Viscount
A Very Reluctant Lady

The Barrington Saga
A Reluctant Debut

To my husband Larry,
Forever and Always

A Reluctant Debut

Chapter One

"What is so bloody urgent that you had me summoned like some imp in need of a good scolding?"

Richard Bolton, the Earl of Belcrave sat behind his heavy Jacobean kneehole desk and looked at his oldest son and heir, Thomas, Viscount Bolton, who stood in a temper admonishing him for disturbing his evening. Thomas was dressed in formal attire wearing a black tailcoat and pantaloons, a white pristine shirt, crisp cravat, and waistcoat embroidered with silver thread. His black cape was thrown over one shoulder to reveal its red satin lining and his tall black beaver hat stood at a slight angle on his head. Even vexed, he was the epitome of a tall, dashing and handsome lord, and was certainly no man's fool.

The earl sighed wishing his younger son, Harry, had an iota of Thomas' sense, and typically blamed his wife for Harry's caring and trusting nature. Regardless of all manner of instruction, Harry still remained too kind a fellow as evidenced by his recent folly. Belcrave returned

Thomas' scowl and waved him to the chair he had failed to take when he entered.

Thomas rolled his eyes, frustrated he would not be taking his leave soon. He looked down at the rectangular oak chair, a remnant from the reign of James the First with its high and stiff back and resigned to having his patience tested. With a flair most bucks coveted, he removed his tall beaver hat and cape with a swing of his arm, dropped his cape over the back of his chair, and placed his hat on his lap as he sat. He immediately tapped a tattoo on the top of his tall hat as he waited for his father to explain the reason behind his summons. The beat of his dancing fingers echoed within the silence of his father's study until his impatience compelled him to ask, "Well, what the deuce is so important?"

The earl sighed again, leaned back in his chair and interlaced his fingers to place his hands on his thickened waist. Streaks of grey marked his black hair and lines creased at his eyes, most likely from all the squinting he did when his temper rose, as it did now. Years of indulgences had turned his once fit body soft and while he was still thought to be handsome, his physique was kindly referred to as robust.

Thomas mirrored his father's manner and reclined back, not an easy feat with a chair designed for a person to sit erect, but he was damned if he would sit like he was about to be reprimanded. He slid down on his seat and stretched out his legs, crossing them at his ankles, while begrudgingly accepting he would not be returning to the opera as he had hoped, or to the activities assured to him by the ever accommodating Lady Selby. The widowed lady had blatantly flirted with him and made an overture he was about to accept when his father's missive inconveniently summoned him. He conceded it was most likely for the best. Widowed ladies who were open to an indiscretion often became troublesome when they expected more for their one night of amusement.

"I need you to fetch your brother and his wife," the earl stated soberly, his features marked with disappointment.

Astonished by his father's announcement, Thomas pulled himself up in his chair. He leaned forward and asked to confirm what he heard, "Married? Harry? My coxcomb of a little brother is married? To whom, and why might I ask was I not invited to the wedding? For my own curiosity, pray, tell me, when and where the happy event took place?"

"I have no bloody idea," retorted the earl angrily. Over the years, the earl had shrugged off his younger son's follies, believing his antics were part of him growing into the man he was expected to be, but marriage to a woman of little consequence, was something the earl never anticipated.

"Are you to tell me your spare eloped and you had no idea?" asked Thomas. "Who is she?"

The earl sat up in his chair and looked down at the letter that lay on his desk. After a quick perusal, he informed, "Rebecca Barrington."

"Barrington, you say?" asked Thomas. "By Jove, he did not marry the daughter of the man who called out Damburten, causing his own and Damburten's death and subsequent scandal?"

"It would have been a tragedy if Barrington's son had not shot Damburten dead," stated the earl soberly.

"Well, Damburten showed no honor in shooting early. His dishonor would have forced him to live abroad. The law forbids dueling and sees it as murder now if there is a death. How in heaven's name did Harry get involved and married to Barrington's daughter?"

"I have no idea," said the earl again. "Last I saw Harry, I sent him to the country to rusticate until he was in funds to pay off his gambling debts. I did not want him to get any ideas of approaching a moneylender. That incident he was in nearly killed him. The boy has the worst luck at cards, mostly because he does not play to win, but to participate without thought to what has been played. Whoever heard of such nonsense?"

"Harry likes people. Always has and loathes to be left out of any kind of play," explained Thomas.

"Well, he has done it now and as usual, I must do what I can to intercede before the news of Harry's nuptials becomes the latest parlour on dit."

"What do you plan to do? The lad is married. Seems to me it is done."

"I plan on ensuring this Rebecca does not make our family a laughing stock by taking her in hand; then, I plan on finding you a wife. It is high time you did your duty and secure the future earldom of Belcrave before the line is tainted by Barrington blood."

"I suggest you worry about Harry, father. I need no assistance in finding a wife, nor do I wish to at this time."

"I don't care what you wish," the lines at the earl's eyes deepened as he steeled them at his impertinent son. In a voice that would brook no rebuttal, he commanded, "I want you married and your wife increasing, but first, I want you to bring Harry and his new wife to me."

Chapter Two

It was easy for Thomas to see how Harry might have crossed paths with Rebecca Barrington as he tooled his phaeton along the road leading to the lady's home in the midlands. It was the same route he would have taken to make his way to his father's country estate. The earl said he sent Harry home to rusticate and somehow, his little brother was waylaid and then captured by a parson's noose.

Since he could not abide being cooped up in a traveling carriage, he drove himself in his open phaeton to find Harry's love nest. The earl had not revealed how long Harry was married, but if the tragic duel was used as a marker, then his brother could have been enjoying marital bliss for the past three months. He hoped Harry was happy, for his brother was always looking to make others comfortable and it would be nice for once to see Harry's needs put first.

However, if his brother had been bamboozled, then the culprits would suffer at his hands. There was more than one way to eliminate a scoundrel without killing him (or her in this case). Thomas inhaled deeply and let out his breath in a long exhalation as guilt overcame him. *How long has it been since I saw my little brother? Or for that matter, inquired into his well-being?*

He could not believe Harry was married. His brother was not one to draw the attention of the ladies, since his only asset in the marriage mart was a connection to an earldom. Second and third sons were overlooked by debutantes who gave little consideration to the merit of their character.

The affront drove many younger sons to reckless behavior to fill their idle time. What else was an aristocratic son to do without industry or purpose to keep him busy? Work was anathema. Aristocrats did not work, nor engage in trade, though many were secretly doing so as tenant rent and sheep farming failed to produce the substantial means to support their lifestyles.

Harry's letter provided an address so it was no trouble to make his way along the country roads to find the cottage Harry was calling home. His travelling coach would follow in two days to bring his valet and to transport the newlyweds to London. Giving him plenty of time to learn how Harry came to be married and whether or not he needed to expend his time and energy to right a terrible wrong.

Thomas conceded he would be in high spirits enjoying the rich and picturesque countryside if not for the purpose behind his trip. The midlands were in full glory. Verdant grasslands quartered by hedgerows burst with bright blue cornflowers, red poppies and white yarrow. Yellow daffodils could be spied near the road and amidst the trees, bluebells colored the ground where clusters of elm and ash trees bordered the open land.

The weather was crisp, but not cold and the sun beamed down on him as if in song. His cattle cantered along the road and he enjoyed the journey until he spied a sign identifying the lane to the Barrington Farm protruding from an untrimmed hedgerow. Mr. Barrington had not been of the aristocracy, possessing no title or rank, but he was a gentleman of property and so it was assumed he was brought up with a modicum of manners and protocol. Thomas hoped Harry's wife was raised as a lady ought and not the country bumpkin his father assumed.

He turned his curricle onto the long dirt lane sandwiched between an apple orchard on one side and some grazing land on the other where a number of milk cows roamed and chewed on the tall grass. At the end of the lane, he spied a two story white thatched cottage of moderate size boasting of eight front windows.

There were no weeds or ivy growing on the cottage to suggest abandonment, yet there was also no sign of industry. He maneuvered his phaeton around the small fountain centered in the drive and stopped his vehicle at the cottage's front steps. He waited for a groom or some other laborer to take care of his horses and when none appeared, he hopped down from his perch and tied his horses' reins to a nearby post. He placed his fists on his hips, looked about the grounds, and wondered, *"Harry, what have you gotten yourself into?"*

Thomas removed his calling card from the silver case he kept in his tailcoat pocket and raced up the steps to drop the brass knocker on the front door. He dropped the knocker again when silence greeted him. He was about to hit the knocker once more when the door opened to reveal a vexed maid, her hair covered in a kerchief. She wore a drab grey dress overlaid with a soiled apron and in her hand was a feather duster.

Thomas gave her no mind and walked in as though he had every right. He removed his hat and greatcoat with a flourish, and then pushed them, along with his driving whip and gloves against the blushing maid who quickly brought her arms up to secure them. He commanded, "Inform Lord Harry, Viscount Bolton awaits him."

"Indeed!" exclaimed the maid, displaying an uncommon exasperation. "No doubt, you want me to ring for tea and sandwiches."

Thomas turned his attention to the infuriated maid, to whom he had given little regard. "That honor, belongs to your mistress whom, no doubt, wonders who has come to call. I suggest you see to your duties, wench, and stop trying to garner my attention."

"I...I...," stuttered the maid.

"Nor I," laughed Thomas who decided to announce himself when the maid pressed her lips and squinted in anger at him after his retort. "Harry," he yelled as he walked further into the house. "Where are you, my lad? Come and greet your better."

A rumbling of steps echoed as Harry hurried down the staircase. Thomas was surprised to see his little brother, not so little. He had filled out since the last time he saw him and no longer wore the clothes of a coxcomb. In fact, he was dressed with no flair or distinction. If anything, he looked like a laborer in his breeches and loose shirt. No coat, nor vest, nor cravat, did he wear. His brown hair was a bit ruffled, but if he was coming from enjoying his wife's company, then his dishabille was understandable.

"My better, more like my elder," returned Harry with a laugh. Thomas was ten years Harry's senior and once he was sent away to school had seen Harry sporadically. They were not close in terms of holding confidences, but they held affection for one another that grew from when Harry was an infant and called him Tom-Tom.

Thomas grabbed Harry by the arms and turned him side to side for an inspection. Harry was no longer a slender youth, but a man who stood eye to eye with him and owned a body honed from physical activity. Thomas knew Harry had engaged in boxing and fencing lessons to sharpen his defensive and agility skills after a moneylender beat him ruthlessly. His brother was determined to never be unprepared again. Thomas shook his head in marvel and said, "What happened to the coxcomb of a brother I shuttered to acknowledge your first Season in London?"

Harry smiled and said, "Do you know, the swells with whom I kept company gave me the cut-direct and called me an imposter when you ignored my greeting. It took me days to fall back into their good graces."

Thomas frowned and replied, "Good lord, whyever would you want to keep their company or their good opinion? I wish I would have known."

Harry laughed, "And what would you have done, Tommy? Thrashed them?"

"Undoubtedly, but for heaven's sake, Harry, what did you expect wearing that impossible suit of striped purple?"

Harry laughed again and shrugged his shoulders, thinking how he had once donned bold and flamboyant colors and spoke in an affected way to fit in with a group of fellows he thought admirable.

Thomas saw his brother's embarrassment and wrapped his arm around his shoulder directing him to a pair of French doors that led outside to a small garden enclosed by a stone wall. The gravel walkways divided the area into quadrants where various, herbs and vegetables grew. Along the perimeter of the wall were a variety of floral bushes blooming bright with red roses, purple hyacinth, and yellow daffodils.

"Those were your salad days, Harry," remarked Thomas trying to ameliorate his brother. "Now tell me about this wife you secured. I want to know if you married willingly. Am I here to bring you both home to present to our parents or am I to reconcile you from the parson's noose?"

Harry unwrapped himself from his brother's arm and explained, "It wasn't like that Tommy. I married Becca freely and am completely devoted to her. Wait till you meet her and you will understand why I love her."

Thomas grimaced. It was worse than he thought. His little brother did not fall into a marriage trap, he jumped. Well, he would be the judge whether "Becca" deserved his little brother's devotion.

"How did you know I was married?" asked Harry.

Thomas' eyebrows rose in shock. He answered, "Why, you wrote father, Harry. Did you expect he would not tell me?"

Harry dropped his head in embarrassment and confessed, "I did not write him."

Confused, Thomas asked, "Then, who did?"

"That would be me, my lord," a voice came from behind him.

Thomas slowly turned and saw the maid who had answered the front door and was surprised to see how a clean face, a simple styled coif and a change of clothes revealed a woman of exceptional beauty. Clearly, he should have given her more than a cursory glance. His inspection had her immediately steeling her light brown eyes and defiantly raising her chin at him. She stood stiffly as if a plank was strapped to her back, glaring at him.

Blast and damnation, he finally thought, *did I just affront my sister-by-marriage?*

Harry shook his head, silently admonishing himself and said, "I should have known it was you, Bella. You did what I ought. Forgive me." Harry turned to Thomas and said, "Allow me to present, Miss Arabella Barrington, Becca's elder sister and mistress of Barrington Cottage." He then turned to her and made his brother's introduction, "Bella, my brother, Thomas, Viscount Bolton."

Thomas pressed his lips in frustration. *How am I to make amends for treating her as a servant? Bloody hell, I arrogantly disregarded her and by her icy glare I have little chance of reconciling her ill opinion of me.*

Thomas noted her hackles like a feral cat were raised and considered what to say. He knew better than to antagonize her further by spouting disingenuous words. Normally, he would keep his distance from an angry lady, but gentlemanly manners forced him to make a courtly bow.

He cautiously stepped forward, making sure he kept his eyes on her hands in case one of her paws struck out at him. The notion of her hand as a paw made him smirk and then the image of her hissing at him made him bellow out a chuckle.

He laughed again when Arabella's eyebrows rose and her nostrils flared in outrage. He expected to receive a heated remonstration from her, but to his surprise her anger quickly dissipated and she laughed, too! Not a maidenly melodious giggle, but a hearty unrestrained chuckle. The tension between them broke as if they accepted the mistaken identity was more amusing than injurious.

Harry was not amused, having come to a conclusion that did not put his brother in a good light. He inquired with a frown, "Do you know one another?"

Thomas and Arabella burst into chuckles again, earnestly waving their hands as if they were batting at annoying flies. They replied in unison a hearty, "No!"

"Then, what is so funny?" inquired Harry.

Thomas opened his mouth and quickly closed it. Arabella blushed.

Harry's eyes opened wide as he chastised his brother, "You didn't?"

"No," Thomas responded sternly, before explaining to Arabella in a whisper, "I do not dally with servants."

Arabella's blush made Thomas grin. Harry was not fooled and said, "Tommy, we will speak of this later."

"Of course," he replied and then using a more forceful voice commanded, "but stop calling me Tommy as though you were still in nappies. I am Lord Bolton, or Bolton to you."

"If I was still in nappies, I would be calling you Tom-Tom," retorted Harry.

To that riposte, Arabella laughed.

"Well then," sobered Thomas and to redirect Harry from any further teasing, asked, "Harry, if your wife is available to receive me, you will introduce me?"

"Of course," responded Harry smiling. "I shall go fetch her and meet you in the parlour."

"Harry," suggested Arabella, "allow me to collect my sister. Why not take your brother to the parlour and offer him a refreshment?"

Thomas noticed Arabella did not even wait for Harry to approve. She turned without a by-your-leave and made her way into the house.

"Come on, then, Tommy, we have our marching orders," remarked Harry.

"Does she often command you, Harry? Have you married into a household of martinets?"

Harry laughed and said, "Heavens, no! But I would easily follow Bella's direction. She has managed her father's home and properties admirably considering they fell into her responsibility with no warning or guidance when he died and her brother disappeared. I expect you heard of Barrington's death and subsequent scandal?"

"Let us seek our dram of whiskey before we delve into deep matters," suggested Thomas. Harry nodded and they both walked back into the house and parlour.

Arabella quickened her pace up the staircase to her sister's bedroom that she now shared with Harry. Heat still crimsoned her cheeks, though now the emotion running through her was far from anger. She was piqued indeed! But her mixed feelings of attraction, intrigue, embarrassment, and downright contrariness were in turmoil. She could not decide whether she liked the viscount or not. He was arrogant and superficial and yet he was not.

Would he have laughed if he was arrogant? Or remained silent about our initial meeting? Why not accuse me of misleading him? After all, I was dressed more like a laborer than mistress and answered my own door. It would be easy for him to put me at fault, but he did no such thing. In fact, he never even mentioned the faux pas and to that, I must give him credit. For what could have come from the disclosure other than embarrassment for the both of us.

As for his superficiality, how else to describe a man for deducing my station by my looks? Well, I shall keep an open mind for the sake of my sister's future happiness. It will do me no good to make an enemy of the viscount. He looks more than capable of making trouble should he wish.

Arabella knocked softly on her sister's door. She quietly opened the door and peeked when Rebecca did not beckon her to enter. The room was simply furnished with a four poster bed, a toilette table, a Queen Anne embroidered chair and two mahogany pedestal tables, one set by each side of the bed. On one wall stood a clothes press that looked like it wasn't being used with the amount of clothes strewn on the floor and over the chair.

Her sister still slept on her bed. Arabella did not think her sister or Harry realized they were to become parents. She would not have noticed herself if her sister's queasiness to certain foods had not alerted her, nor the realization of what had been missing from the laundry. She quietly made her way to sit on the mattress next to her sister. Gently, she shook Rebecca's shoulder as not to scare her and whispered, "Becca dear, you must wake, we have company."

"What?" she grumbled before settling into slumber again.

"No dear," chastised Arabella as she shook her sister again. "Wake up! Harry's brother is here and wants to meet you."

Rebecca's eyelids shot wide open and she immediately sat up trying to reconcile the news. "Harry's brother is here? For Heaven's sake, why? Is Harry to leave me?"

Arabella reassured her sister, "Never. Harry is yours for all time."

"Then, why is Lord Bolton here? Harry promised me he would not inform his family until I was ready to be presented. I begged him," she whined as her face paled with worry.

Arabella gaped realizing she had done Harry an injustice. She had railed at him for treating her sister like a mistress hidden away instead of a wife fully acknowledged. Even so, Harry had not revealed Rebecca's confidence. Instead, he had taken the blame to protect her.

Arabella soothed, "He did not fail you, Becca. It was I who wrote to the Earl of Belcrave. I am sorry to cause you grief, but you must be acknowledged. If Papa was here, he would have had the announcement in the London papers. It's been three months and I began to worry the earl might contract a marriage for Harry and then have him wed in absentia. Our keeping quiet might make him a bigamist."

"Can that really happen?"

"Of course," explained Arabella. "The earl could stand proxy for Harry if he has a legal document giving him permission, but who is to say he doesn't have it. Come on, let's tidy you up and then I want you to greet the viscount with all the manners you possess."

"Is he very high in the instep, Bella? Will he not like me because I am plain Rebecca Barrington?"

"I do not know his bias toward class, Becca, but you are not plain, nor are you a Barrington anymore. You are Mrs. Harry Bolton."

"Not Lady Bolton," frowned Rebecca.

"No, Harry's address is simply a courtesy title. However, you could become a countess one day, but only if Harry's brother died and he begat no sons."

"Oh," gasped Rebecca. "Harry and I would never wish Thomas ill. Harry is very fond of him."

Arabella laughed and said, "Harry likes everyone. Come on, let's not keep them waiting."

Chapter Three

Thomas flipped the tails of his coat out of the way to sit in one of the two leather winged chairs with scrolled arms, while at the mahogany side table his brother poured them each a dram of whiskey. His eyes took in the Barrington parlour with a single glance. The room was simply appointed with an embroidered floral sofa stitched with pink, blue, and green threads.

White crocheted doilies covered the pedestal tables situated by the sofa and the winged leather chairs. On top of them were a number of wooden wildlife figures, smoothed over from constant handling. Glass jars filled with sea shells were displayed on the marble fireplace mantle and on the shelves of the built-in bookcase.

There were books of the popular variety, like Walter Scott, Jane Austen, and Mrs. Radcliffe, but also books regarding agriculture, pomology, and animal husbandry. The unique selection and weathered spines negated any notion the books were purchased by the yard to fill the shelves.

The parlour window faced the front of the cottage and offered a view of the small fountain in the center of the circular gravel drive. Floor-length blue brocade tiers, in need of replacement, framed the window. A large rectangular hand-tufted floral rug covered the floor on which the furniture sat and brought cohesiveness to the cozy room.

Thomas looked up at his brother when the glass tumbler Harry extended to him came into his view. He took it and dubiously eyed the suspicious pale liquid masquerading as whiskey before raising his eyebrows in astonishment.

Harry was quick to admonish him, "Don't be so discriminating, Tommy. Barrington was a man of property, not wealth. The whiskey is not as bad as it looks. Take a sip."

Thomas' nostrils flared the moment he brought the glass under his nose. His raised brows would have sufficed to dismiss the foul concoction from his sight had he been at his club, but leave it to his brother to rebuke him for being persnickety. The liquor had none of the full-bodied, caramel-colored, smoky characteristics he expected in a well-aged whiskey. He shook his head, knowing he had no other recourse but to relent and reluctantly took a sip. His pride kept him from gagging on the liquid burning his throat, but his good sense had him quickly placing the tumbler as far away from his person as he could on the nearby pedestal table. He looked to see his brother's reaction to the brew as he asked, "Tell me how you came to be wed, Harry?"

Harry barely put his glass to his lips before he set it down next to Thomas' glass. He looked guilty for not actually drinking the brew and uncomfortable with the question. He fumbled with his loose sleeves to collect his thoughts and his words. "I am not sure how to begin."

"Begin at the beginning," suggested Thomas. "Father said he sent you home to rusticate. Somehow, you met Miss Barrington. Tell me about how you met her."

"Oh," smiled Harry, his eyes bright with the memory. "She caught my attention right away, Tommy. As you know I was on the road, making my way home when I saw her, reins in hand, pulling on a horse attached to a gig. I didn't notice the gig's wheel was cracked for my eyes were focused on her beautiful face framed with rich chocolate brown curls.

"She wore an expression of stubborn determination that bowled me over. Never have I seen such a beautiful young lady put forth such effort. She was alarmed when I first stopped and offered my help, but once I suggested she unhitch the animal and leave the carriage behind to be fixed later she relaxed. Naturally, I dismounted, unhitched her horse; all the while keeping up a conversation with her. She wouldn't let me escort her home, so I watched her lead her horse away, but not until she agreed to let me have her gig fixed. I promised to leave it at the rectory for her to retrieve."

"You fixed the wheel?"

"Well, I did not fix the wheel, Tommy, but I am quite capable of getting someone else to fix it. I am not without funds, you know."

"I thought you were and that was the reason behind father sending you home."

"No," replied Harry. "He just doesn't like me losing money at the tables. He is afraid I will seek out a money-lender again, as if I did not learn my lesson the first time. I am no gambler, Tommy. I no longer bet more than I can afford to lose, not even to accommodate my friends as I once did."

"Thank goodness," responded Thomas. "And friends do not encourage their friends to indebt themselves. I am glad you do not associate with that crowd of coxcombs anymore."

"As am I, Tommy."

"I did not mean to lead you astray, Harry. Continue your tale. What happened after you came to your fair lady's aid?"

Harry chuckled and said, "She is more than fair, Tommy. Wait till you see the beauty I have won."

Thomas admonished, "None of that foolishness, Harry, finish your story."

"Well, I did not want to leave the area until the gig wheel was fixed and I was assured the conveyance was sent to the rectory, so I stayed in the village and attended the festival going on there. That evening, I saw Becca arrive in the company of a woman I later learned was her sister Bella, and one thing led to another."

"You danced with her, Harry?" asked Thomas in a manner that suggested he inferred something different.

Harry crimsoned at the innuendo and answered, "Of course I wanted to dance with her, but I came to her aid instead."

Thomas raised his brows before dropping them to form a "v" and scowl. "Explain," he demanded.

"She had barely stepped a foot inside the meeting hall when she was accosted. I could not hear what was said for I was across the room, but I heard Bella yell at the scoundrel to keep his hands off Becca. Before I knew my own intentions I strode to Becca's defense and had the villain assaulting her on his backside. Once free, Bella removed Becca from the premises and then all hell broke loose. You will be proud to know I held my own."

"How," pressed Thomas, "did your gallantry lead to marriage?"

Harry grinned and replied, "Providence was with me. I learned where she lived and the next day I went to call on her. I only meant to inquire on her health, but before I knew it I was down on my knee proposing. No, don't look at me Tommy like I was mad to do such a thing. I tell you in that moment I knew she was the one. I have no regrets. These last months have been heaven. I never knew my life's purpose until I wed Becca."

Thomas shook his head, then asked, "Be honest, Harry. Did you know of the scandal attached to her name before you proposed?"

Harry frowned and retorted, "None of it is true, Tommy. She did nothing to encourage Damburten's advances and if not for her brother's intervention, she would have suffered more than a torn sleeve from the man."

Confused, Thomas asked, "I thought her father, not her brother asked for satisfaction from Damburten."

"He did, but that was after he learned of the assault," explained Harry. "Damburten had spread tales about Rebecca even before his attack and until our wedding Becca had suffered from the most malicious taunts. It was sheer pride that brought Bella and Becca to the festival. They had refused to let the gossipmongers dictate where they could go."

"So, Harry, you came to the rescue and wedded the lass?"

"She rescued me, Tommy," insisted Harry.

"From what, dare I ask?"

"Sheer idleness and boredom," replied Harry. "I can't wait to give you a tour of the property and show you our plans for it."

"It will have to wait, Harry," Thomas announced with a sigh. "Duty calls. We must present your wife to our father and mother."

A gasp and soft ruffle drew their attention to the open door in time to see Rebecca slide to the floor. Harry ran to his unconscious wife's side and collected her in his arms. He looked up at Arabella and she had the where-withal to tell him to carry her to their room while she went to fetch the village doctor. Thomas suggested he go in her stead and asked for directions. He sent Arabella to look after her sister and took his leave.

Thomas stood at the parlour window, his eyes transfixed on the landscape as his mind reflected upon his brother's tendency to aid the downtrodden, be it beast or brethren. He could not tally the number of injured animals or desperate people he had helped, be it with tender care or his quarterly allowance.

Harry had a soft heart and tended to think the best of everyone until he was proven wrong. Thomas hoped his marriage to Rebecca Barrington would not be an instance where Harry misjudged. The sound of footsteps entering the parlour turned his attention the door. His brother's worried expression prompted him to ask, "How is your wife, Harry?"

"The doctor requested I leave so he could examine her and said he will apprise me of Becca's condition once he is done. Bella must have read my mind for she intervened before I could tell the good doctor what I thought of his suggestion. I only left because Bella convinced me Becca would be fine," replied Harry begrudgingly.

Thomas went and picked up the tumbler of whiskey Harry failed to drink and brought it to his brother. Harry shook his head to refuse the offer, until Thomas teased, "Now who is being judgmental. I am assured by the best of brothers the whiskey is not as bad as it looks."

Harry grinned, accepted the tumbler and took a fortifying breath before sipping the toxic brew. He let the burn in his throat caused by the potent whiskey diminish before he confessed, "I promised Becca she did not have to be presented to our parents until she was ready. As you know I did not write to father having ceded to Becca's wishes and while I am happy to have the news of our marriage known, I will not subject my wife to the scrutiny of the *ton* until she is ready."

"You would make our mother answer to the gossip-mongers?" queried Thomas angrily. "It will not do, Harry. You are a Bolton and we are not fodder for the rumour mills. You will bring your wife to London and allow our mother to bring her up to snuff. Your wife will make her curtsey to the Queen Mother and present herself to Society as expected of any member of nobility."

"My wife is common, Tommy. I doubt very much the Queen will receive her and I will not subject Becca to the snub. She has suffered enough. Her own townspeople slurred her good name and made her the villain in her father's and Damburten's death. I will not see her injured further. Besides, we are quite happy. I see no reason to disturb ourselves for the sake of some mealy-mouthed matrons."

"Harry, you are the spare and therefore it is very possible the title might descend to you and then your son should you beget one. Will you have him unprepared? Will you not give your children every advantage our good name has to offer? Or will you bind them to the life of a commoner?"

"You would snub my family, Thomas?" asked an incredulous Harry.

"Don't be ridiculous, Harry, but one day they may regret not having a choice where they wish to settle themselves because you decided for them."

The sound of voices approaching had Harry stand shoulder to shoulder with his brother to view the parlour's entryway. Both the doctor and Arabella entered speaking in hushed tones to one another. Harry anxiously interrupted their discourse and asked, "How is Becca?"

"Your wife, my lord," answered the good doctor, "is simply overwrought."

"Then, why did she faint?" pushed Harry.

"It is not uncommon, my lord, for one in her condition to faint when she has failed to break her fast or is overwrought."

"What condition?" interjected Thomas before Harry could ask.

"Why, my lord, Mrs. Bolton is with child."

Thomas saw his brother sway and he quickly brought his arm around him to prop him up until he regained his composure. Within seconds, Harry was standing proud, beaming a smile ear to ear and declaring,

"A baby, I am going to be a father. Did you hear that Tommy? You are going to be an uncle and the earl and countess grandparents."

"Oh, Harry," sighed Thomas. "Well, that settles it. Talk to your wife. We leave in two days.

"I think not, Viscount Bolton," countered Arabella.

Thomas opened his eyes wide in surprise. No commoner had ever countered his orders. He waited for an explanation for her impertinence.

Arabella read the anger and question in Thomas' eyes and remembered the good doctor who would be happy to share their contretemps with the village, so she suggested to her audience at large, "Allow me to see the good doctor out and then we can continue our family discussion in private."

Thomas waved her to do as she pleased and then watched a very disappointed doctor take his leave.

Arabella returned, nervously massaging her hands until she realized the activity had drawn the viscount's attention. She knew she had only one chance to see her will done and steeled herself for a confrontation. Bolton was not the type to be managed like his amiable brother and she did not think the viscount would abide postponing their trip unless she had a sound reason.

"My lord," she began rather obsequiously before cringing. The sight made Thomas raise his brows and retort, "Do not choke on the address, Miss Barrington. If addressing me so is too much of a mouthful then simply call me Bolton."

"How about Tom-Tom," retaliated Arabella.

Thomas looked sternly at her and warned, "Do not think I will allow any disrespect to my station, Miss Barrington. Only a fool would provoke my temper."

"Leave her be, Tommy, and let her speak," admonished Harry. "What is on your mind Bella?"

Arabella turned her attention to Harry and spoke. "Becca needs time to fortify herself with rest and food before she can make the journey to London. She is overwhelmed learning she is with child. Even if she was not *enceinte*, she is still recovering from Damburten's attack. The memory revisits her when she is under duress and I tell you she is worried. Can you imagine how frightened she is of meeting another nobleman bearing the same manner Damburten had toward ladies of our class?"

"Our last venture into the village did nothing to diminish her fears. She is not yet ready to enter society; especially a biased one who will not think kindly of her for marrying you. Besides," she finished with an exhalation, "I need time to find someone I can trust to oversee our property before I can leave."

"You are going somewhere, Miss Barrington?" smirked Thomas.

"Indeed," responded Arabella irritably. "I go where Becca goes. I will not leave her to battle the *ton* on her own."

"You think her husband and his family inadequate protection?" Thomas asked, insulted by the implication.

"Í hope not, Bolton, but never the less, I will accompany her," she insisted.

"And where will you reside?' he pushed.

As expected, his query made Arabella gape. Before he could take satisfaction in his shot, Harry put him to shame by announcing, "She will reside with us, Tommy, as you well know. Bella is family, my family now and wherever I am welcome, so is she, or are you of a different opinion, Tommy?"

Thomas looked at Harry, astounded by his brother's backbone. His little brother was committed to this marriage and to a code of conduct that made Thomas proud. He wondered if Harry's strength of character was always there and whether his disposition to please others had stifled it. The notion Harry no longer needed to be watched over not only astounded him but amused him.

"Well?" pressed Harry.

Thomas smiled at Harry and then replied, "Not at all, Harry." He turned to Arabella and said mockingly, "You must forgive me Miss Barrington for failing to welcome you into the family. I shall give you a week, no more, to settle your affairs and prepare your sister for travel."

Arabella smiled and before taking her leave, replied, "Thank you, Bolton."

Chapter Four

Arabella held up a sprig muslin day dress by its shoulders, one of her sister's favorites, and shook her head as she assessed its suitability for their trip to London. She and Rebecca were in her room inspecting their clothes. Rebecca had grabbed the lot of her wardrobe from her dresser and brought them to Arabella's room where they began to grow two mountains of clothes on Arabella's bed. The largest of the pile was deemed unsuitable; their clothes were either too worn or too unfashionable for Mayfair society. Even their newest and best dresses were at least two years old for they had willingly sacrificed their clothing allotment, so their father could pay the back taxes and debts associated with the farm they inherited from their father's cousin.

Barrington Farm was once an unentailed asset attached to Baron Damburten's Estate. The previous baron believed their father's cousin had acquired the property unfairly and upon his deathbed made his son promise to return the property to their holdings. It was the baron's dying wish and his son thought to fulfill it easily by purchasing the farm at a cost more than it was worth. He did not expect the man to die and leave it to a family member who had no interest to sell, no matter the asking price.

In addition to his festering anger over Barrington's refusal to sell, Damburten's rage was inflamed by Rebecca's rejection to his overtures. Rebecca had caught the baron's eye when the Barringtons first moved into the community. At first, Damburten thought Rebecca was overcome with shyness. After all, he considered his overtures more than she deserved being below him in consequence.

He looked for a dalliance, but after being rejected and snubbed, his ire rose to a certain madness. The idea a chit beneath him in title and wealth would refuse his advances made him lash out at her with lewd propositions. He made sure her family did not hear his vulgar suggestions, so they would not call him to account, but the villagers knew he was behind the tales that questioned her innocence, calling her a tease, and even worse, *Haymarket ware*.

The gossip took root and gave him the notion on how to force Barrington to sell. He spread vicious tales to sully Barrington's good name and turn the community against him and his children. His actions were excessively cruel considering Barrington had never injured, nor spoke false of him, nor been responsible for any injustice toward a villager. Nevertheless, the villagers were dependent upon the baron's patronage and did not dare question the validity of Damburten's accusations or act in defiance of his wishes.

In spite of Rebecca's continuous rejections to the baron's vulgar suggestions, he continued to harass her and before long, she sought refuge by isolating herself at home. It was the only place she felt safe and could easily be happy at home with industry, leisure, and the company of her family.

She liked to read and often took a book to the apple orchard where she sat with her back against a tree trunk with branches so full they formed a canopy of shade. She would get lost in the story until her brother or sister collected her for their midday meal.

She had smiled when a pair of boots planted themselves before her, knowing she was about to receive a well-deserved scold from her brother for her tardiness. Her cheerful features fell at the sight of Damburten standing over her looking like he was about to throttle her.

She instinctively pushed herself away from him, but was hindered by the tree. Her heart pounded and her body shook knowing she was trapped. Damburten laughed at her fright and then he reached for her.

Rebecca opened her mouth and screamed. Damburten recoiled expecting someone to come running to her rescue, but when no sound reverberated, he laughed. Fear had made her mute.

Rebecca cried out in alarm when she woke and was quickly consoled with soothing words from her sister. She was overcome with relief to be in the safety of her home and then the horror of Damburten's attack made her wail. She hurt all over and it took her a moment to comprehend what her sister asked.

"Do you hear me, Becca? Where do you hurt?"

She couldn't speak to say she hurt all over. All she could do was cry until exhaustion pulled her into sleep.

Three days later, she came to her senses to learn her father was shot dead by Damburten and her brother was in hiding for killing him. The grievous news made her shake. The grief of what transpired because of her brought more tears. Was she somehow responsible for Damburten's attack? She cried until again sleep overtook her.

Arabella looked at the piles of clothes on her bed and remarked, "These will not do, Becca. We must acquire at least a couple of fashionable dresses before we meet the Earl and Countess of Belcrave. I will not have them think we are country bumpkins. We may not be titled, but our dear departed mama raised us properly. I will not have us judged by our fashion."

"It is impossible, Bella," reminded Rebecca. "You know Harry used up his quarterly allowance to pay our village debts. Even the costermonger would not sell us any goods unless we paid with coin."

"Indeed," responded Arabella, "but this dilemma is because the Earl of Belcrave summoned you to London and therefore, the costs of our clothes are his to bear. I will speak with Bolton."

"Why not Harry?" asked Rebecca.

"He would not know of what to ask. Unless of course, he was in the petticoat line and I do not think it of him. Your husband has a kind heart and is much too sensitive to play the game many gentlemen engage to satisfy their base needs."

"Really, Bella," asked Becca, "when did you become so coarse and how do you even know of such things?"

Arabella raised her brows, opened her mouth, and then shut it in exasperation. She replied, "I am not the green girl you were Becca before your marriage. Mama spoke to me of many things, mostly for my own protection and to prepare me for marriage. I feel deep regret I did not do the same for you."

"My attack was not your fault, Bella," offered Rebecca sadly.

"Neither was it yours, Becca. You must heed me in this, Damburten was evil. His actions were all his own and had nothing to do with you. You must forgive yourself and allow yourself to be happy with Harry."

"He does not know, Bella," said Rebecca. "How can I be happy deceiving my husband; especially now I am with child?"

"Neither do you know, Becca," argued Arabella. "The only person who knows is our dear brother and he left with our papa the moment he settled you in my care to demand satisfaction from Damburten. You were unconscious from a bump on your head, or maybe from being choked. I don't know.

"Bruises were forming everywhere on your body when Nathaniel brought you home to me. There was a pool of blood on your torn dress, but once I removed it I discovered it was not yours. I do not know the extent of your assault because I did not have time to ask Nathaniel, since seeing to your injuries was my greatest priority."

"I don't know which is worst, knowing or not knowing," replied Rebecca. "Why didn't you summon a doctor to see me after the attack? He would have known if Damburten did his worst."

"I was trying to protect you from ruin," Arabella answered. "No one saw you until the night of the festival, not even the pastor's wife when we went to visit because you chose to turn tail and return home before we even reached the rectory. I was forced to go on foot alone.

"Thank goodness, too, or else you would have never met Harry and captured his attention. By then, the swelling and bruising on your neck and face were gone. There was nothing to suggest why papa demanded satisfaction from Damburten. Even now, it is believed the baron in a pique tore your sleeve when you refused his addresses. Harry certainly believes it to be the truth."

"I would rather have suffered ruin than to have papa dead and our brother gone," whimpered Rebecca feeling sorrowful and guilty.

"Well, they would not and you must stop blaming yourself," Arabella argued. "Papa and Nathaniel knew the risks and consequences. Papa could not let the assault go without satisfaction. To do so would leave us both vulnerable. Every man would think us wanton and up for grabs. You must not let their tragedy go for naught. Providence blessed you with Harry, Becca. Do not take the gift lightly. He is a good man whom I thought you held dear. Am I wrong?"

"No," Rebecca admitted. "I was surprised I did not fear Harry considering what Damburten did to me, but the minute I met Harry I knew he was a gentle soul. He has been most patient with me and since there is genuine affection between us nothing enters my thoughts when we are together. I only shudder when I think of the attack. I would forget it ever happened if I could."

"I wish that as well, Becca" said Bella with empathy. "I would see you happy. Tell me, do you love Harry?"

"I do," she answered with a grin.

"Then, be happy and leave your past behind," counseled Arabella.

"I will try." Rebecca rummaged her hand through the pile of dresses and asked, "Bella, do you ever feel guilty we are not honoring papa with proper mourning?"

Arabella raised her brows in surprise and pressed her lips tight to quell her temper at the idea of sacrificing more than they had already. She answered, "Becca, we do not have the luxury of dying our clothes black to grieve papa. What would we wear when we came out of mourning? I do not feel it necessary since our society is nil to none. Besides, except for essentials, we rarely go to the village. We only attended the festival to quell the gossip and you saw how that turned out. Thank goodness Harry was there and might I remind you, if we were following protocol, you would not have been able to marry Harry for at least six months after papa's death. We needed Harry's protection, so I was only too glad that you wanted to marry him."

Rebecca's mouth turned down and then her lower lip pushed forward in a pout as she said, "Both Harry and I would know the truth of this baby if we had waited six months."

"Stop borrowing trouble, Becca," Arabella scolded. "Now, I will leave you to return this mountain of clothes to their proper dressers while I seek out the viscount and put our request before him. Wish me luck."

Arabella left her sister to her task and went to find Harry's brother. Ever since the viscount resigned himself to staying, he allowed Harry to show him what made up the Barrington Farm. There was not much to see, but Harry had grand ideas and was excited to share them with his brother.

Arabella knew if they were not inspecting the property she could find the viscount in the parlour with a snifter of brandy, poured from a bottle he had brought from his own reserves. Bolton was a wealthy man with no need of a quarterly allowance, unlike Harry who depended on his father's benevolence for his living expenses. She discovered the viscount owned an estate not far as the crow flies from the Barrington Farm. She could not deny the viscount intrigued her or that she sought information about him.

Even though she had been the victim of his arrogance, she easily admitted to herself she liked how he had no qualms to publicly show kindness and affection to his brother. Their interactions amused her. No matter how often Harry called his brother Tommy, instead of Bolton, the viscount rarely took a haughty manner with him.

Harry seemed to think his brother more bark than bite, but Bella had seen the steel behind Bolton's eyes when he thought she had disrespected him. She would not make that mistake again, but she had no quandary to tease him. A challenge seemed to amuse him and she was more than capable of sparring with him. Her current request was sure to annoy him and the idea made her smile.

She did not know if she was pleased to see Bolton a man of routine or not. Regardless, he was in the parlour where she expected him to be, enjoying his brandy with a book placed on his lap where he sat. She announced her arrival by asking, "Bolton, might I have a word with you?"

Thomas looked up to see Arabella looking quite young and mischievous bouncing into the room like an excited puppy. She was wearing a simple high-waist jonquil day dress with puffed sleeves that had seen better days. The dress looked weary even improved with the bright green ribbon around her high-waist. She had left her long brown hair loose, except for the few strands she pulled away from her oval face and secured with pins. Most likely she forgot it was down, or had not styled it into a coif because she gave him no consideration in regards to her appearance. It seemed he had fallen into the rank of family. He took no affront as it was something he was used to with three sisters living at his father's home.

Looking at Arabella he easily saw the same beauty Harry boasted of his wife. Their features were similar, though Arabella's frame was tall and slender to Rebecca's shorter and more voluptuous one. Both ladies had almond shaped eyes enhanced by long curling eyelashes and framed by naturally arched brows. A straight nose rounded at the end and full lips completed their similar features, but while Arabella owned light brown eyes and brown hair mixed with strands of auburn hair, Rebecca's hair and eyes were a deeper and richer brown.

Their similarities and differences reminded Thomas how much Harry favored him and how much he didn't. Their physique and coloring were slightly different. Thomas was slender and sinewy while Harry was broad chested and muscular. His hair was almost black where Harry's hair was brown. Thomas favored his father with blue eyes while Harry's features could be traced to their mother and her hazel eyes, but no one doubted they were brothers. The same would be true for the Barrington girls and he wondered whether their brother Nathaniel favored Arabella or Rebecca.

He had to keep a sober expression so as not to reveal his amusement at seeing her display her feminine wiles. Upon her entry, he immediately set his book on the small pedestal table next to his tumbler of brandy and rose as required of a gentleman when a lady entered a room. He needed to control the chuckle he felt bubbling up within him and waved her towards the matching leather wing chair across from where he had sat. He waited for her to sit before returning to his seat and asking, "How may I be of assistance, Miss Barrington?"

"Oh, good, Bolton," Arabella responded cheerfully. "I am glad you are in a mood to be of assistance for that is exactly what I require." She did not allow Thomas to speak, but sped on like a runaway horse. "I know both you and Harry want your parents to find Becca worthy of the Bolton name and in that end, I want to give my sister every opportunity to make a good first impression. I am sure you agree first impressions often give credence to what people surmise of one's character."

Bella paused for breath. Bolton nodded and gave her a pointed look to get to the point.

She continued. "Oftentimes, what one wears leads to that first impression."

Thomas shook his head and said, "Miss Barrington, is there a point to this lesson of first impressions?"

"Indeed!"

"Then," retorted Thomas, "by all means enlighten me."

"We have nothing to wear!"

"And?"

"And since it is your wish for us to travel to London and present ourselves to esteemed society, I say it is your obligation to see we are presented in a manner that now fits my sister's station!"

"Are you asking me to purchase a wardrobe for you and your sister, Miss Barrington?"

Arabella blushed and dropped her head in embarrassment. She had come in full righteousness to demand what was proper and now under his scrutiny, she found she could not look him in the eye. She had become more beggar than crusader and the notion pushed her to want to run out of the room.

She had not heard him rise from his seat, nor any idea her eyes had watered until he pressed a fine piece of linen into her hand. She should not have been surprised. She had thought him kind and now to make her feel better he placed the fault and the burden of her request upon himself by saying, "You are quite right, Miss Barrington. I have been derelict in my duties. Fear not, I will see to resolving the need of a new wardrobe for both you and your sister."

"But how?" she asked.

Thomas grinned. "I have my resources, Miss Barrington."

Arabella nodded, rose and left with the notion Lord Bolton was most assuredly in the petticoat line.

Chapter Five

Rebecca swiped her hand at the errant hair tickling her nose and heard a chuckle. She opened her eyes and saw her husband in bed next to her, lying on his side with a strand of her rich brown hair in his hand.

"Time to wake up, sleepyhead," he announced.

Rebecca grinned at him and stretched out her arms and legs like a feline cat waking from a nap. Her movements made Harry smile in appreciation and she blushed. She would never have imagined after suffering Damburten's attack she could have found wedded bliss, but Harry had proved she could.

From their first meeting, she did not fear him. He was kindness personified with gentleness and a caring nature that drew her to him like a bee to nectar. He called upon her the day after the festival and then surprised her with a proposal so sincere she had accepted without any further consideration. It was an instinctive response to his blatant show of tender affection. He was so sure of their union that when she opened her mouth to answer, she found she had said yes.

Perhaps, it was his gallantry in aiding her with her gig, or coming to her rescue at the village festival that led her to accept, or maybe it was simply his unwavering belief they were meant to be. She could not deny she loved him now, or that she had betrayed him by not confessing the whole of Damburten's attack. The baby would reveal the truth and in that revelation would be the death of her marriage when he learned he had not been her first. The loss of him would be impossible to bear, but so was keeping the truth from him.

"What is it Becca?" asked Harry. "You look sad. It was not what I intended when I woke you."

Rebecca turned on her side and wrapped her arms around Harry's neck and cooed, "What did you expect Harry?"

"This," he replied bringing his lips down upon Rebecca who welcomed his kiss and embrace.

"How long ago did you say Harry left to wake Becca, Bolton?" asked Arabella.

Thomas replied with a grin, "Not long by their standard I am sure. They are newly married after all."

Arabella blushed and rose from her seat, not wanting to be the brunt of Bolton's amusement. She took to strolling around the parlour until her flushed face cooled and then returned to where Thomas sat to ask, "Tell me again, Bolton, the plan you have to provide a wardrobe for Bella and me. And why that wardrobe cannot be purchased in London?"

"We cannot introduce you to London society until you are properly attired. First impressions, Miss Barrington, are formed by more than my parents. Shopkeepers are notorious gossipmongers. Their tidbits are part of their appeal. Modistes are the worst for they keep their clients happy with speculation while they measure and pin them. Trust me; Lord Harry Bolton's wife would be the juiciest morsel of gossip a modiste could share."

"Then if a London modiste is not to dress us, then whom? I hope it is someone who is aware of the latest fashion trends and who has the skill to create the finery of haute couture we need."

"Dear me, Miss Barrington," replied Thomas. "Do you intend to be a fashion arbiter?"

Arabella blushed again at the idea Thomas saw her vain. She might have slinked away had she not noticed her discomfort amused him. She rallied and retorted, "Are you saying I am incapable of being admired for my good taste?"

"Your good taste, Miss Barrington?" countered Thomas. "I expect it will be my good taste that will set you in the peak of style."

"And what makes you," Bella stopped midsentence as realization struck that Bolton was most likely a rake of the first order and thereby was very knowledgeable about lady's fashion. She stiffened her straight arms, closing her hands into fists as if in a temper. Squinting, she assessed his character.

"You were saying, Miss Barrington?" pressed a steely-eyed Thomas who took affront at being under her scrutiny.

His stern expression did not intimidate Arabella. She responded by raising her chin, pointing her nose up in the air as if she was the Queen Mother addressing her minion and asked disdainfully, "You are in the petticoat line, Bolton?"

Thomas smirked at her attempt to reproof him and retorted, "Are not all men, though even I admit there are some who prefer other men."

Arabella dropped her jaw in mortification. This was not a decent conversation for a lady and Bolton knew it. He was toying with her and she did not like it! She would not be teased for her unworldly experience. She chastised, "You know what I inferred, Bolton. It is un-gentlemanly, even unkind to embarrass me, much less make me feel foolish."

Thomas did not like being put in his place, certain-ly not by a country maiden. He responded sternly, "You should expect such remarks if you request personal knowledge of a bachelor's activities. I do not kiss and tell, Miss Barrington, nor do I answer to anyone. I suggest you keep your indiscreet thoughts to yourself; especially when we enter London society. The *ton* takes affront easily to outsiders daring to question their behavior."

Duly chastised, Arabella went and stood by the window where she could collect herself. She gazed upon the lane leading to her home and saw an approaching conveyance. *Is this the steward Bolton recommended to oversee the farm while I am away?*

She turned to make her way to the front door to greet her arriving visitor, but Thomas' reprimand in the form of a question stopped her. "And where are you going, Miss Barrington?"

"I expect your hearing is as good as my own, Bolton. We a have visitor and I am going to answer the door."

"Pray, do not. My man will see to the door. He is most obliging to do whatever I require of him and while I am here without sufficient staff, he will see to the door."

Arabella's eyes opened wide, angered by his audacity to tell her what she should do. She admonished, "You forget yourself, Bolton. This is my home and I determine the managing of it!"

"Actually, Miss Barrington, Barrington Farm belongs to your brother, to which must be rectified. I should hope you know how to contact him."

Arabella paled. It was true the laws of primogeniture made Nathaniel the heir and that she and Becca lived here at his beneficence. *Good lord! Is the property entailed? Is our future not safeguarded should something happen to Nathaniel?* She felt herself stumble and found support from Thomas who rose when her face drained of color.

"For heaven's sake, do not lose your fortitude now," scolded Thomas. He took hold of her arm and led her to a seat and went to the side console to pour her a splash of his brandy. "Here," he commanded as he handed her the glass. "Take a sip and prepare yourself to greet your steward. We will discuss this matter later."

He no sooner finished speaking when the parlour door opened and Mr. and Mrs. Higgins were announced. Thomas waited for the man to approach him and make his salutation before offering his own greeting and introduction of Arabella. He informed, "Higgins, you and your wife would likely appreciate a short respite before we delve into your duties. There is a small apartment on the first floor. I expect it once belonged to a housekeeper and is now at your disposal. I hope you do not mind staying in the house, but it would be the most convenient of all options while we are away. Shall we meet in the small study in an hour?"

"Thank you, my lord. I appreciate the time to settle ourselves and will present myself in one hour."

The Higgins left guided by Bolton's valet.

Arabella rose from her seat and haughtily asked, "Am I to be part of this interview where you speak of the managing of my farm?" Her face flushed when it looked like Bolton might refuse her, so she reproved, "and do not say it is my brother's. I was left in charge and the duty of managing the farm is mine to fulfill."

Thomas shook his head at Arabella's outrage and the tediousness of it all. He said, "You are most welcome to join us, Miss Barrington, if you mind your tongue. I will not pay for a steward with no industry at hand and the duties I plan to discharge upon him have already been agreed upon by Harry and me."

"Without my counsel?"

"It was my understanding you and Harry already discussed what you wished to improve upon the farm. I am only seeing it done."

"But, with what funds? Am I to be indebted to you without benefit of knowing the cost? I think not, Bolton," she ranted.

"The improvements are my wedding gift to Harry and his wife and have been accepted as so by them. If you take issue with my gift I suggest you speak with them. You have an hour, so do not dawdle by remonstrating with me."

Bolton picked up his book and left the parlour, leaving Arabella with her mouth gaped.

"But Bella," inquired Rebecca, "I still do not understand your anger behind Bolton's gift? Both Harry and I thought it most generous."

"It is generous," retorted Arabella, "too generous."

Harry left his seat beside his wife to stand before his sister-by-marriage who was canvasing the area rug of the room he shared with his wife. The room was far from a suite and so Bella's to and fro was a short trod that made her movements look like a fish swimming in a small bowl. Harry stopped her pace, held her by both arms to gain her attention and asked, "I can tell there is more, Bella. We cannot help unless we are privy to all the details. Tell us."

Arabella let out a long exhale and explained, "I feel foolish not realizing the farm does not belong to either me or Becca. Even more so for not looking into whether my father had a will. What if the property is entailed? What happens to our home if something happens to my brother? Why even bother to fix the farm if we cannot be assured it is ours to keep?"

"Tommy will learn all the answers, Arabella," he assured. "And I know my brother, he would not invest in something he did not expect to prosper. Wait until there is reason to worry, for now let my brother be the overbearing viscount I admire and let him guide us. I trust him Bella. I ask you to do the same."

"Oh, all right, Harry," harrumphed Arabella, "but I shall sit in that meeting and assure myself he has not added anything to what was agreed upon."

Harry smiled and said, "Then, I suggest you be on your way for the hour has passed."

Arabella flew down the staircase and barely came to a stop before what was once her father's study. The door was closed and she had to bite her bottom lip from releasing an anathema at the idea they had started without her. She tugged and straightened her muslin skirt, smoothed her hair, lifted her chin and knocked. She chastised herself for waiting to be bid enter and not walking in as she had every right to do.

Bolton's "come" was clear and commanding. She entered and the sight of him sitting behind her father's desk in her father's seat froze her at the door's threshold. It took her a moment to catch her breath and soothe the ire she felt at the viscount's audacity to usurp her father's chair, but then she remembered her father was gone and everything that once was his was no longer.

Sheer will kept her sorrow from bursting forth. Nothing in the study had changed to eradicate her father's presence. His mahogany kneehole desk with account books and papers on top of it held center court in the dark wood paneled room. The bookshelves against one wall were still filled with his books; while on another wall hung a seascape picture above a stone fireplace.

Behind the desk was a window draped with long crimson brocade tiers, each curtain pulled back with a golden cord to swag the material and let in the light that illuminated the room. The bright rays softened Bolton's contour making him look ethereal. She almost grinned at the notion of a sainted Bolton, until she saw two embroidered seat chairs, situated before the desk as though one occupant was inferior to the other in importance.

The inheritance of the farm had seemed like a godsend to her father when he first learned of it. He had no qualms to pack up his children and belongings to move. They were all grieving over the loss of his wife and their mother who had died days after delivering a still-born boy.

Their home was cloaked in sadness. Memories floated like dust motes and the recollections were too much to bear; especially for their father. Everywhere he looked he was reminded of what he had lost, and he told his children he viewed the inheritance as a fresh start for all of them. She and her siblings were hesitant to leave the small cottage where they had industry and friends, but the notion of elevating their father's position to a man of property persuaded them to move. They never expected prejudice to assail them.

Barrington was a man of faith and believed in the good will of man. He was confident the community would come to welcome him and his children; especially since they had always been well-liked. He encouraged his children to turn their cheeks to any affront made them until Rebecca was assaulted. Then, nothing stopped him from demanding satisfaction from the man who hurt his daughter, and ultimately, his death and the exile of his only son.

One moment Arabella and Rebecca had a father and brother to care and provide for them and the next moment, they were left unprotected and burdened with debt. They had no one to counsel or help them, until Harry entered their lives.

"Ah," exclaimed the viscount upon seeing Arabella, "you have come to join us, Miss Barrington."

"As you see," she retorted at his glib observation and took the empty seat placed outside the realm of conversation behind Mr. Higgins. The blatant positioning told her she was expected to be a spectator and not a participant. Out of mischief, she wanted to scoot her chair forward, but refrained herself from so doing. She sat demurely and saw how her subdued nature made Bolton raise his eyebrows in astonishment. She almost laughed at seeing him taken aback by her manner.

Thomas turned his focus to the man whom his steward had recommended for the job and asked, "You are settled, Higgins. Is there anything not to your satisfaction?"

Higgins grinned, knowing the question was made from a drilling of manners than real sincerity. He did not know of a lord who cared a wit for his comfort, though some had said Bolton was of a different nature. Certainly, Bolton's steward, the man who recommended him for the position, praised his character. "Everything is quite satisfactory, my lord, thank you."

Thomas squinted at the man to determine the truth of his answer. He hoped he was not a sycophant looking to win favor with flattery rather than industry. He relaxed his inspection remembering he trusted his steward and thereby should trust this man until he was proved wrong. "You have my authority to resolve any problems or fill any needs you find; especially in completing the work I have assigned to you."

Arabella listened and could not find fault with anything discussed: a new thatched roof, fresh paint for the cottage and fences, a scythed lawn, trimmed hedgerows, pruned apple trees, an apiary, and a sundry of other maintenances required on a working farm. Higgins was to hire laborers and other servants to see to the work. Bella rolled her eyes at the money being spent, but kept her tongue tied. She would speak with Bolton alone. Why hire a cook? The woman would only lose her position when they all returned. The farm did not profit well enough for hired help; especially when all debts were called in upon the death of her father. Any reserves they had were spent to keep them out of debtor's prison. Besides, she had her brother to consider. She had no idea how Nathaniel was faring, but surely he was in need of funds.

Higgins left with a sheet of paper listing all the tasks assigned to him. Bolton said he expected weekly updates and that he might add to the list if he remembered something or if Harry requested something. She continued to sit even when Bolton stood and rounded her father's desk to lean against the front of it. Taking her measure, he asked, "Is there something you wished to ask me, Miss Barrington?"

Arabella looked him straight in the eyes and said, "Yes, thank you." Silence weighed between them as if he knew how vulnerable she felt. She continued, "Harry told me to trust you and I told him I would. My brother is undeservingly exiled. Is there a chance he will ever return to call the farm home once again?" Arabella thought she meant to speak of cooks and sundry and had surprised even herself by her question. She looked hopefully at Thomas and added with a sad grin, "Harry said you would know the answer."

Thomas sighed and explained, "Your brother shot a peer in cold blood among witnesses. There is no chance of him being acquitted of the crime unless those same witnesses said your brother shot Damburten in self-defense. No one has come forward to suggest the tale, so I do not believe it to be the case. No, Miss Barrington, your brother will never call this farm home again."

Arabella's lips trembled in sadness and once again she found Bolton close at hand to give her his square of linen. "You must think me a watering pot," she said.

"You need not apologize, Miss Barrington," replied Thomas. "I am happy to answer your questions."

"Your wedding gift reminded me how singularly my life is, now my sister is wed. Harry said you would not invest in our farm unless you expected it to prosper. I realized you see it as Harry's future. Are you looking to buy the farm for him from my brother, since Nathanial can never live here again?"

"You are very astute, Miss Barrington," he replied. "First, let me assure you I need not buy any property for Harry. He has his own trust set aside for him when he turns five and twenty or marries, so he is quite able to buy the farm if he wishes. He might intend to look for another property. I guess it would depend on whether the Barrington Farm is entailed or if your brother wishes to sell it, providing we can locate him. Harry needs a place that bears his name and not someone else's."

Without thought, Arabella gasped, "What about me?"

Sympathizing, Thomas said, "I am sure you will always have a place with Harry and your sister, but may I suggest you find yourself a husband while attending the Season with your sister. There is a reason it is called the marriage mart. Every eligible lady and gentleman will be in the city for three months."

"Marry? Me?"

"Indeed," replied Thomas. "You are not quite on the shelf and with my guidance you could attract any number of gentlemen."

"Indeed, Bolton," replied Arabella heatedly, "but may I remind you I am no doxy looking for a protector."

"No," agreed Thomas grinning at her attempt to shock him, "but definitely a lady in need of a husband and there is no better place to look than in the environs of the Season."

"Surely, you jest," she retorted.

"Not at all," he replied. He made his bow and left, leaving Arabella flummoxed at the idea of putting herself forward for marriage at the advanced age of four and twenty years.

Rebecca ran into Arabella's room in a flurry of excitement and asked, "Is it true, Bella, are you to join the gaggle of ladies searching for a husband in London?"

"Who are you calling a goose?" complained Bella until she compared how ladies flocked together like a gaggle of geese, both primping and making a lot of noise. The notion made her laugh.

"I knew you would get the pun Bella," Rebecca giggled.

Arabella asked, "Who told you I was going to seek a husband."

"Oh, Harry mentioned it. He said Lord Bolton thought it the best solution to see to your future."

"Indeed!" huffed Arabella, angry to be thought a problem to be solved.

"Oh, don't let your feathers get ruffled," laughed Rebecca at another pun at geese. "I don't care if you join the marriage mart or not, but I am happy I will not have to suffer the social events by myself."

"Harry would be with you, Becca," reminded Arabella. "I might even hinder your acceptance for I carry the Barrington name."

Rebecca admonished, "Do not be foolish, Arabella. You are no hindrance and I am not sure I can manage without you. Promise me you will not desert me, unless of course, a man of distinction catches your eye."

Arabella grinned and changed the topic to tomorrow's departure, "Bolton says we leave bright and early in the morning and should arrive at his manor within two days of travel. Do you feel up to the journey, Becca?"

"Oh, yes. Harry says Bolton's traveling carriage is well-sprung. We are to have warmed bricks, lap blankets and a basket of food to break our fast with Bolton's coat of arms displayed on the doors. None will dare to accost us or impugn our good name. I hope the village people choke on their surprise when they see us riding in it."

Arabella hoped as well. She had grown tired of turning the other cheek.

Chapter Six

Dusk settled as Bolton's traveling carriage stopped in front of the busy George Inn where other travelers were debarking and making their way inside. The courtyard was a flurry of patrons and ostlers maneuvering to assist the travelers and earn coin for their help. The whinnies and stomps of horses, the stench of their sweat, the heated exclamations of weary travelers and dust whirling around filled the air. Thomas' coachman yelled from his perch for one of the lads seeking coin to grab the lead horses' headgear and hold them steady among the crowd. The boy who was outmaneuvered for the job ran to the mounts where Harry and Thomas sat. Both gentlemen preferred to ride their horses rather than travel in the closed carriage and were ready to dismount and give the care of their horses to the eager stable boy.

No sooner did Harry hand over his reins to the lad than he rushed to help Rebecca from Bolton's traveling carriage. Thomas stayed behind to give instructions to the boy for the care and feed of their horses. Once finished, he went to join his party and marveled at how his brother used the upmost care to bring Rebecca safely to the ground.

Harry held her hand in one of his, used his other hand at her waist to steady her stepping from the foot stool to the ground until she was surefooted. He then wrapped his arm around her shoulder as if to shield her from any ruffian that might run into her while they waited for Arabella to debark.

Thomas silently admitted it was heartwarming to see the love shared between his brother and wife and while they cooed at one another Thomas stepped forward to assist Arabella. She had stretched out her arm from the dark carriage, wiggling her fingers when no one came to her aid. Gentlemanly manners prompted him to offer his hand; especially since, he was the only one paying attention. He almost laughed when Harry finally took notice and gave him a pointed look as if questioning his motive for his gallantry.

Heated shouts emerged from some gentlemen in the courtyard and both Harry and Thomas searched the area for a possible threat. Rebecca paled spying the altercation and Harry, tuned into his wife's every emotion, quickly escorted her away and into the inn. Arabella stood nonplussed waiting at the carriage door.

Thomas offered his hand again and with no other choice Arabella accepted his help. She placed her fingers in his palm, but quickly pulled them back and massaged her fingers as if she had been singed. The surprise written on her face made Thomas want to chuckle; especially when she gave him an assessing gaze. *Does the chit think Cupid's bow has struck?* Thomas could not count the number of times the electrical phenomena caused by friction had put the silly notion into a lady's head and he was ready to refute the idea should Arabella suggest such foolishness. To her credit, she did not, though she did blush, suggesting the thought had crossed her mind.

He assured, "You may take my hand, Miss Barrington. The shock you felt will not repeat itself."

She nodded and cautiously placed her hand in his and when nothing happened, took a firmer grip, stepped down onto the carriage stool and then to the ground. She removed her hand, looked into Bolton's eyes and finally inquired, "You felt it too, Bolton?"

"Indeed," he replied without further explanation. He winged out his arm to offer his escort and she took it. They walked into the inn and up to the desk where the publican was already offering a key to Harry. Thomas asked his brother, "You secured rooms, Harry?"

"Yes," Harry replied. "Three rooms, one for me and Becca and then one each for you and Bella."

Surprised, Thomas asked, "You think it is wise to let Miss Barrington sleep alone, unprotected?"

Arabella's temper rose at the notion Bolton thought she was a child in need of a nanny. She retorted, "I am quite capable of sleeping alone, Bolton. Please do not inconvenience my sister and Harry."

Harry grinned, relieved to not be encumbered with his sister-by-marriage for the night and happy to see Arabella at odds with his brother. Before anything could change, he quickly maneuvered his wife towards the stairs to find his room, informing his brother, "We will be taking a small respite before our meal, Thomas."

"Thirty minutes," Thomas called after his brother scurried away like a mouse abandoning ship. "The day is long gone and we all need food and rest."

Thomas returned his attention to Arabella and asked, "Would you like me to see you to your room, Miss Barrington?"

"No," she answered tartly. "I can manage." She procured her key, turned and made her way to the stairs.

Thomas returned his focus to the owner to ask for a private dining parlour to be made ready in thirty minutes. He was about to inquire into the evening's menu when Arabella's scream and shout made him bolt to her rescue. She stood a few steps up on the staircase admonishing the attentions of a gentleman or so the man's attire suggested. She was eye level to her accoster who still held a piece of her skirt in his hand. The man's chuckles proved his actions were far from innocent.

"Keep your hands to yourself, sir," Arabella scorned as she batted his hand to release her skirt. Her face was crimsoned and when the man reached out to grab her arm her eyes widened in distress. She recoiled, but had no need for the man's hand was stopped and then turned back on its wrist.

"Bolton," she gasped in relief. "I am glad you have come."

"Indeed," he replied as he placed her with his free hand behind him. "He applied a bit more pressure on the man's wrist he held in his other hand and said to its owner, "I believe the lady requested you to keep your hands to yourself. Do I need to offer further evidence of how uncomfortable unwanted attention can be?"

"No," the accoster shouted.

Thomas let go of the brute's hand and asked, "Your name, sir?"

"Elwood."

"Not," stressed Bolton, "the heir."

Elwood shook his head side to side, grimacing from the pain radiating from his wrist.

Thomas reprimanded, "Then, you are the spare. I suggest you consider this a warning to watch your manners around a lady."

"Lady?" Elwood queried in disgust as he rubbed his tormented wrist. "I heard her name and Miss Barrington is no lady."

Bolton jabbed Elwood on the jaw hard enough to place him on his backside. His head hit the floor and dazed him. Thomas turned and addressed the owner watching the proceedings and ordered, "See this rubbish is taken outdoors. His smell offends me."

"My lord," the owner appealed frantically. "He is an earl's son."

"As am I," retorted Thomas, "but unlike him, I am a viscount who you will not wish to offend." Thomas took out a sovereign from his waistcoat and tossed it to him. The publican caught the gold coin in his hand, smiled and said, "I will see it done, my lord."

Thomas turned to Arabella and suggested, "Perhaps, Miss Barrington, you will now accept my escort to your room."

"Yes," she replied and slipped her hand through his arm.

Harry hustled his wife through the door into their room, laughing along with her as he slammed the door and locked it behind him. They both began to fumble with buttons, ribbons, and stays until their clothes lay in a heap on the ground and they tumbled onto the mattress. Harry pulled her into an embrace and silence fell between them while they gazed into each other's eyes. In the quiet they spoke reverently of their love. A tender kiss came next and then more to seal their vows.

Harry flopped on his back and then pulled Becca into the side of his body, cuddling her into his warmth. He placed his head on hers and cooed, "Becca, tell me your greatest wish."

Turning her face to his, she replied, "I already have it."

"And what is it?" pressed Harry.

"You."

"Ah," he grinned and kissed her nose. "Our greatest wishes have been fulfilled." He kissed her again, this time on her mouth. "Tell me another wish I might grant when we go to London?"

"London?" she queried and tossed the idea around in her mind. "To be accepted among those important to you."

Harry shook his head and said, "You will have to choose another wish for that one is assured."

"Well, it is my wish."

"Request another," he pressed. "Ask me to squire you about for I want to be congratulated on my good fortune. We can eat an ice at Gunther's; ride through Hyde Park in the afternoon with the rest of the *ton*; see a performance at Astley's Amphitheatre; enjoy the opera at the Royal Theatre; shop on Bond Street; ascend in a balloon from Green Park; see the menagerie at the Tower of London; walk amongst the flowers at Kew Gardens,.."

"Oh stop, Harry!"

"None interest you?"

"Everything interests me as long as I am with you." Rebecca sobered and asked, "Harry, do you suppose you can love me no matter what might transpire in the future?"

Harry saw the worry in Rebecca's face and asked, "What are you afraid of Becca?"

"Can you answer me without knowing, Harry?"

Harry turned to hover over her and answered, "Without a doubt, my darling wife. I will love you no matter what might transpire in our future."

Rebecca drew her arms around him and hugged him, hoping it was true.

Thomas rolled his eyes at his brother and wife. They were *smelling of April and May,* whispering sweet nothings and grinning like fools. Lord, how he hoped he never behaved that way...again. He had vowed to never be foolish enough to trust in love. He caught Arabella smiling at his annoyance and to distract her inspection of him, asked, "Is the fare to your liking, Miss Barrington?"

"It will do, my lord."

Thomas could not offer a different opinion. The food was dry and flavorless. The cook was either out of herbs or else had no knowledge of them. At least the ale was of good quality and he was able to wash down the poor meal. It was obvious, since his brother and wife were too busy giggling amongst themselves, that manners required him to engage Arabella in conversation. He remembered her earlier assault and asked, "Does your name often bring such ungentlemanly attention?"

"It was usually directed at my sister in the village," replied Arabella. "Damburten had spread malicious tales about her. I did not realize the vile talk had spread further than our village, or that I might be ruined through association. I knew the scandal of the duel was widespread, but not that my family's name put me in peril."

"The gossip surrounding the duel is indeed parlour on dit," he confirmed. "I am sorry you and your sister must deal with being assaulted because of it."

"And you do not think gossip upon one's reputation an assault?" she retorted.

"I misspoke, Miss Barrington," replied Thomas soberly. "I very well know a lady's reputation is all that keeps her from ruin. Your sister was lucky to marry Harry."

"Harry would argue he was the lucky one," she countered.

Unknown to them, both Harry and Rebecca were keenly listening and Harry could not keep quiet when the conversation became heated. He opined before Thomas could respond to Arabella, "Indeed, I would Thomas. If there was any luck involved then it was on my side. I am most grateful Becca trusted me to say yes to my proposal."

Thomas asked Rebecca, "Did your trust in Harry compel you to accept him?"

Rebecca looked Thomas in the eye and replied, "It took trust on both our sides, my lord."

Thomas wanted to inquire "How so," but was kept from asking when the cook entered to solicit compliments for her meal. She offered blancmange for dessert, but Thomas felt they had all suffered enough and after seeing the shakes of everyone's heads, declined the cook's offering. He suggested the ladies retire, while he and

Harry took a night cap at the bar. Before Arabella left, he commanded with authority, "Lock your door, Miss Barrington, and scream if anyone attempts to disturb your sleep. My room is not far from yours and I sleep lightly."

Arabella smiled, nodded her head in agreement, and left.

Chapter Seven

Thomas and Harry brought their cantering horses to a sedate walk having left the carriage a hundred yards behind them. They had turned onto the lane taking them to Bolton Manor and in their rush to finally reach their destination had spurred their horses ahead of the carriage. Bolton's lands were extensive and so it was not until they journeyed over a small rise that his estate situated amongst groomed lawns and gardens came into view.

"Tommy," exclaimed Harry in delight, "the place looks magnificent."

"Thank you, Harry," replied Thomas with a grin looking upon his property with pride. He purchased the manor home almost seven years ago when he turned five and twenty, and his own trust funds became available to him. Before then, the estate was left to a caretaker with little means to do anything aside to ensure no one came into the traditional red brick house to steal what the owner left behind. Thomas had found the extensive property and manor enchanting. He purchased the house and its lands and then allotted the necessary funds to return it to its former glory.

The three story red brick manor offered an elegant scalloped outline trimmed and quoined with white brick against the bright blue sky. Three ogee gables made up each wall with tall square turrets topped with ogee caps at each corner. The manor was an architectural design of elegant arches and sharp lines. A central white bell clock tower emerged from behind the central ogee gable to rise above the corner turrets.

The front of the house was symmetrical in design. Matching dormer windows protruded from the flat walls on each side of the central arched entry and were ornamented with Tuscan columns and Victory figures in its spandrels. Above the entry was a twelve pane window decorated with more carvings of the winged Victory in its frame and railing. Multiple pane windows graced every floor and a pediment topped the long narrow tower windows at each corner.

From the steep roof rose multiple chimney stacks. Verdant and groomed yew trees and hedges covered the base of the house and the contrast of white window frames and white embellishments against the traditional red brick made an impressive and stately sight for any passerby.

"Are they expecting us, Tommy?" asked Harry.

"I sent a messenger to alert them of our arrival today," Thomas answered and then in a voice suggesting he had been affronted by his brother's question added,

"But even if I had not, Harry, I keep the manor fully staffed with standing orders to ensure they are always prepared for my arrival. You will find no Holland covers or rooms closed off."

Surprised, Harry exclaimed, "But the costs, Tommy?"

Thomas replied curtly, "Since when do you worry about fiduciary matters, Harry?"

"Since I acquired a wife and assumed responsibility for her sister. My allowance only goes so far."

Thomas' annoyance subsided at Harry's reply and with sympathy he reminded his brother, "Your trust will keep you in funds, as long as you properly invest. Do not be overindulgent like a horse eating his oats, wondering what happened to his feed when the bag becomes empty."

"You will help me, Tommy? I confess I am worried about money. Before I married I simply retired to Belcrave to rusticate until my allowance set me in good stead, but now I do not have that luxury. Both Becca and Bella look to me to see to their welfare."

Thomas frowned, but Harry interjected before his brother could give his opinion on the matter. "I am not complaining, Tommy. I am only saying that I want to do right by my wife and her sister. I do not want them to worry, nor do I want to squander my inheritance. I want to do what you have done and make my money grow; and to do that I will need your guidance and expertise."

"As you wish, Harry," replied Thomas. "My first counsel would advise you to stop investing in a property that is not your own."

"Then, why are you making improvements to the Barrington Farm?"

"Who is to say you will not call it your own? Besides, the village is suffering from the loss of Damburten's largess which is probably the reason behind the villager's continued hostility against your dear wife. The farm's improvements will be doubly served by coaxing their good will through employment. Do you desire the property if it can be sold?"

"I do not know. It is true Becca and Bella have been impugned by the village gossip and I have often found Becca looking overwrought with concern. I have wondered if the farm is a constant reminder of Damburtern's attack. I did not believe I had any option other than to reside there until you reminded me of my trust and I must admit the idea of starting fresh has a strong appeal. I also do not like the idea there is no adjoining land to grow the farm if I could buy it. I have grander plans than a small farm. However, I do not know if Becca would move without her sister and Bella has too much pride to live on my benevolence. I could see her managing the farm on her own for her brother. I know she worries he is in need of funds."

"I have seen your Arabella's stubbornness in action, Harry," laughed Thomas. "Perhaps, she will take advantage of the Season and become someone else's problem."

"Unkind, Tommy," chastised Harry. "Bella is no problem. She has been unbelievably strong and resilient these last months. She is also a great comfort to Becca; especially when she falls in one of her moods."

"She is moody, Harry?"

"Not exactly," Harry replied while contemplating how best to describe Rebecca's emotional turns. "She seems distracted at times, as if she is worried over something. I am constantly reminding her not to scrunch her brow. Oftentimes, I smooth it out with my finger which gets her to giggle." Harry grinned at the recollection.

Thomas rolled his eyes, amazed how foolish Harry looked whenever his mind turned to his wife. He asked, "Have you asked her what worries her? Sometimes a direct approach results in a speedy and accurate answer to a question. Secrets, even small ones, can cause havoc between a husband and wife."

"Who says she has a secret?" retorted a piqued Harry.

Thomas counseled, "What other reason would keep her from confiding in you?"

Harry sobered immediately wondering if Thomas could be right. The pounding of hooves reminded them both to heel their horses into a run before the traveling coach barreled into them. They raced up the front drive and before they could dismount a flurry of servants burst out the manor's front door to present themselves to their master.

"Oh Bella," exclaimed Rebecca peering out the coach window with her sister for their first look of Bolton's property. The coach had turned onto a private lane marked by its gravel topping and she had been searching the green pastures and nearby forestry for his home. Not until they came onto the rise of a small hill did the red brick manor with its white bell clock tower reveal itself.

"Oh, is right, Becca," grinned Arabella. "I had no idea Harry's brother was so wealthy."

Shocked by her sister's indiscretion, Rebecca chastised, "You must never say so, Bella. In fact, I am surprised to hear you comment on a matter society considers vulgar."

"I was not speaking in public," Arabella retorted, "but really, had you any idea Bolton was so flush with funds?"

"His father is an earl, Bella," reminded Rebecca, shaking her head in disbelief her sister did not deduce the obvious.

"True. But title and wealth do not always go hand in hand," remarked Arabella smugly. "Most marriages of convenience negotiate wealth for title. Many common families are elevating their status through marriage."

"As I have, Bella," whispered Rebecca guiltily.

"Don't be a goose Becca," scowled Arabella. "Yours is a love-match. Do not have any doubt on that account."

Rebecca grinned and agreed Bolton was a wealthy man by pointing out, "He does have a lot of windows."

Arabella laughed. Britain's window tax was forcing homeowners to brick up many of their windows to reduce the property taxes they had to pay.

"I am glad this is not Harry's," remarked Rebecca. "I do not think I would care to be responsible for the management of all this."

"Do not sell Harry short, Becca. Your husband has grand plans and I expect you will one day find yourself in a situation greater than Barrington Farm. You will manage quite well when that day comes."

"Why would Harry and I leave our home, Bella?"

Arabella replied, "Well, technically, it is not ours. It belongs to our brother and I do not know how long Harry will be satisfied as caretaker."

The carriage stopped and the door opened before further conversation could continue. Harry and Thomas were there waiting to help them make their exit. The ladies smoothed out their skirts and straightened their bonnets. Thomas turned to speak with his housekeeper, so Arabella maneuvered to stand behind her married sister who now took precedence over her.

She was taken by surprise when Thomas grabbed her hand and pulled her forward. She tripped and without his strong grip she might have tumbled. He had brought her to his side, granting her the honor of greeting his household staff with him. Manners had compelled him to not leave her unescorted and his gentlemanly overture made her blush; especially when her sister grinned at her.

Thomas gave each servant his lordly approval and proceeded into his home as if the fanfare his servants presented was a common sight. Arabella followed in his steps and tried to greet each servant as if she knew them personally, but Bolton's departure from her side made her rush to keep up with him.

They barely crossed the threshold when Bolton's butler presented his master with a silver salver full of urgent messages. Bolton grabbed the multiple missives and drew his brows together after a quick perusal. He apologized he could not welcome his guests properly explaining business demanded his attention. He ensured them his housekeeper, the redoubtable Mrs. Jenkins, would see them to their rooms and provide them with anything they needed and then he left.

Mrs. Jenkins was a small slender lady of middling years who wore her greying brown hair pulled back in a tight bun. She presented an austere appearance with her stiff posture and grey service dress buttoned up to her rounded white collar, and if not for her twinkling light blue eyes, her friendly nature might have been over-looked.

She led them up the central staircase that broke off at the second floor like the letter "y" and took them to the side called the West Wing. His lordship, she informed, had his suites in the East Wing as he liked to watch the sunrise. She regaled how guests in the West Wing were treated to a beautiful sunset.

She opened a door and Bolton's guests saw the walls were papered in yellow silk with a running sprig motif. A four poster bed covered with a jonquil brocade satin cover showed prominently. Light filtering through the window made the gilt furniture glow. Mrs. Jenkins informed them the room was for Arabella and closed it with satisfaction once she saw the ladies' eyes round in awe. Harry was not as affected. He had visited Thomas before, though he stayed in the East Wing near his brother. As an earl's son he was used to lavish decorated rooms, having lived in one and been the guest of others.

Mrs. Jenkins stepped quickly to the next door and opened it. She stood to the side and held the door open for them to enter. She announced the suite was for Lord Harry and his wife. The top half of the walls were covered with blue striped silk paper, while the bottom half was paneled with white pinewood. A large multiple pane window draped with blue brocade tiers pulled back with corded ties revealed a view of verdant lawns and fields, and a number of serviceable buildings dotted the land-scape.

The suite consisted of two rooms. The sitting room where they stood housed a brocade rose sofa, a number of gilded chairs with lion's feet, a low mahogany oval table, a marble side table with gilt legs, and an elegant escritoire. The connecting room designated for sleeping was not visible, but Mrs. Jenkins assured Harry he would find no fault with the room's appointments or comfort.

She informed them a platter of small sandwiches, cheeses and fruits would be sent up shortly and asked them what they preferred to drink, offering ale, lemonade, or hot tea. Rebecca and Arabella opted for a pot of tea while Harry ordered a pitcher of ale. They decided to break their fasts together in Harry's suite and then retire to their respective beds to nap. They ate quickly, surprising themselves with their voracious appetites. Rebecca was the first to yawn and on that cue, Arabella left them to seek her own room and bed where she immediately fell asleep.

A series of taps pulled her from slumber. The notion she had overslept and was now late for dinner put her in a panic. She threw off her cover, jumped out of the bed and rushed to answer her door. A maid made her curtsey and presented a note sealed with the viscount's mark.

Arabella took the note and quickly broke the wax seal to read it. She asked the maid if her sister had also received one. The servant affirmed his lordship sent one to Lord Harry, not to her sister. Rebecca informed the maid she had no response for Bolton, and then pulled her door close, before hurrying to her sister's room.

Harry answered her knock and upon seeing his brother's note in Arabella's hand guessed why she had come. He informed, "I think I shall just have a tray sent to our room, Bella. Your sister is spent and I cannot think having her rise and dress will do her any good. Do you mind terribly?"

"Not at all," assured Arabella. "I must admit I am still tired as well, and shall follow your lead and take my dinner in my own room. The staff will be quite pleased not to wait on my singular person. Besides, how dull it would be to keep my own company," she chuckled.

Harry grinned and remarked she was a good sport. Arabella returned to her room and realized she would not suffer to spend the night alone amidst such splendor. Her room at home was very comfortable, but her guest room was an indulgence she had never experienced. She had no trouble believing Rebecca still slept; for she would still be asleep in the warmth and comfort of her bed if the maid had not pounded on her door.

The notion of being at leisure where she could leave the industry and worry of chores to someone else had her diving into her bed as if it were a lake. The downy mattress crested like a wave and then cradled her body in softness. She wallowed in the luxury of it, turning on her back and stretching her arms and legs out as if she was making a snow angel. The plastered ceiling caught her attention and she spent the next half hour admiring the crafted squares each depicting a bucolic scene. One square revealed a maid milking a cow; another showed a shepherd watching over his sheep. She marveled over their craftsmanship and then was reminded of all the exquisite furnishings and art decorating her room. The room was a treasure trove.

She jumped out of bed and took in the appointments as if she was in a museum, approaching each piece of gilded furniture and wall painting with consideration to style, era, and the name of the artist. *Did any of this furniture once belong to a French aristocrat before he met his fate?* Many aristocrats were killed by *Madame la Guillotine* or displaced by the madman who had warred with her country. Her own paternal grandfather and his family escaped to England at the onset of the French Revolution.

She tried to recall what she learned from her mother who had visited the London museums before her marriage and had often shared her knowledge of classical works and artists with her children. Arabella studied the landscape hanging on the wall before her and tested what she remembered. *Is it a Gainsborough?* The artist loved to paint the noble at leisure, so her mother tutored. *I will have to ask Mrs. Jenkins if my guess is right.*

Arabella could not remember the last time her mind was not clouded with responsibility. Nothing was required of her for even a maid had seen to putting her clothes away and filling her ceramic pitcher with warm water. Knowing she only had to pull on the bell cord if she required anything made her giddy.

Chapter Eight

Arabella was summoned early in the morning by a housemaid to her sister's suite. She found Rebecca's head over a porcelain chamber pot with her body convulsing. A distressed Harry swabbed his wife's forehead with a dampened square of linen. Arabella rushed to his aid and quickly replaced him in his administrations. She soothed, "You are done, Becca. Come to bed. A bit of dried toast and a short nap will improve you."

Harry helped his wife to bed while Arabella ordered the housemaid who had followed her to bring toast and a cup of mint tea for her sister. Harry stepped away from the bed after tucking in his wife and whispered to Arabella so as not to alarm Rebecca, "Is this normal? Her spasms were quite violent. Do you think I should send for a doctor?"

"I do not think a doctor is necessary, Harry," Arabella soberly replied. "I am no midwife, but even I have heard 'morning sickness.' strikes the *enceinte*."

"For how long?"

"I do not know, but I suggest you wait until we get to London to find your physician for they would be more in the know than a country doctor."

"Very well, Bella," he answered. "I will heed your advice unless her symptoms worsen. Will you stay until she falls to sleep?"

"Of, course."

Arabella knew the moment her sister breathed steady and deep she was asleep. She rose from her chair and took a closer look at Rebecca before she was satisfied she fulfilled her promise to Harry. She hurried out of the room fearful her grumbling stomach might wake her sister. She was not dressed to be seen, having thrown a well-worn dress over her head in her rush to come to her sister's aid.

She had not even taken the time to coif her hair, letting it hang down her back and now because her stomach required sustenance, she was forgoing decorum to venture downstairs to pilfer some nourishment. Surely, she could grab some tea and toast, and be back in her room before anyone saw her.

She practically raced down the hall to the central staircase, only to come to a frantic stop when she saw Lord Bolton descending the stairs from the East Wing. He looked quite dashing in tan riding breeches and a superfine brown tailcoat. His white cravat was expertly tied, worn with a crisp white shirt and a brown embroidered waistcoat. His black riding boots glistened. She immediately crimsoned in embarrassment over her appearance, but had too much pride to retreat knowing he had seen her. She continued down the staircase and met him at the apex where the central stairs formed a "y."

Arabella responded with a curtsey to his morning salutation. He extended a compliment to which Arabella cringed and then remarked upon it by saying, "I am far from looking fine Bolton."

Thomas raised his brows at her curtness and offered, "I did not mean to offend, Miss Barrington."

"Oh, I beg your pardon, Bolton," she apologized. "You have caught me..." she blushed.

"About to steal the silver," he chuckled. "Come now, Miss Barrington, what has made you witless?"

Arabella's cheeks flushed hotter. She had too much pride for him to think he had somehow flustered her, but the truth was just as embarrassing. Realizing she could not dissemble without insulting him, she finally confessed, "If you must know I am ravenous."

Concerned, he asked, anger tinging his voice, "Did my staff not provide dinner last night for you, Harry or Rebecca?"

Arabella gasped at being misunderstood and quickly explained, "No, Bolton. I am sorry to imply such a thing. We were so tired we decided to order trays sent to our rooms for dinner, but I never did, being so full from the meal Mrs. Jenkins ordered for us when we first arrived. I am embarrassed to say I fell asleep before I could inform your staff I would not come to sit at the dining table. This morning, I was diverted from breaking my fast because Harry summoned me to help with my sister. I beg your pardon for insinuating differently. I am not at my best when I am hungry."

Learning Rebecca was in need of her sister pressed Thomas to ask, "Is Rebecca sick?"

Bolton's concern made her grin. It pleased Arabella to know he cared for Rebecca's health and answered, "She is suffering from being with child, no more. I understand mornings are difficult for the *enceinte*."

Thomas nodded and let the matter pass since he feared the information was more than he wished to know. He gestured they continue their descent and informed, "The staff is prepared to serve as early as seven in the morning as I often break my own fast before I head to my stables or study. You may have a full meal if you wish."

"That sounds delicious, Bolton," replied Arabella. "And forgive my appearance. I tend to my own needs at home and thought only to sneak down to secure some tea and toast before returning to my room to fix my hair. I did not expect anyone else to be up."

"Why did you not ring for service?"

"I had already requested a tray for Bella and did not wish to inconvenience your maid again."

"My servants are happy to please, since I am rarely here to justify their employment."

"Why not reside here more. I would love to call Bolton Manor 'home'." Bella blushed, coming to an abrupt stop at hearing her impertinence. She turned to Bolton to explain it was the house she desired, not him, but before she could, he teased, "Do you, indeed?"

She angrily waved off his gibe and rebuked, "You know what I mean. I am no *romp* trying to ensnare you, Bolton."

"Your use of cant is extraordinary," he remarked disapprovingly.

Bella's cheeks bloomed brighter as she apologized, "Oh, I must beg your pardon again, Bolton." She looked quite contrite for her insolence until she came to the conclusion he owned half the burden. Then, her eyebrows drew close in anger. She scolded, "I am not the only one at fault here, Bolton. You do have a way of raising my hackles. In either case of who is at fault, I did forewarn I have a temper when I need sustenance."

Thomas laughed at her scowling face and replied, "Yes, Miss Barrington, you did." He motioned her forward and added, "Might I suggest we move quickly to the dining parlour before you assail me again with it."

Arabella did not rise to his taunting, but hurried forward. She stopped after entering the dining parlour when he did not follow her, and asked, "You do not break your fast with me, Bolton?"

It had not occurred to Thomas to do so. He planned to ring for his meal once he was in his study. He had work to complete before they left for London. The first report from Barrington Farm arrived which he did not expect for another few days and he was anxious to learn the reason.

In addition, he had his regular estate business to review and multiple reports from his other investments. The enormity of the work ahead of him made him wish he had thought to bring his secretary with him. While his steward was capable of attending to the manor's estate business, he was neither inclined nor astute enough to deal with the array of problems associated with Bolton's other ventures. He considered Arabella's silent request and remembered he needed to inform her of the modiste he hired and decided he might as well attend to it now. He replied, "I would be happy to join you, Miss Barrington."

Thomas motioned her to the table, watching her reaction to the room's décor. Her ardent appreciation pleased him. The dining parlour was the first room he had commissioned for refurbishment. Before its transformation, the walls were papered in red silk to display the previous owner's hunting trophies and paintings. The man was an avid sportsman and the whole manor reflected his love for the killing of prey. Thomas could only shudder with revulsion before he changed it to reflect his own good taste. He could now sit at his table without feeling as if the animals with their open mouths and sharp teeth were about to exact revenge.

He had chosen cream paint for the walls and red satin for the drapes and chair upholstery. The colors contrasted beautifully, and with the gilt frames and appointments, the room spoke of elegance. One side of the room provided a view of the outdoors and let in light through its three long windows. Aside from the gilt-framed mirror hanging above a white marble fireplace, every other wall space was covered with wall-sized gilt-framed landscapes.

The ceiling was decorated in the neo-classical style with gilded medallions and a gilt motif border. A crystal chandelier hung from the center. Gilt sconces hung on the walls and crystal candelabras sat atop white marble and gilded console tables to provide extra illumination when needed. The oval dining table was covered in white linen and the chair frames were made of mahogany with legs ending in claw and ball feet. Twenty chairs vibrant with their red satin seats were tucked in around the table. A red and cream leaf area rug covered the floor.

Rebecca's eyes were still wandering in admiration when Thomas pulled out the seat to the right of him reserved for honored guests. He had to prod her to sit which made her utter an "I beg your pardon," before she thanked him for his gallantry. She sat, placed her hands on her lap and sat straight so her back did not touch her chair like her mother had taught her. Thomas waited until she was settled and then took his own seat. With proper decorum he lifted the silver bell before him on the table and rung it for service. His footman appeared looking surprised to see him. "My usual, Joseph," Thomas commanded, adding, "And whatever Miss Barrington desires."

"What is your usual, Bolton?" she asked with enthusiasm.

"Three eggs, a beefsteak, toast, and coffee."

Arabella turned to the footman and astonished her host by requesting the same. Then, she turned her attention back to Thomas and brazenly asked, "Well, Bolton, when can Becca and I get our wardrobes?"

Thomas shook his head at her impertinence. Her audacity reminded him of his sisters and so he informed her, "You are as bad as my sisters. Have you no patience at all?"

"Of course," retorted Arabella grinning, "but that does not mean I do not want to be informed." After a pause, she asked with surprise in her voice, "You have sisters?"

"Three," he answered, adding, "and all of them are very demanding and as impertinent as you. Has Harry not mentioned them?"

"Harry does not speak much of his family to me and I am not impertinent, Bolton," she explained with conviction. "Some might call me bold, but I like to think of myself as resourceful."

"How so?"

Arabella considered Thomas' question thoughtfully before she answered, "I like to think that I find ways to get things done."

"Well," replied Thomas, "I cannot argue since you have managed to get me to sponsor your presentation in London."

"I would not go that far," Arabella argued. "Becca and I only want to make a good impression with your parents."

"Well, you will do so and much more. In answer to your question, I have a London modiste, Mademoiselle

Lavigne, and a couple of her assistants put up at the village inn. They will move their belongings here later this morning. Both you and Rebecca will be measured and then can review the fashion plates Mademoiselle has brought for your consideration. Mademoiselle Lavigne and her assistants will work tirelessly to sew a traveling ensemble, a variety of other dresses, and all the necessities a gentleman does not mention in mixed company for you and your sister. Then, mademoiselle will return to her shop in London to complete the whole commission of walking dresses, riding habits, evening dresses, and ball gowns. When we arrive in London, both you and Rebecca must make yourselves available for fittings and under my mama's guidance you will shop for shoes and the numerous other accessories needed to complete your wardrobes."

Arabella's mouth gaped open in astonishment. She countered, "It is too much, Bolton. I did not expect you to go to so much trouble and expense."

"It will be adequate and nothing more, Miss Barrington," he explained. "It is what is proper for Harry's wife and since you will be keeping your sister company, you must also meet the rigid standards of *ton* fashion. My parents would expect nothing less. Trust me; I have merely begun what my dear mama will no doubt finish."

Arabella could not argue his reasoning. She was so engrossed listening she almost jumped when the footman placed a serviette on her lap and then arranged a place setting of silverware on the table for her. Another footman saw to his master's tableware, while two more servants followed in their stead to put plates of food before them.

The aroma made her stomach rumble and she dove into her meal with gusto. She ate heartily, savoring every bite until her plate was clean. Her hunger had urged her to eat like a glutton and not until she dabbed her mouth with her linen, did she realize she had not engaged in polite discourse nor eaten delicately as behooved a lady. She turned to face Bolton hoping he had not noticed, but the smile on his face proved otherwise.

Thomas asked with amusement, astonished at how much food a slender girl could partake, "Shall I ring for another serving, Miss Barrington?"

Arabella shook her head and replied, "No thank you, Bolton. I am quite full and you might as well wipe that lopsided grin off your face before my good humor turns. I should beg your pardon for not displaying any social skills during our meal, but I did warn you I was hungry."

"Indeed, you did. Remind me to ensure you eat something before we attend any social events. Heaven forbid your hunger should unleash your temper on any unsuspecting peer."

"Your wit leaves me speechless, Bolton," she rebuked. "I shall take my leave to inform my sister of our upcoming appointment. May I ask how I may take my leisure while I am here?"

Thomas stood to help Arabella to rise and then answered her question. "There are walks for your amusement if the weather permits: garden walks and of course, the Nature Walk which taken in its entirety will bring you around the lake. If you are a fishing connoisseur there are poles and hooks in the boat house, though there are little fish to catch. Lawn games are also available.

"If you prefer to stay indoors, there is the library, and the long gallery with the various landscapes I collected hanging on the walls. This is not an ancestral house so for portraits of my antecedents you would have to travel to Belcrave. I have a pool table, a music room, and an assortment of card games. I suggest you tell me what you would like to do and I shall see it done."

"I am astounded, Bolton, to have the world at my feet," she laughed. "Who would have thought a simple question could cause an answer to be difficult to make. I would enjoy the Nature Walk, but on another day when I am not needed. With your permission, I shall peruse your long gallery after I speak with Becca, and in that way, be within summoning distance when your modiste arrives."

Harry placed a piece of dried toast to Rebecca's lips when her eyelids began to flutter. She took a nibble and then another until she raised her hand to grab Harry's wrist to stop him from pushing the toast into her mouth. She opened her eyes and Harry asked, "Are you feeling better?"

"Oh, Harry," she sighed with embarrassment. "How perfectly horrendous I behaved. You must think me very ill-mannered not to have sought my privacy when I became sick."

Harry was shocked by her apology and assured her, "Don't be a goose, Becca. I do not think you ill-mannered. It is not as though you made yourself ill. Why some would argue I am the culprit." He grinned at his cleverness; especially when Rebecca's lips turned up in a grin.

"Now who is being silly," Rebecca responded, adding, "We are both the culprits for the little one inside me." Her words caused her to sober and her cheerful disposition turned glum. Harry recognized the quick mood change and asked, "What is it that worries you, Becca? I cannot help, nor reassure you if you do not confide in me."

"I am tired is all, Harry." She turned away from him to lie on her side and closed her eyes. Harry had no wish to upset her further. He left her and went off to soothe his own disappointment and rising temper.

Chapter Nine

Arabella could not believe she allowed her hunger to take her downstairs without thought to her attire or grooming, and ate without a modicum of manners. *Heavens be! I ate like a glutton*. The idea Bolton thought her uncouth made her blush.

Harry was used to her whim of jetting in and out of the parlour at home in her night clothes to break her fast with nothing more than a wrap for modesty. The idea she was comfortable to behave in like manner in Bolton's home boggled the mind.

Bolton said her impertinence reminded him of his sisters and while she argued she was not impertinent, the reprimand made her think of her brother Nathaniel, who on more than one occasion delivered the same scold. In that moment, Bolton became dear, and while he likened her to a sister, she was not sure the feelings swirling inside her were of one.

She saw the maid who helped tend her sister earlier walk towards her down the hall and before the servant could press against the wall and drop her eyes to become invisible to her, she asked, "Is Lord Harry with my sister?"

The maid dipped a short curtsey and raised her eyes to reply, "No miss." When no further instructions came, the maid asked, "Do you need anything else, miss?"

Arabella blinked. Wrapped up in her own thoughts she had forgotten the maid and dismissed her curtly. She reprimanded herself for being rude. It was not the maid's fault she was not paying attention, and she might have apologized if the servant had not hurried off.

She continued to her sister's room and entered without knocking knowing Rebecca was alone. She quietly made her way to the bedroom and hoped her sister was awake. The window curtains were pulled back with cords to let the light in to brighten the room. Rebecca lay awake staring at the ceiling.

"What are you doing, Becca?" Arabella asked as she climbed onto the downy mattress to lay down by her sister's side. She stretched out on her back, straightened her twisted skirt and then looked in the same direction as her sister. The ceiling capturing Rebecca's attention was designed with a geometrical symmetry of squares, arches, and beads.

"Oh!" Arabella exclaimed, "Your ceiling is different than mine. What possibly enthralls you?"

Rebecca sighed and replied, "Until you burst into my room I was counting the beads."

"Why?" Arabella asked.

"It was something to do. I am not inclined to rise, yet I have no wish for contemplation. I took to counting instead," she answered.

Arabella frowned at her sister's woeful response. A number of retorts popped into her head, but she let them fly like a swarm of bees leaving their hive. "First of all," she argued. "I did not burst. I was quite considerate in my entrance, making as little sound as possible in case you slept. Second, what thoughts are worrying you to keep you from rising, and last," she added with a grin, "how many beads are there?"

"I do not know," sighed Rebecca.

"Don't be absurd, Becca. Surely, you are astute to know the number of beads you counted and the reason for doing so," chastised Arabella.

Rebecca sat up in bed and Arabella joined her, both of them pushing themselves up against the mahogany carved headboard. Rebecca revealed, "Harry is angry with me."

Surprised, at her sister's confession, she asked, "Why? Where is Harry? He rarely leaves your side for long."

"I do not know, Bella. He left rather abruptly. He did not even offer me a kiss goodbye which is what he always does when he takes his leave of me."

"I know." Arabella rolled her eyes and grinned. "The man is completely head over heels in love with you."

"I expect not for long when he learns I have been faithless with him."

"Heavens to be, Becca, what have you done?"

"I am not being honest with him, Bella. He asked me what I worry about and I told him I was only tired. He knows I am withholding and he is hurt because I will not confide in him."

"You are making yourself sick over something of no importance, Becca. He knows of Damburten's attack."

"He does not know if I carry the baron's child," Becca argued.

"Neither do you, nor do you know if it is possible," she counseled, "but if the guilt of not knowing what transpired between you and Damburten is more than you can carry, then share the worry with Harry."

"I cannot. I could not stand his disappointment in me for accepting his proposal with the knowledge I might have been soiled goods. He will leave me and I do not think I could bear it."

"I do not think you give your husband enough credit, Becca. I think you have yet to reconcile you had nothing to do with Damburten's attack and until you do, you will suffer from this undeserving guilt." Arabella rose from the bed and walked around it to help her sister to do the same. She scolded, "Becca, are you going to let that scoundrel Damburten ruin what you have with Harry? I know Harry, being an earl's son, has forced you to enter a society that frightens you, but can you do it to find happiness with Harry?"

Rebecca jutted her chin out in defiance and proclaimed, "I am not afraid." Her proud demeanor quickly dropped and she revised, "Well, I am not afraid of Harry or Thomas. In fact, I was quite comfortable on our journey here. No one assaulted me."

"No, only me," Arabella interjected. She gave a chuckle upon spying her sister's horror. "It came to naught Becca, but you must consider a lady is rarely accosted under a gentleman's protection. What happens when you make the rounds visiting with his mother, the countess, or when we are out about shopping? How will you manage the unwanted attention of passing gentlemen? You must reconcile yourself or else, others might misread your timidity as guilt. You must find the strength to protect yourself as you did with Damburten."

"I did not protect myself, Bella," she reminded her sister.

"You did well enough; especially considering the blood on your dress was not your own."

"I bloodied Damburten's nose with my book," confessed Rebecca, "and received a sound slapping for it."

"You never told me," remarked Arabella sympathetically. "Well, you did not speak of your beating at all, other than to acknowledge it happened."

"I was terrorized and could not speak of it without reliving it. At the time, I was glad I lost consciousness, but now I wish I knew what happened."

"You are better now, Becca," stated Arabella. I think stronger. You no longer weep at the memory."

"No, but I am afraid of being accosted."

"We could learn to protect ourselves," Arabella suggested.

"What do you mean?"

"I am not sure," she replied. "The words resonated of their own accord, but the notion is appealing to me. I must admit I worry about my own safety, now the Barrington name incites transgressions against my person. Bolton came to my rescue at the George Inn because I was of his party. I do not know if he would have done the same if he had not known me."

"Harry would have rescued any lady in need," proclaimed Rebecca. "I am evidence of that since it is how we first met. I know Bolton is arrogant, but he does not seem to be uncaring. Look how he is helping us. I would like to think he, like Harry, would come to the aid of any lady in distress."

"Well, Bolton came to mine when that rude man grabbed me and seemed to think I was fair game because my name is Barrington. After the incident, I had wished it was I and not Bolton who turned that man's fingers back on him, bringing him to heel like a dog. I admit I felt quite vindicated to see that villain at Bolton's mercy." Her eyes lit with amusement and she enthusiastically exclaimed, "I know what we should do! I will ask Bolton to teach us how to do what he did!"

"Are you insane, Bella? I am with child and am not going to endanger my baby by engaging in fisticuffs."

"Not a fight, Becca, just a defensive move to remove us from harm."

"I do not know, Bella. I will have to speak with Harry."

"You do that and I will speak with Bolton. We won't let that vile representation of a man, Damburten, ruin our future happiness."

Arabella left her sister and went to search out Bolton, but turned into her room when she remembered she had yet to style her hair. She considered whether she should put on one of her better dresses, then discarded the notion after remembering she would be undressing to be measured by the modiste. She grinned imagining herself wearing something new and stylish. It had been way too long since either she or her sister purchased anything other than a necessity. Even this new wardrobe would not be at their expense. She absolved herself from her burgeoning guilt with the knowledge Bolton had more blunt than necessary to purchase the clothes for them.

A knock at her door redirected her thoughts and she opened it to find the housekeeper Mrs. Jenkins. "Miss Barrington," she announced, "my lord requests the appearance of you and your sister in the solarium. I am to escort you there since it is unknown to you."

"Oh," replied Arabella surprised at the immediacy of the request. She did not think her sister was ready to comply having not yet broken her fast. "Can you come for us in an hour, Mrs. Jenkins? My sister has not yet dressed or broken her fast?"

"As you wish, Miss Barrington," the housekeeper replied and was about to leave when Arabella asked, "Will his lordship take offense, Mrs. Jenkins? I know it is wrong to inquire after your master, but I do not want him to think us ungrateful. I could come with you now if you think best."

Mrs. Jenkins smiled and replied, "His lordship is all consideration, Miss Barrington, and would want your sister to take whatever time she needs. I am surprised you have not discovered this of his character."

Chapter Ten

Harry strode into the room his brother used to conduct business and found him sitting behind his desk. Thomas looked up from the letter he was reading when Harry demanded, "Where is my wife, Tommy?"

The hostility Thomas saw quite perturbed, then vexed him. He replied, "Where is your civility, Harry? Do you accuse me of something? If so, I suggest you make done and then be prepared for a thrashing if you think I have done anything with your wife."

Harry plopped, and then slouched down into one of the comfy upholstered chairs with padded scrolled arms situated before his brother's kneehole desk. He tilted his head and placed his cheek on the bent arm of his fist. He sighed knowing he had behaved badly and quickly apologized, "I am sorry, Tommy. Becca is not in our room, nor in the dining parlour, nor in any other room I can think she might have wandered. We had words this morning and I am worried." His concern turned into a pique when he remembered why they argued. He railed, "Thanks to you!"

Thomas steeled his eyes at his brother and asked, "How so?"

Harry sat up in his chair, leaned forward and explained, "I asked her to confide in me as you suggested and when she did not, my temper rose and I left."

"Well," he corrected, "you cannot blame me for any bungling you did, nor for losing your temper. In future, I suggest you count to ten and consider your words before you speak."

"Very funny," he replied. "Now, where is Becca?"

"She is in the solarium with her sister where they are being measured for their new wardrobe."

Surprised, then angry, Harry stood and exclaimed in a rising voice, "Are you mad, Tommy! They will be in their unmentionables and on display for every gardener and laborer to take an eyeful. What could you have been thinking?"

"Harry," Thomas rebuked softly, but sternly, "You are trying my patience. My servants know better than to ignore my dictates. No one is allowed within spying distance of the solarium. I assure you the ladies' modesties are well-protected."

"Why not use a guest suite where their privacy is assured?" asked Harry.

"Not that I need explain myself to you, but I will if it will get you to desist with this tedious conversation. I am not ignorant to the fact seamstresses suffer when their light is poor. The solarium provides the best illumination being more glass than structure; especially since there are several seamstresses at hand."

"Well, that is extremely nice of you, Tommy," Harry relented and then he grinned knowing his brother did not like to be considered nice. "I don't question how your blunt drew a modiste away from London, but I am curious to know whom you hired? Our dear mama is quite discriminating."

"She will find no fault with Mademoiselle Lavigne," Thomas assured returning his focus to the letter he was reading when his brother burst into the room. He was tired of explaining himself and diverted his attention to the letter hoping to force Harry to cease hounding him.

Harry's mouth gaped in surprise before he asked, "Camille is here? Is that wise, Tommy?"

Thomas looked at his brother vexed he would have to explain himself, again. He forgot Harry once met Camille and knew of his history with her. "She is an accomplished modiste, Harry, and the only one I trust to be discreet." His impatience made his voice rise when he said, "Of course, it is wise to have her here. The ladies must have something appropriate to wear when presented to our parents."

"You know what I meant, Tommy," retorted Harry with a grim expression.

Thomas sighed and replied, "I am afraid I do and it disturbs me you think I have any purpose other than the wardrobe I commissioned for your wife and Miss Barrington."

"You have not always called Camille, Mademoiselle Lavigne," Harry reminded his brother.

The dark-haired beauty was under Thomas' protection three years ago before their arrangement petered out after six months. It was believed Thomas ended the affair because he came to admire Camille too much to keep her as his mistress. Thomas had often spoke of Camille's intellect and talent, so Harry was not too surprised when his brother turned from protector to investor by buying a building where Camille could open up her dress shop.

Harry remembered the transition was not as smooth as his brother hoped. Thomas suffered his peer's crude jests about the talents mademoiselle must possess to be worth making an investment. His brother never let the insult stand and whether through the power of his fists or his influence, the slander stopped; especially after the Duchess of Winsberry became the talk of Mayfair wearing one of Camille's creations. Then, every lady who craved to be an arbiter of fashion flocked to Camille and their aristocratic husbands had no choice but to forget Mademoiselle Lavigne was ever Bolton's mistress.

Thomas retorted with an edge to his voice, "But I do call her Mademoiselle Lavigne which should be enough explanation for you, Harry. Now desist and take a lesson from me. Leave the past in the past, nothing good ever transpires from rehashing it."

Harry gave a nod acknowledging he heard his brother's message loud and clear and then turned to make his exit. Thomas raised up the letter he had been reading and asked his departing brother, "Where are you going, Harry. I have a letter from Higgins and I thought you would like to read it."

"Later," replied Harry. "For now, I seek my wife." He strode out the door with the same determination he entered it and made his way to the solarium where he neither announced nor asked permission for entry. There were a number of seamstresses seated working on needle-work and furbelows for the commissioned apparel who gasped on behalf of the ladies exposed in their chemises.

Arabella, aside from her head not flopping to the side, stood like a scarecrow with her arms outstretched, while Rebecca froze at seeing him. The modiste did not let his interruption pause her work. Most likely, she was used to people barging into her sessions to give opinion or to entertain her clients. She moved about Arabella swiftly with a length of cord to measure the length and breadth of her, recording her findings in a tablet at each interval.

Harry dropped his head and steeled his eyes on his wife, striding towards her as if she was the only person in the room. No one else mattered. Arabella was not a stick-ler for propriety around him; however, being spied in only her underdress was another matter and if she took affront or embarrassment to his barbaric intrusion then he would ask for her forgiveness later. He would make his apology as she deserved after he assured his wife all was well with them.

Harry hoped Camille was finished measuring Rebecca for he had better things to do with her than see her outfitted. She looked sorrowful and he did not like it. Rebecca took things to heart. No doubt, she blamed herself for their dispute and then worried over his absence. He had taken his horse for a hard gallop and once his temper cooled he remembered why he instigated the conversation with Rebecca in the first place. His intent was to ease her burdens, not create new ones and so he was determined to make right what had gone terribly wrong this morning.

He recognized and picked up her dress lying across the back of a chair and put it over her head. He heard her gasp and then bat at his hands to take over the task herself. Her words muffled until her head broke through her clothing to ask him, "What are you doing, Harry? I am in the middle of a fitting."

"Have you been measured?" he asked.

"Yes," she replied. "But I still have to make my selections." She pointed to the table with illustrated cards piled in various groups and another table stacked with fabric swaths.

Harry pulled his wife to the table of pattern cards and Rebecca watched in wide-eyed wonder as he shuffled through them and picked out a traveling dress, a walking dress and a number of other gowns for day and evening wear. He then went over to the fabric table and made appropriate selections. Camille nodded with approval and within minutes, Harry was pulling Rebecca down the hall. She was having trouble keeping up, so Harry lifted her in his arms and carried her up the main staircase and down the hall to their room. By the time they entered and shut the door behind them he was out of breath and they were both laughing.

"I should be angry, Harry," confessed Rebecca. "This is the first new wardrobe I have had in over two years and I did not have a say in the matter."

Looking chagrined, Harry apologized, "I am sorry, Becca, but I could not wait to speak with you. There will be more opportunities very soon for you to commission new clothes and I promise not to interfere."

Rebecca studied her husband and did not see the anger from this morning. She asked, "You are not mad at me any longer, Harry?"

"No," he replied. "It was never my intention to quarrel with you. I only wanted to unburden you. You often look sad and I thought I could make it better, but I think I made things worse. We are happy together, are we not?"

"Yes, we are very happy, Harry."

"Well then, let us continue to be happy and should your troubles ever threaten you or our happiness, then, please trust me to carry the mantle. I am more than capable, Becca."

Rebecca could not hold back her tears. Harry's gentle and caring nature never stopped surprising her. He should be angry. If she thought he withheld from her she would not be as generous as he, but how could she confide something that would destroy their happiness? "Let us continue to be happy," he had said. *Could it be that easy? Is Arabella right and I am worrying needlessly?*

Only her brother knew the truth of the injuries she sustained by Damburten, even so, she would never have any peace until she learned it herself, *but how?* Harry said Bolton could take care of anything. Could her brother-by-marriage find Nathaniel so she could ask him if Damburten had taken her innocence? Harry said to trust Bolton and she decided she would. She would seek his help to find Nathaniel, or maybe she would ask Bella to inquire.

Her sister liked to match wits with the viscount and thus far she had been successful in getting her way. She persuaded him to take her to London, purchase new wardrobes for them and no doubt, would get him to agree to teach them self-defense lessons. *What could one more request matter? I can't ask Harry to find Nathaniel for then I would have to confess why I so urgently needed to speak with him.*

Who knew if she would get to talk to Nathaniel? Most likely, a letter would be carried to him and a response returned to her. Harry would want to know what the letter said as was his right. The whole plan was full of risks, but it offered her a respite from her guilt. She would do anything not to hurt Harry for she loved him. She reached up and wrapped her arms around Harry when he brushed the tears off her face. She grinned and brought his head down for a kiss. Harry needed no further motivation. He picked her up and took her to bed.

"Harry," asked Rebecca as she snuggled close to him, "Do you suppose we shall ever take leave of our room? I have yet to tour the manor or its grounds."

Harry laughed and replied as he nuzzled her neck, "Not if I have my way."

A knock to their door had Harry rising and donning a silk banyan to answer it. A servant handed him a sealed note. Harry opened it, read the message and laughed.

"What is it, Harry?" asked Rebecca.

"It is from Tommy. He said if we want to eat, we best hurry ourselves down to the dining parlour for he and your sister are starting without us."

Arabella and Bolton sat in the drawing room waiting for Harry and Rebecca to arrive. Arabella unable to sit any longer rose from the sea blue camelback leather sofa and began to stroll about the mint green painted room adorned with white pilasters on its walls. The ceiling was plastered in white and from its center hung a crystal chandelier. A myriad of Adam furniture featuring gilded running mouldings, carved ram heads at jointures, and ram's hoofs at the end of each leg filled the room. On the floor lay a medallion carpet made of blue and red threads.

Heat radiated from a white marble fireplace and mint green brocade satin drapes crowned with tasseled swags hung over the windows. There were a number of classical paintings, along with a gilt-framed mirror and sconces on the walls. Knickknacks decorated the fireplace mantle and the mahogany tables throughout the room.

Bolton, upon watching Arabella pace, stood and announced how they would wait no longer for their truant siblings.

"I do not mind waiting, Bolton. This is not the first meal where Harry and Becca were tardy," she remarked.

"And most likely not their last time, Miss Barrington," he countered. "However, neither you nor I will suffer for their...their tardiness."

Arabella grinned at the viscount's stutter. She did not think his response was intended to be so tame. In truth, she was happy they were not going to wait for she was hungry. The revelation made her ask, "Bolton, did you mean our appetites will suffer or you will suffer if we do not eat readily?"

Keeping a sober face, Thomas answered, "You did warn me this morning of your temperament when you are hungry. Let us not test the theory." He winged his arm and after Arabella took it, escorted her into the dining parlour and sat her to the right of him. The footman poured wine into her crystal goblet and Thomas rang his bell for their first course to be served.

The *consommé* was being removed and a course of *duck á l'orange* was being placed before them when Harry and Rebecca joined them looking flushed from hurrying. The giddy couple took their seats quickly, while Thomas instructed his footman to inform Cook to plate courses for the new arrivals.

Awkwardness rose as everyone knew why the couple was late. Harry grinned unperturbed, while Rebecca blushed and fiddled with her linen, until her sister came to her rescue by diverting everyone's attention with her remark to Bolton, "Your modiste said with the additional seamstresses our dresses should be ready in three days. I do not think she will need us during that whole time, so how shall you amuse us, Bolton?"

Thomas raised his eyebrows at Arabella with a look of surprise that she expected him to own responsibility for her amusement and then his features softened at her audacity. She spoke to him as an equal with no thought to his consequence or her common station. Normally, he would take umbrage, but for some reason he did not. She treated him as a brother-by-marriage, rather than an aristocrat, and so he responded in kind, "What would you like to do? I believe I already assured I would provide you with whatever is necessary for your entertainment."

"Oh, indeed you did," she laughed. "I remember there were too many choices. Help me decide by telling me how you would take your leisure? And do not say you have too many responsibilities to partake and therefore can offer no choice."

Before Thomas could reply, Harry answered, "He would fish. When we were boys we would wake every morning and hike out to the lake at Belcrave before our governess dragged us back to the nursery."

Thomas interjected, "I doubt your wife and Miss Barrington would find pleasure in such an excursion."

Rebecca and Arabella grinned. Arabella informed, "You would be wrong, Bolton. Papa's family hail from Dover and are fishermen. Papa taught us to cast a line once we started walking. At least I know that to be the case with Becca. He never left us behind when he and Nathaniel went fishing."

Rebecca nodded her head in agreement and then asked her sister, "What say you, Bella, shall we test our skills against the men to see who of us are more successful?"

Grinning, Thomas shook his head and reminded his guests, "I have not stocked our lake, Miss Barrington. I fear the effort would be for naught. May I suggest the Nature Walk?"

Arabella retorted with good humor, "You will have to rectify your lack of fish, Bolton for when we visit again." She blushed realizing she had just invited herself for a return visit and stuttered an apology, "I...I beg your pardon, Bolton, for sounding presumptuous. I would never impose myself upon your hospitality without benefit of invitation."

"Would you not, Miss Barrington?" Thomas retorted sternly.

Arabella gasped, but before she could take umbrage, she remembered how she had foisted herself into Bolton's party in order to accompany Rebecca to London. For once, she could not retaliate nor speak and that made everyone, aside from herself, laugh.

Chapter Eleven

Arabella suffered the lip quirks and side jokes made at her expense, but the minute dinner was over she excused herself claiming exhaustion. Before retiring, she sought out the housekeeper, Mrs. Jenkins, to order a meal to be sent to her room in the morning. She refused to be teased again; especially while she broke her fast. She would rather eat alone in her room, than suffer further embarrassment. At the time, she had no idea challenging Bolton on how she would never impose herself, would become trivial, in light of what later transpired.

Who would have thought she could transgress further from Bolton's good opinion. Her initial embarrassment might already be forgiven and forgotten by all, since it intruded on no one's discomfiture but her own. However, to be found eavesdropping was another matter and she had no idea what Bolton would do to her when next they met.

Sleep failed her when she went to bed, and so she considered every remedy. She rang for a cup of chamomile tea; she put drops of lavender on her pillow; she counted sheep and meditated to banish the mortification torturing her mind. Nothing worked and so she rose to pace the floor. Back and forth she went, until she remembered Bolton's library.

She had no reservations about trespassing since Bolton offered its use as a choice of amusement. A good book was her last hope to taking her mind off her embarrassment and to falling sleep. She did not bother to change out of her cotton nightdress knowing the household was retired and undoubtedly asleep. She donned a wrap, knowing the unused rooms would be cold without a fireplace alit to warm them, and picked up the sterling candleholder by her bed to light her way. She knew the staff extinguished the wall sconces before retiring.

A sense of urgency drove her, or perhaps the eerie darkness and the shadows cast by her candle sent her scurrying down the staircase in haste, as if an apparition might appear at any moment. She entered the library and finally released the breath her rising fright held captive in her chest.

She took a minute to inspect the room with her single flame, moving the candle from one direction to the other. The walls were paneled in wood with floor to ceiling inset shelves that were filled with books. There was a sterling silver candelabrum atop a round mahogany table in the middle of the room and she went to light its multiple candles with her single flame.

The room brightened sufficiently for her to read the titles, so she left her candleholder on the table to peruse Bolton's collection. She had just started her search for something to read when she heard his voice. Surprised, she turned to see from where it came and saw a door left ajar.

The door connected the library to the room where Bolton conducted his business, apparently late into the evenings, where it seemed he liked to indulge in speaking to himself. She went to make herself known and to apologize without fanfare or witness for her earlier presumptions. She had just grabbed the doorknob when the sound of a woman's voice stopped her from opening it.

She had not felt like a trespasser until that moment when she learned Bolton was not alone. He was with a woman whose voice she recognized immediately. *What is Camille doing with Bolton in the middle of the night?* Her better sense told her to release the doorknob and to quietly leave the library. Nothing but awkwardness would occur should her presence become known; especially for her. She was taught better than to eavesdrop; but an emotion she had trouble identifying kept her feet glued to the floor and her ears pressed close to the door's opening.

Thomas looked at Camille and could not deny she was a temptation. She was wearing a black laced negligée designed not to be seen out of the bedchamber for it held no secrets. He was wont to scold her, but with the household asleep he chose to enjoy the view, even if he had no intention to act on her invitation. He always made a point to cut off relations with a woman when her feelings began to show. Camille began to act more like a wife than a mistress after being in his protection for six months and so he had severed the relationship.

However, rather than settle her with jewels, he purchased a building for her to realize her life ambition of opening a dress shop. He never expected to make a profit from the venture, but Camille had an astute eye for design and once he convinced the Duchess of Winsberry to wear one of her fashions, Camille earned the fame and success she deserved.

He had immediately thought of Camille when he agreed to supply a wardrobe for Arabella and Rebecca because he knew he could count on her discretion. However, he had not counted on his one-time mistress to misconstrue his motive. Soberly, he inquired, "How may I assist you, Mademoiselle?"

"My lord," she cooed, "Are we to fall to rank then? We are no longer Camille and Thomas?"

Thomas replied with a soft, yet chastising tone, "We have not been so for many years, Mademoiselle. Why are you here, dressed as you are?"

"I thought you might seek me out for old time's sake and when you did not, I sought you," she confessed in a sultry voice.

Thomas had trouble keeping his face stern at a woman whose company he once enjoyed. Regardless, he had no wish to start a relationship he had taken great care and great expense to end. He rose from his chair to escort Camille out of the room and was momentarily distracted by a flickering light. The door connecting to his library was cracked open and he went to close it, making a mental note to extinguish the candles before he went to bed. He would inform the housekeeper in the morning and have every confidence the dereliction of duty would be addressed with the negligent servant.

There was resistance when he pulled on the knob and he had to give it a swift jerk to close it, immediately discerning the eavesdropper's identity for neither his staff, nor his brother would be brazen enough to spy on him. The guilty party was assuredly Miss Barrington.

Annoyed by her audacity, he grabbed Camille by her hand, pulled her out of the room and sent her on her way with a push. His brusque manner made Camille frown, but she took her leave graciously and made her way to her room alone. She knew better than to try his temper. Thomas shut his office door loud enough for Arabella to hear and then he leaned against the wall to await her exit from the library.

Arabella didn't know whether to hide or run to make her escape. Her eyes kept turning from the joining door to the library door, anticipating to be found. Her heart raced and then when she thought she had no choice but to reveal herself, she heard the door shut to Bolton's office as the occupants left. In her relief, she promised herself she would never be so foolish as to eavesdrop on another person again and focused on slowing her speedy heart.

No sooner had she composed herself than her temper began to rise. *Why am I in the wrong? I was not the one being indiscreet.* Her pique did not last long for she realized she was not safe from being discovered. *What if Bolton returns?* Her renewed fear drove her to flee like a jack rabbit racing for its burrow. Frantic, she ran out the library door and smack into Bolton's chest.

Thomas moved away from the wall the minute the library door opened. He did not expect to see Arabella racing out and barreling into him. He expected more sleuth from the lady who chose to interest herself in his affairs. The impact propelled her backwards until his two firm hands gripped her arms.

It took her a minute to catch her breath and another minute to lose it when she saw his anger. He steeled his eyes upon her and kept his grasp tight on her. She looked astonished and embarrassed, but whatever fear initially drove her to run out of the library diminished from whatever she saw in his features. Exasperated, Thomas shook her and demanded, "What the deuce are you about, Miss Barrington?"

Arabella's own temper rose at being manhandled and she rebelled with equal ire, "Release me, Bolton!" Then, in a softer voice she whined, "You are hurting me." Mortified, Thomas released her immediately. Arabella stepped back, checking the grin that wanted to widen on her face for having taken advantage of his character. Holding onto her outrage, she asked, "Perhaps, Bolton, it is not me, but you who should explain what you are about?"

Completely astonished, he said in a very soft but livid voice, "I do not answer to you, Miss Barrington. You are my guest, but you are not at liberty to trespass on my privacy, nor wander all hours of the night in my home for your amusement. Should I check the silver or have my staff inventory the household to see the results of your mischief?"

The accusation first embarrassed then angered her. She rebuked, "Shame, Bolton! You know I would do no such thing. I came to find a book to read. I saw your light and sought your company, but quickly realized you were engaged with someone else. How dare you insult my character?"

Arabella began to stomp off, but Thomas grabbed her arm to stop her and asked, "Why did you seek my company?"

"Another time, Bolton, I am in no mood to suffer it." Arabella replied irritably. She pulled her arm free and walked away. She did not look back, not even when she heard Bolton laugh and realized how her remark sounded as if she had sought an assignation with him. *Heavens be!* Completely mortified she wondered how she was ever to face him again.

Arabella bid "enter," expecting to see a maid with her morning meal, not her sister creeping into her room. Concerned, she asked, "Is something amiss, Becca?"

Her sister jumped, turned around and then blushed. Rebecca bit her bottom lip and replied with an unbelievable, "No."

Arabella grinned and remarked with humor, "Are you acting guilty because you left your ardent husband in bed and hope to return before he discovers your absence?"

Rebecca laughed. "You are too funny, Bella. Harry is out riding with Bolton. I am not sneaking behind his back." She paused, considering her words and then added, "Not exactly."

Arabella frowned and suggested, "Take a seat Becca and explain yourself. What, not exactly, are you doing behind your husband's back?"

"I have made a muddle of simply wanting to ask a favor of you." Rebecca waited for her sister to say "what favor?" and when Arabella did no such thing, she continued, "Will you ask Bolton to search for Nathaniel?"

"Whyever for, Becca? Our brother is in hiding and I do not think our trying to ferret out his location will be of service to him. If he thinks it wise to communicate with us then I am confident he will."

"I did not consider the risk to him by having Bolton find him," she responded sadly.

Arabella crouched next to where her sister sat, gave her a hug, and asked, "Why do you want Nathaniel?"

Sighing, Rebecca answered, "I must know the truth, Bella. I cannot in good conscience keep my worries from Harry. He said he had no need to know what they were as long as they did not threaten our happiness. I fear they do and I am now afraid my refusal to give him my confidence will cause him greater hurt than the truth."

`Arabella stood and paced, examining the particulars of Rebecca's request and possible outcome. She finally returned to stand in front of her sister and said, "Bolton would not keep this confidence from Harry. He would feel disloyal to his brother, believing it to be Harry's right to be your gallant and confident. You must ask Harry to find Nathaniel. He most likely will seek Bolton's assistance."

"What if he asks for the reason why?"

Arabella urged strongly, "You must confess to Harry now, Becca, if this is your course. He will be sympathetic with your plight; however, if you do this without his knowledge and seek another's help, then he will see it as a betrayal. Not only did you not trust in him, but you trusted another and acted without his counsel. He will not take the affronts lightly."

Rebecca sobbed, "I am afraid he will renounce me."

Arabella bent over and hugged her sister. She asked, "How can I have more faith in Harry than you? Do you not know the man loves you?"

Chapter Twelve

The area preceding the main staircase was known as the Grand Hall and it was here that visitors were welcomed and distinguished. Guests of common birth were asked to take a seat on one of the neo-classical backless wood framed and dark blue upholstered sofas, while the butler inquired to whether his master was at home. Noble guests were escorted into the drawing room and offered refreshment.

Rebecca sat on one of the sofas waiting for Harry. She wore a sprig muslin dress with a blue spencer and blue gloves to warm her from the brisk day. A straw poke bonnet decorated with matching blue satin ribbons were tied in a neat bow to the right under her chin and she sat with a stiff back as a lady should. Her ankles and knees touched; and her hands were clasped on her lap.

Her anxiety to speak with Harry had her legs bouncing on the pads of her feet and then as if she was startled, she turned her head to look at the basket next to her, as if she feared it might be gone.

She had made up her mind to confess all her worries to Harry and the wait was testing her bravery to do it. The notion Harry could renounce her and her child made her tremble. Legally, her baby would be Harry's for the birth would come after their marriage, but that did not mean Harry had to acknowledge the baby. It was known to happen among noblemen who believed their wives cuckolded them, making the poor child suffer for their mother's indiscretion. Her mind considered the worst outcomes and then quickly naysaid them, knowing Harry could never be so cruel. Regardless, she felt she had misused Harry terribly for never correcting his belief of what she had suffered under Damburten's villainy.

A burst of wind assailed her when Harry and Thomas finally entered through the front door. Her worried expression had Harry rushing to kneel by her side and his concern choked her with emotion. Thomas looked embarrassed to infringe upon their intimate moment and quickly left once he acknowledged Rebecca with a nod.

Harry took his wife's hands into his own and began to rub them. He asked, "Are you not well, Becca? Is it the baby?"

Rebecca silently chastised herself for ever doubting Harry and answered, "I am well, Harry, just beginning to worry my idea for a picnic would not please you. I did not consider you might need a respite after your morning ride."

Harry's relief was seen in the disappearance of his frown lines and widening grin. He rose from where he knelt, pushed the picnic basket out of his way, and took the seat next to his wife. He tugged on her hands so she would turn towards him, lifted her chin to see her face under the large brim of her hat and tilted his head to gain access to her lips. "Becca," he said after kissing her, "I never need a respite from you. I admit a picnic was not in my plan for when I returned, but I find the notion that it was of your own making pleasing to me."

Surprised he had made plans, she asked, "What was your plan, Harry? Is it something we can do later?"

Harry laughed and said, "Most assuredly."

Rebecca frowned and then her brows rose as she discerned his meaning. Her cheeks crimsoned further and in retaliation for the embarrassment she suffered, she swatted Harry on the arm. Harry laughed and rose from the sofa to help her to stand. He winged his arm out to her and then picked up the basket of food to lead her down the long hall to exit from the back of the house where it was a shorter walking distance to the lake.

As they walked Harry stopped a passing footman and ordered a quilt, some cushions and a lap blanket to be brought to the lake for he did not want Rebecca to take a chill from the cold ground. They walked down the long corridor until they came to a door to exit. Harry, with a bit of muscle, pushed the door open and they were both immediately beset by a strong breeze.

The brim of Rebecca's bonnet turned up and she reached up with her hand to hold it in place, while Harry shielded her with his body from the swirling spring wind. They laughed at the unexpected bluster and pushed forward to the sock-shaped blue lake. Harry had no wish to tire his wife by journeying too far afield. Besides, Harry had no intention of keeping Rebecca outdoors any longer than to satisfy her need to picnic; regardless of the picturesque view on display. Spring flowers grew wildly and dotted the lush grass with colors of blue, yellow, and white. Clusters of trees and shrubbery added texture to nature's canvas as did the repeating ripples crossing the lake marking it a fine day to take out Bolton's two-person sailboat.

The footman met up with them not far from the manor and quickly spread the quilt on the ground, placing the cushions and lap blanket on top before taking his leave. Rebecca accepted Harry's help to lower herself onto the quilt and then raised her arms for Harry to hand her the basket. No sooner had he given her the food than he worked to make her comfortable by arranging the pillows to support her back. He wanted to wrap her up in the wool blanket, but Rebecca shook her head and said, "Later, Harry, I can neither serve nor eat bundled up like a newborn babe. Truly, desist with your coddling for I am fine. Why not settle yourself and share any news Bolton gave you."

Harry did as bid and stretched out on his side with his head held up by his bent arm and fist. He watched his wife put more food on his plate than hers and remarked, "Need I remind, you are the one eating for two?"

Rebecca smiled. It was nice to have Harry attentive to her and she hoped after her confession his ardent affection would not diminish. She replied to his concern by saying, "I will get more later, Harry. Tell me whether Bolton has news."

Harry's eyes twinkled and he replied cheerfully, "Tommy received an update from Higgins. Can you believe it? We have not been gone a full week and the man has already sent a report of his progress. Even Tommy thinks his diligence remarkable."

Surprised, she asked, "Higgins has completed one of the tasks on his list? If so, that is indeed remarkable for none of them were small."

Harry laughed and explained, "It was an update to inform us he had no trouble hiring laborers from the village. Tommy was aware of the hostility your family suffered within the community and was not sure if any of the men would take employment from us. It seems they no longer feel obligated to snub you with Damburten dead. Higgins is also inquiring to our preference for a cook and is asking if we prefer simple home fare or someone who can produce sauces and other culinary delights seen in French cuisine."

"Harry, I do not even know how we can afford to hire a cook, much less, determine the type of food we prefer; especially when I have never tasted French food."

"Well, that is easily settled for we will have plenty of French food to sample at all the numerous events we attend while in London. The *ton* love to brag about the French cooks they steal away from other households."

Harry pulled himself up to a sitting position when Rebecca's complexion paled. He momentarily had forgotten how nervous she was about being presented to the *ton*, even he knew the task she faced was daunting; not only was she a common girl with no connection to nobility or wealth to recommend her, but she was tainted by scandal. He took her hand and was about to assure her all would be well when she squeezed his hand and offered a pathetic grin.

"Harry," she started, "you told me to trust in you; especially if our happiness is at risk. I have not been forthcoming with you and it has weighed heavily on me. The more I think about it, the more I realize the great injury I have done you. Please forgive me."

Her eyes teared up and droplets fell marking a path down her cheek. Harry brushed them away with his fingers and then wrapped his arms around her, pushing the poke bonnet off her head. He had no idea what she was talking about, but could not stand to see her grief-stricken. He pulled himself back and moved the plates of food out of his way to gather her up in his arms. Once situated with her beside him, he asked, "Tell me, Becca, so I can make all well and you can put your mind at ease."

She cried and Harry brought her in his arms to lie back on the quilt. He kept her cuddled to his side and let her sob. There would be time later to learn all, but for now he let her release the flood of emotions she had kept refrained for so long.

They did not touch their meal. He left everything behind for a servant to clear and carried his sleeping wife to their room. She had exhausted herself explaining how she did not know the extent of Damburten's assault. Her guilt cut him to the core. *How can she believe she did anything to justify Damburten's attack? And how can she fear I would love her less if the villain had his way.*

He would kill the baron himself if he was not already dead. He had to press down his raging emotions when Rebecca began to shiver as she told her story. The last thing he wanted was for her to believe he was angry with her. The villain was Damburten and now was not the time to indulge in his hatred for a man long dead.

For now, he assured her the baby she carried was their own; regardless of what they learned or not from Nathaniel. Rebecca fell asleep and when it looked like she would not wake, he cradled her in his arms, carried her to their bed and settled her gently under the bed cover. He made sure she slept at ease before he searched out his brother.

Thomas rose from his seat the moment Harry entered his office. The evidence of Harry's rage pulsed from his throat, burned in his heated face and shot daggers from his eyes. Thomas had never seen his warmhearted brother look like he wanted to kill someone and he hurried around his desk to come to his brother's aid, "What has happened? You look as if you are about to commit murder."

Harry responded in clipped words as he tried to speak calmly. "I wish I could, Tommy, but the villain is already dead. I need a favor of you while I take my leave for a few days. Can you care for my wife and her sister, ensure their protection and comfort while I am gone?"

Worried his brother was in trouble, Thomas asked, "Where are you going, Harry?"

"Can you not just promise me, Tommy? If you must know something, then I go to fulfill the request my wife asked of me."

"Can I help, Harry? I have resources to aid you."

"The duty and honor are mine alone, Tommy. It is enough I leave knowing my family is in good hands."

"Dear Lord!" exclaimed Thomas. "You are not to demand satisfaction of someone, Harry. If so, then being second is my right and honor. You must confide in me and let me assist you."

Thomas' exclamation distracted Harry from his anger. He apologized, "Do not be offended, Tommy. I am not about to duel." He did not know what to tell his brother without knowing the truth. His conscience struggled with what was right. If he and Rebecca bore a son, then the child could accede to the earldom if Thomas did not beget his own son. As the spare, Harry's children were next in line after him to inherit; which seemed possible since Thomas had no wish to marry. *Could I deceive my family to protect my wife and child from slander?* He was too angry and would keep his own counsel until he had his emotions in check. He told his brother, "I will confide when I learn the truth, Tommy. Until then, do I have your assurance to care and protect Becca and Bella?"

"Of course, Harry," replied Thomas soberly. "You need not ask, for what is precious to you is also to me. Do you leave now, without a bag, Harry?"

Harry's features softened as the particulars of his travel came to light and he realized in his fury he had planned to mount his horse and go. Thomas' inquiry made him sensible enough to answer, "I shall do so now, Tommy. Thank you."

Thomas said he would call for Harry's horse and return to see him off. What he did not say was that he planned to order two of his grooms to follow and keep his brother in their sights without Harry knowing. Thomas would not allow Harry to stumble into trouble with no one to come to his rescue. One groom would be duty-bound to report, either through messenger or in person, Harry's location and activities; the other would stay close at hand to come to Harry's aid if needed.

Arabella was not sure what to say to Bolton regarding her eavesdropping so she had stayed hidden in her room all day. She was too embarrassed to face the viscount, much less apologize for overhearing the private affairs between him and his one-time mistress. *Good heavens!* The recollection made her blush.

She would have continued to keep to herself and not attend dinner if doing so would not raise concern with her sister. Not once had she complained of feeling unwell and if Rebecca learned she had not left her room since she saw her, then her sister would press Bolton to send for a doctor. She doubted Bolton would think her ill, but he could not refuse Rebecca's request without explaining why. Arabella had no choice but to attend dinner and face Bolton.

Her fretting eased when she realized Bolton would not introduce the subject. How could he without explaining his clandestine meeting with his one-time mistress. *Ha! I am not the only one to be embarrassed!*

A tap to her door brought her out of her musings. She found the maid on the other side of the door. "Miss," she informed, "if you please, the modiste needs you in the solarium."

Arabella hoped she would not run into Bolton on her way there, or that she would reveal to the modiste she knew of her relationship with the viscount. She had no wish to explain herself to Camille or to cause any awkwardness between them by revealing she knew Camille was once Bolton's mistress. The idea mortified her.

The moment Arabella arrived, Camille rushed toward her and without a by-your-leave, briskly turned her around and undid the buttons on the back of her dress.

Within seconds, a new dress was placed over Arabella's head and fastened. Camille straightened, tugged, pinned, and when she was satisfied, exclaimed, "Magnifique, Miss Barrington. Lord Bolton has exquisite taste."

It was not until Camille's praise that Arabella realized the dress was not of the design, nor the fabric from which she had selected. She looked down at the net overlay, the exposed skin of her shoulders and arms, and silently exclaimed, *Heavens be! My ankles are even exposed!*

She had to check her anger when she concluded Bolton had his hand in her wardrobe and while she could not blame Camille for doing as Bolton wished, for it was his blunt that paid her commission, she could be mad at Bolton for not requesting her permission to make the changes. Camille noted her fury and quickly asked, "You do not like, Miss Barrington? Be assured, you look very fashionable and pretty."

"I have no qualms with your talent, mademoiselle; however, this is not the dress I ordered. Can you explain why?"

Camille had the temerity to grin. "Ah," she replied, "His lordship did not inform you of the changes. Be at ease, Miss Barrington. The dress is *a la mode*. Even the raised hemline is of the latest fashion. All who look upon you will seek to learn your modiste's name. They will be impressed it is I who you retained for I am much sought after for my original designs."

"But it is not the pattern I chose," she argued.

"No," replied Camille with remarkable patience. "However, you must let his lordship guide you for he has exquisite taste. The style you requested is very outdated."

"Then why offer it to your patrons if you believe it outmoded."

"I serve my customers, Miss Barrington, and some do not easily accept the new modes of fashion. They want what they want and I serve to please."

"Yet," she countered curtly. "You have not served to please me!"

"No, miss, I served to please his lordship who commissioned my services," Camille responded with heated vexation. She walked over to a table where another dress lay. She picked it up and showed Arabella some details that were the same as the dress she wore. The dress had the same short waist where the skirt fell directly from under the bosom and flared at the hem, unlike her older clothes where the bodice was longer and the skirt dropped straight.

The dress she held also used pleats to puff out the short sleeves instead of being gathered. The pleated process used less material and therefore the line of her arms flowed from the sleeves with elegance. There were a number of trims and furbelows that put the dress in the first stare of fashion which she honestly would not have noticed having no knowledge of current fashion.

However, the point was the *ton would* notice and Bolton had done her a favor by making sure she was up to snuff as she entered Mayfair's elevated society. Regardless, she still planned to give the man a scold for not consulting her. "That dress you are holding is too short for me," Arabella rebutted, simply to be right about one thing.

Camille corrected, "This one belongs to your sister. Lord Harry also has a keen eye for fashion and made the selections for your sister. You both have been well-guided, Miss Barrington."

Sufficiently chastised, Arabella finished her fittings and then went in search of Bolton, so she could make him suffer for underhandedly changing her wardrobe without consulting her. In her eagerness to banter words with him she forgot her embarrassment and how she wished to stay out of his sight. She practically bounced on her way to his study. She could not explain why she was drawn to the man like a magnet, especially when in a pique.

Bolton was not in his study, so Arabella headed to the drawing room, but found him instead in the Grand Hall. Before she could greet him, she saw Harry walking down the staircase with a bag in his hand. She rushed forward to inquire where he was going, but was halted by his stern features. She realized her sister must have finally confessed her fears to him. Her question sounded more statement than inquiry, "She told you?"

"Yes," he replied soberly and then added with affection, "Becca still sleeps. I would not wake her for she needs her rest. Tell her I have gone to fulfill her request and will send word when I can. Take care of her Bella, and remind her not to worry."

"Of course, Harry," she replied before leaning in to whisper, "You will tell our brother he is in our thoughts and prayers."

Harry nodded, turned to Thomas and offered his hand. Thomas reminded him to send word. Harry nodded, thanked his big brother and then took his leave.

Thomas turned his attention to Arabella. He had heard what she whispered to Harry and while his brother's leave was still a mystery, Thomas felt better knowing one piece of the puzzle. Somehow, Nathaniel was a major character and information about the duel must be the circumstance that took Harry away. He would learn the all of it, whether from the Barrington sisters or from Harry himself, though he had little patience to wait upon Harry. He asked Arabella, "You wish to have a word with me, Miss Barrington?"

Arabella was thrown by Bolton's question. She was sure he was going to ask her what Rebecca told Harry. It was not her news to share and so she was steeling herself from having to answer his questions. The man was a conundrum. She never knew what to expect from him. She gathered her wits and responded, "I have just seen the dresses you commissioned for me and my sister, Bolton. Imagine my astonishment to see they were not of my selection."

Thomas grinned.

Arabella's nostrils flared in temper. *The cad! He doesn't deny or make apologies!* She chastised, "In the future, Bolton, I suggest you consult with me. I do not take kindly to having my own choices negated; especially in favor of one who does not know me. You are lucky I did not dislike the dresses for had I not, be assured I would not wear them!" Her voice had begun to escalate as Thomas' grin widened into a smile. His amusement at her tirade made her turn and take her leave before she began to screech at him like a fish wife.

"Where are you going, Miss Barrington," Thomas asked cheerfully.

"I go to my sister, though it is no business of yours," she replied curtly.

"I fear your business is mine, Miss Barrington, as Harry has commanded it," he explained smiling still. He added more soberly, "I would remind you Harry wants his wife to sleep and gain rest."

Chapter Thirteen

The red drapes were closed to keep the dark night from intruding into the brightly lit dining room. The candles in the crystal chandelier and in the multiple wall sconces radiated and reflected against the cream walls and white table linen. Any other time, the room's warm glow and elegance would have drawn marvel from its guests, but tonight's party was deep in thought with worry.

Thomas helped Rebecca to the seat which would be to the right of where he sat and then assisted Arabella to the chair on his left side. He rang the dinner bell. The china, silver, and crystal place settings sparkled, as if in greeting to its user, and within minutes while silence continued to reign, the first course was served.

Thomas watched the ladies choose to move their food around their plates rather than to speak of trivial things. They were all worried about Harry. No word had arrived from him or from Thomas' grooms, but Thomas knew better than to expect anything so quickly. He would not anticipate news until late in the evening and he planned to keep vigil until it came. He could not help his brother until he knew what troubled him, nor could he settle the awkwardness with the sisters unless their secrets were revealed. He could be patient when needed; especially when it came to the business of discerning the truth. He excelled in his business ventures by delving into people's pasts and reputations. Usually, the direct approach manifested the best results, so letting intuition guide him, he broke the silent meal as casually as if he was speaking of the weather and asked about the Barrington's family history.

"It is a shame there are no fish in the lake for it would help distract us from Harry's absence," he remarked. "I would enjoy seeing how many fish you could hook. You did say your paternal grandfather was a fisherman, did you not?"

One side of Rebecca's pressed lips turned up to form a lopsided grin as if in appreciation for her brother-by-marriage's attempt to distract her from her worries. She answered his question with a "yes," and then her eyes darted towards the ceiling as if she had a recollection.

Her features softened, her lips turned up into a full grin before flattening again into a fret. She said, "You will think Bella and I are unique in not knowing much of our family history, Bolton. You see, we never met my mama's family and only saw my papa's family when they came to visit. Our grandpapa and uncles did not come often when we lived in Truro, but when they did they brought gifts, of which, my papa always seemed to frown upon, but never the less, he allowed us to accept them."

She continued, "It is through those visits and tidbits of overheard conversations that we have some understanding of our relatives. As children, we never thought to question our parents; or perhaps we had and were discouraged from inquiring again. I believe Nathaniel knows more about our relatives because I once overheard him arguing with our papa. I remember papa refused him from taking work from our uncles. Our brother wanted to earn some 'ready blunt' and was assured by them he could do so on the coast, but papa refused Nathaniel from going, insisting the danger to him was not worth the cost of some *ready blunt*. Papa did not like my brother using cant phrases and underscored his dislike of it by repeating the phrase back to my brother."

"It is odd to know so little of one's family, Rebecca," remarked Thomas, turning his inspection from her to her sister for verification.

Arabella shrugged her shoulders in reply to Thomas' silent inquiry and confirmed, "It is the truth, Bolton. We do not know much; therefore there is little to tell. Our family led a quiet life before moving into Damburten's sphere. Our grandfather lives on the Cornwall coast and by trade is a fisherman. Papa had an academic mind and could envision other possibilities for himself; however, he often admitted he would not have ventured forth if not urged on by his papa and brothers."

"Barrington is an uncommon name for a family of fishermen," Thomas remarked.

"I never said my grandfather was born into a family of fishermen," responded Arabella a bit peevishly and then laughed. "Good heavens!" she exclaimed. "Until this moment, I never realized how many marriages in our family took place without parental approval."

"How so?" asked Thomas in amusement.

Rebecca interjected earnestly into the conversation, chuckling her answer as if was a great lark, "Our papa and grandpapa also married without parental approval just like Harry and me. Grandpapa fell in love and married a young girl against our great-grandmama's wishes. It is reputed he raged he cared not one whit for her approval. If you ever meet our grandpapa, you will think him gentry for he has the manners and air of one. The locals call him Squire Barrington in jest because he can be quite lofty. I have heard even the smugglers use the title to show him proper respect."

Arabella blushed and abruptly halted her sister's discourse with a scold, "Becca, desist! Bolton did not ask for grandpapa's story." She was surprised to hear her pitched voice and felt her blush deepen. A part of her felt her sister just betrayed their father who had aspired to elevate their station by becoming a landowner. Now, with a loose tongue Rebecca marked their whole paternal family among the lowest of people: thieves, cutthroats, and lest we not forget fishmongers.

"Do not reprimand her, Miss Barrington," rebuked Thomas. "I am very much interested in every level of your family history. I understand why you felt it necessary to halt her discourse. It should never be revealed to the *ton* in such a manner."

"I am not ashamed of my family, Bolton!" Arabella flared before Thomas could finish.

"Bella," interjected Rebecca, "of course, we are not ashamed. I did not mean to suggest our grandpapa was a smuggler, but you know everyone on the Cornish coast lends a hand now and then, even the women and children, and they all receive a bottle of French wine or bit of lace for their troubles. I expect many of the silks and scarves grandpapa gave to us came from such a bounty and the reason our papa did not approve of them."

"I am not judging, Miss Barrington," intervened Thomas in a voice that sounded more consoling than tempered. "Nor did I say you were ashamed. However, may I remind how you demanded a new wardrobe so as not to be judged on your less than fashionable clothes? Would you now have the aristocracy use their prejudices to judge you? Trust me, the *ton* can be quite rude when inquiring about the background of those unknown to them. They pride themselves in rooting out the mushrooms, those people who show up out of nowhere claiming nobility."

"Well, we are not mushrooms, Bolton, but we are common," argued Arabella sadly.

"As are most of them," soothed Thomas. "Not everyone who regards themselves as good *ton* holds a title; however, most assuredly, everyone who does is connected to someone with a title. Even a distant connection to nobility can give one entrée to the *ton*. Allow me to guide you through the intricacies of parlour talk. Neither Harry nor I would set you or your sister up for failure. Continue your story, Rebecca. Tell me how your father met your mother."

Rebecca looked to her sister for permission. Arabella said, "I cannot disagree with his wisdom, Becca. Tell papa's story. We shall do as Bolton suggests and allow him to guide us."

"Thank you, Miss Barrington, for your trust," replied Thomas.

Trust him? Do I? Arabella was astonished by his reply and then upon further reflection, was surprised she did trust him. Her cheeks bloomed into a blush when other emotions rose to the surface. Feelings to which would not benefit her one iota and would certainly become an embarrassment should anyone deduce she held them. She blinked when Thomas raised his brows at her.

Heavens be! She had fixated her eyes on him and now the man was silently inquiring to what she was thinking. *Does he think I am besotted? Did he ask me a question? No, not a question, but nevertheless, he expected a response for his gratitude.*

Too embarrassed to give a belated reply she searched for a safe haven and found it when her eyes met her sisters'. She hoped Thomas would not press her for answers now that she no longer looked at him and was significantly relieved when he turned his attention back to her sister, "Continue with your story, Rebecca?"

Rebecca began, "Our papa emigrated with his father and brothers at the beginning of the French Revolution and settled in Cadgwith along the Cornwall coast, Bolton. He did not take to the industry of fishing and made his way to Truro to find work as a clerk since he was good with numbers and kept very good records. Truro is a big city in Cornwall and papa was sure he could find work." Rebecca's eyes opened wide and she laughed heartily. She turned to her sister and explained, "Bella, mama met papa much like I met Harry! He also came to her aid."

"How so?" asked an amused Thomas unable to keep his lips from turning up when Rebecca chuckled aloud.

She turned her focus to Thomas and explained. "Mama's side of the family is a mystery because they did not approve of papa. Both Bella and I think they disavowed her, but we are not sure. We think mama came from gentry for she had remarkable manners and those talents for music, drawing and dancing for which are of little use to our class, though Bella learned to play the pianoforte, along with other girls whose parents paid mama for lessons. Anyway, we do not know if our mama was visiting Truro or whether she lived nearby when she met papa, but she was driving her gig and the spoke of her wheel cracked. Papa came upon her, on foot no less, and helped her to unhitch her horse and get her to town. Papa always said he fell in love with her on sight. They married without her parent's approval."

"Do you know your mother's maiden name?" Thomas asked.

Both Arabella and Rebecca turned their heads to each other for the answer. Arabella was the one to voice their astonishment, "How could we not know?"

Thomas offered, "Do you know where they married? There would be a church record of your mother's name."

Rebecca replied, "We assumed it was in Truro, but we do not know for sure. They could have married over the anvil for all we know. Why do we need to know?" Rebecca's rising anger marred her words, "I am sure Bella would agree we have no wish for a relationship with grandparents who would cast their only daughter aside because she dared to love our dear papa!"

"Because Miss Barrington, your mother's family may have the noble lineage to ease both you and your sister's entry into Society," explained Thomas. "Would you repudiate the connection which undoubtedly would please your mama's family or use it to your advantage and their ongoing displeasure?"

Both Arabella's and Rebecca's eyes widened at the notion, and then gleamed in mischief. Arabella took the lead after a nod from her sister and gleefully said, "By all means, Bolton. Let us discover how best my mama's family may help us."

"And your brother as well," he added. "Does Harry know to look for your brother in Cadgwith?"

Rebecca's jaw dropped in astonishment, while Arabella's surprise took the form of a question, "How did you know Harry went to search for Nathaniel?"

Thomas frowned as though working something out in his mind and asked, "Was it a secret? If so, pardon my inquiry."

Rebecca asked nervously, afraid of how much her brother-by-marriage knew, "Did Harry tell you?"

"No," answered Thomas softly before turning to give Arabella a pointed look.

The implication she had revealed where Harry went ignited her temper, especially when she realized she was the culprit. She exclaimed in accusation, "You heard me!"

"I was in your company, Miss Barrington. I was not outside a door straining to hear your conversation. If you meant for your words to be private, then you should have withdrawn from my presence or asked me to leave," rebuked Thomas.

The reference to her own eavesdropping added to her guilt for revealing her sister's request to find Nathaniel. She explained to Rebecca how she had whispered to Harry, never meaning to reveal Harry's purpose and then apologized to her.

"It is of no consequence, Miss Barrington," Thomas stated looking weary from the outburst of female emotions. He had no time for sentimentality. He needed answers if he was to help Harry and stressed to refocus their attentions, "What is important is whether Harry knows where to look for your brother."

Both sisters sobered and nodded in agreement. Rebecca opened her mouth and then paused in thought. Her eyes darted about as if recalling every conversation she ever had with her husband about her family, before saying, "I do not believe I ever mentioned Cadgwith, Bolton, but Harry knows to look on the Cornwall coast."

"Ease your mind, Rebecca," he soothed seeing her creased forehead. "I will send a messenger to direct Harry where to go once I discover where he has settled."

"You think you will hear news soon, Bolton," asked Rebecca anxiously.

"Most assuredly," he replied, his focus turning inward as his brain mulled over the information and voiced his thought, "Did you mention Cadgwith to the runners when they came looking for your brother? We might be on a wild goose chase if they already found him."

Arabella spoke first, "No runners came looking for Nathaniel. Should they have?"

"When did you last see or hear from your brother?" he asked instead of answering her. He did not want to alarm her any more than he had with his careless remark. Was Nathaniel in prison? If so, where was the gossip regarding his capture? The tragic duel was still parlour talk and any news about Nathaniel's capture would have been the latest on dit and if it wasn't, whyever not?

Arabella answered, "I last saw him after he brought Becca into my care. He and papa left directly to call Damburten to account for his villainy."

Thomas asked, "How did you learn of the duel's outcome?"

Arabella's voice dropped in sorrow. She barely rasped the words out as she held back the sob wanting to burst forth, "Papa took the wagon. He had no skill with guns as far as we knew. I never saw him shoot one, though he practiced swordsmanship with Nathaniel. He was a clerk, not a soldier or a gentleman who practiced his accuracy with a target. He might have held his own in a fist fight for he was quite fit, but I don't know if he understood the ramifications of dueling. He only knew honor and love for his daughter demanded he call out Damburten."

"I think he believed Damburten would shoot to wound, not only because dueling is illegal, but because he gave me no fond farewell or instructions on what to do upon his death. Why else would he take the wagon unless he expected to be injured? Nathaniel was in a rage, so I received no direction from him either. I remember my brother sitting tall on his own horse, impatient with our papa to move the wagon forward, or maybe it was because he was taking the wagon and what that might mean."

"We were not *plump in the pocket* as my brother would say, but papa made sure my brother had his own mount as behooved a gentleman. After the duel Nathaniel fled, but he did not leave the city until he found a carter to collect and bring our papa to an undertaker and then home for burial. When the carter arrived he explained he was hired by my brother and then informed me who was in the coffin. We have not heard from Nathaniel since."

Arabella could not withhold her sobs. Her body convulsed. She dropped her head and covered her mouth with her hands when she could not stop her tears from flowing. Rebecca pushed back from her chair and rushed to comfort her sister, her own eyes dripping tears.

Rebecca had not known how much Arabella suffered having to receive and take responsibility for their dead papa. Sadness and guilt assailed her as thoughts of how Damburten's fixation on her had brought nothing but hardship and loss to her family. She dropped to her knees and hugged her sister. Together they cried and consoled one another until Thomas could take no more.

He rang the dinner bell to call the servants to clear their plates and then rose to gather up the sisters. He said, "Why don't we retire to the drawing room and fortify ourselves with a nightcap before retiring for the evening."

His strong and caring voice stilled their tears and Arabella rose, bringing her sister up with her. She apologized, "I am sorry Becca. You should not be on your knees to console me. How are you feeling?"

Through gasping sobs, she replied, "As well as you, dear sister."

Thomas shook his head. He did not like to see women cry. The sight was an abomination and something he took great pains to avoid. He took each sister in hand and escorted them to the drawing room where he situated them on the sofa and then went to the side console table to pour them each a cordial of sherry. He was glad they each had their own linen to swab their tears for he only carried one and he was not sure to whom it should be offered: to his sister-by-marriage or her elder sister. Who took precedence? Surely, Rebecca as a married lady claimed the right of superiority, but he was sure Rebecca would refuse the offer and then emotions would emerge again.

He rolled his eyes at the absurdity of his thoughts and served himself a snifter of brandy and gulped a mouthful before passing out the other drinks. He waited for each sister to sip their cordials before he asked, "Where was the duel fought?"

"In London," answered Arabella. "Damburten fled to his townhome after he assaulted Becca. It was days before I knew what happened. I was in quite a state worrying and then when the carter brought papa home and I saw the coffin in the wagon bed I crumbled. I think my anguish was too much for the man for he was about to unhitch his horse tied to the back of the wagon and take his leave.

"Thankfully, I rallied enough to stop and ask him to take papa to the church cemetery once he spoke with the pastor. My papa and the pastor met regularly to discuss scripture and had become friends, so I knew he would see to papa's burial since I could not leave Becca alone. She was prostrate in bed after her assault.

"The whole time it seemed as if I was in a nightmare from which I could not wake. I was assailed with grief, anger, and helplessness, dealing with Becca's injuries and papa's death. I could not even take the time to mourn him for the creditor's came knocking on our door the moment papa's death was learned and to add to all our burdens, the villagers viciously blamed us for the loss of Damburten's patronage.

"They slandered us and some refused to sell to us. I had no idea how to come about or who to ask for help. There was no word from Nathaniel and it never occurred to me to write our grandpapa for aid. He was an occasional visitor, so it never crossed my mind to ask for his help. I am not sure how we would have managed if not for Harry."

The devastation and sorrow these ladies suffered made Thomas silently vow to never let them suffer again. For the first time, he was glad Harry fell into their world and was there to give them succor. He would stand by them with Harry. The Barrington sisters were now family and under his protection. He would ferret out the secrets and discover whether they were assets or liabilities. He would do whatever it took to ensure Harry was happy and the Barrington sisters were free of worry.

Chapter Fourteen

Bolton's butler entered the dining parlour with a silver salver and Thomas immediately set down his fork next to his plate. Worry over Harry had him grabbing the letter off the plate his servant proffered and breaking the seal without notice of the insignia pressed into the wax.

His butler informed, "A messenger just arrived, my lord. He is in the kitchen breaking his fast awaiting your response should you so desire."

Thomas cloaked his disappointment when he saw the writing was too flowery to be his brother's or one of the grooms he commanded to watch over him. He recognized the script with its teardrop loops belonging to his mother and the letter's signature confirmed it was from her. He took a moment to soothe his frustration knowing Arabella and Rebecca were watching him.

"Is it from Harry?" asked Rebecca anxiously.

Thomas shook his head and he suggested they continue with their morning meal when they looked crestfallen. He reminded them it was too early to hear anything, which Thomas realized was true even though he held vigil for word last night. Sound reasoning reminded him neither Harry nor his grooms would send news if there was nothing to report. Harry would write when he found Nathaniel, while his servants would report once Harry arrived at his destination and began his search.

The grooms he sent were well-trained for covert operations. He recruited them and a number of other veterans after the war ended when many soldiers were looking for work. The men were perfect for the multiple assignments involving reconnaissance, guarding, and delivering the messages he required for his personal and business ventures. His men worked in the stables at his manor and at the mews of his townhome. Thomas had multiple men stationed at various inns along the king's highway, working as grooms so he could relay messages or discharge them at will. He had earned the men's loyalty through fair wages and treatment, so he never worried about them gossiping or accepting bribes about his private affairs.

Thomas returned his attention to his mother's letter and contemplated how best to address her concerns. Her letter troubled him.

Belcrave House, London

Thomas,

I hope this letter finds you and brings you, your brother and his wife to London, post haste! The invitations

to the ball were delivered and are garnering more specu-
lation than responses. "Why did Harry marry the Barring-
ton girl? Wasn't she the one who caused the duel and death
of her papa?"

The gossipmongers are wagging their tongues and I
cannot do anything about it without taking the girl in hand
and introducing her around. I expect she needs to be out-
fitted and coached. The earl is vexed and causing an uproar
in the house calling Harry's wife a country bumpkin without
sense to make a proper curtsey. Is this true? Are we to be
humiliated?

You must bring Harry and his wife immediately. I do
not even know if anyone will come to the ball if I cannot
contrive to present her to a few of our peers and win them
over. I shall never live down the shame should that happen.
Please send a reply with my messenger. I am all asunder.

The Countess of Belcrave,
Your dear mama

"You look concerned, Bolton?" queried Arabella.

Thomas waved the letter and replied, "It is from
my mother. We are running out of time. The invitations to
the ball were delivered and there is still much to do. You
are needed in London, Rebecca."

Rebecca exclaimed, "Not without Harry! He said I
did not have to suffer the Season alone and I will not go to
London without him."

Thomas saw her color rise and feared her pique
might hurt the baby. He soothed, "Be calm. If you won't go

without Harry to London, then I shall retrieve him. Will you put your quest in my hands to relieve Harry of his promise to you?"

"I can't," answered Rebecca. "It is a private matter that only Harry can fulfill."

"Then, we are in dire consequences, Rebecca," he replied sharply. "If I don't get you to Town to be outfitted and introduced to key members of the *ton* to counter the gossip feeding the rumour mill, then the embarrassment my mother suffers will never be reconciled. Any chance of a favorable relationship with her and my father will be doomed."

"Becca," suggested Arabella. "What if I went with Bolton so Harry could return to you? I could speak to Nathaniel privately on your behalf instead of Harry. I am already in your confidence and would not betray it."

Thomas stared wide-eyed at Arabella. His nostrils flared as if she had just spoken impudently. He said, "If I didn't know better I would say you were trying to entrap me into an offer of marriage."

Arabella gaped and then snapped her mouth closed forcing her lips to turn down and her eyebrows to scrunch. She admonished in a temper, "You would be lucky if I ever accepted an offer from you!" Then, like the mimes that wave their hand across their face to change their expression, Arabella laughed and exclaimed, "Heavens be! Bolton, you have a way of vexing me. I have no designs on you, so put your wild presumptions to rest. I am trying to ease Becca's mind. Surely, there is a way for us to travel together without impugning any of our reputations. Why I have been traveling with you this whole time!"

"Yes," he replied with impatience, "but your sister and Harry were with us which made it respectable. I cannot travel days with you without a family member at hand. Your reputation would be ruined."

"And yours elevated, no doubt." Arabella heard her sister gasp at her audacity, but she was too distracted to acknowledge she had spoken brazenly. She chewed her lips in thought, her eyes racing as if searching the corners of her mind for an idea when her face broke a smile.

"Well," sighed Thomas having taken no affront this time to her impudence. He was getting used to her bold retorts and was more interested to discover what notion had risen in her mind to make her smile. "What hare-brained idea are you ready to suggest?"

"But, Bella," whined Rebecca. "I thought you would be by my side as Harry's mama launched me? How can you leave me when I need you most?"

"Becca," replied Arabella. "I am serving you a high-er purpose. Remember, our mama brought us up proper and we are more than capable to socialize with any peer. We are no country bumpkins. Besides, Harry will be with you and once they see the two of you together no one will ever doubt your marriage is anything but a love-match."

Thomas was impressed. The Barrington sisters would fare well if they considered themselves equal to any lady in society. Those that felt inferior were treated poorly, but if these sisters could give as good as they got, then they might very well succeed, much like Beau Brummel who came from humble means and came to call the Prince Regent his friend. Hauteur was respected among the *ton.*

"I will do it," proclaimed Rebecca sitting a bit taller in her seat after heeding her sister's words. "I will show everyone we are equal in manner to any lady."

He was glad he did not have to finagle Rebecca's compliance and hoped his sister-by-marriage would put sense into Arabella's notion to travel with him. He needed to get Rebecca to entrust him to find her brother and then learn whatever secret he held.

Rebecca's expression turned from excited to concern as she asked Thomas, "but who will accompany me if you are to travel with Bella? Surely, I will not stay alone overnight at an inn?"

"Indeed, not!" exclaimed Thomas. "Harry would skin me alive," he added half in jest. "No, I will ask the pastor's wife to act as companion for both you and Miss Barrington. She has a sister who lives in London and would consider it a great boon to accompany you both."

Arabella asked, "Bolton, why can't you acquire another respectable lady so we can travel together?"

"Because, Miss Barrington," Thomas replied in a sigh, vexed he had to repeat himself, "It is not respectable. Besides, I travel to find your brother who is wanted for murder. I do not think it wise to announce my quest for anyone to relay. I, for one, have no desire to place myself before a board of inquiry for aiding and abetting a fugitive."

"Dear me, Bolton," responded Arabella. "I was not thinking clearly. Then, it seems my plan is the best. I shall travel with you disguised as a man."

Rebecca and Thomas both shouted simultaneously, "What?!"

Arabella opened her mouth to explain, but Thomas held his hand up and ordered, "Stop! I have no time for such foolishness. I must write and send out messages and then speak with Mademoiselle Lavigne regarding her immediate departure. I will select a pattern for your ball gowns and have her begin to make them the moment she returns to Town." Arabella steeled her eyes at him, prompting Thomas to add, "With your permission, of course."

Arabella again opened her mouth to speak, but he stopped her as if he knew what she was about to say. He remarked in an amused voice, "I did ask, Miss Barrington."

"No!" exclaimed Arabella. "You informed, Bolton, but do as you must for I know you will."

Rebecca chastised, "Bella, where have your manners gone? Forgive her impertinence, Bolton. We are all anxious. However, we appreciate your beneficence and thank you for your generosity."

"Oh!" gasped Arabella and then apologized, "Indeed, Bolton, pardon my outburst."

"Meet me in one hour in my office for I need answers to questions I believe will aid me in finding your brother," he ordered the sisters and then left.

Rebecca looked at her sister wide-eyed as if she had just seen an apparition. "Bella," she asked, "did I not make myself clear that I would not entrust him to speak to Nathaniel?"

Arabella soothed, "Yes, you did, but do not concern yourself. I WILL accompany Bolton for I will do as I must. He will see us stand firm when we meet with him in an hour." Arabella saw her sister's expression wane. "What is it Becca?"

Her voice trembling, she asked, "What if someone forces their attentions on me in London?"

"You will have the earl's protection and with Harry by your side, no one would dare accost you, but I will ask Bolton for some defensive moves. I did not have the opportunity before."

"Will he grant this request made of him, Bella? He does not seem to be in the most accommodating mood right now."

Arabella grinned for she liked it best when she could match wits with Bolton. "Let us finish eating and then we can discuss how best to proceed."

Thomas pressed his signet ring onto the hot red wax to seal his letter and sat back in his chair at his desk.

He finished his mother's letter, but needed to write a line or two more to his secretary before he sealed it. His man needed to know where to send his report and he realized he had no idea where he would be.

He might well be back in London by the time his secretary completed his investigation into the warrant against Nathaniel Barrington and to the death of Damburten. He could not remember any particulars on the duel, other than the gossip painting Nathaniel as a bereaved son. Damburten had not taken his mandatory ten steps before turning to set and fire. He had turned early and shot Barrington in the back. The shot was fatal and Nathaniel ran to his father's body, picked up his pistol and shot Damburten dead, so the rumours went.

He picked up the letter addressed to his mother and tapped it against the desk. She would not be happy to learn Rebecca came alone, without benefit of Harry or himself, but at least she would have her daughter-by-marriage in hand. She would see for herself Rebecca was far from a country bumpkin.

He grinned realizing his sister-by-marriage was someone his mother might have selected for him if Rebecca owned a title and wealth. After all, she was pretty, petite, and shy; alluding she would make an obedient wife. He did not think obedience was a trait the Barrington sisters had in their gene pool. They seemed to do as they pleased, ignoring convention to live on their own and managing their property until Harry came into the picture.

Arabella and Rebecca insisted there was no one for them to turn, but indeed, they had a grandfather and uncles, who based on past generosities, would have at a minimum offered guidance if not their home for them to live. After all, the Barrington property came through the Barrington line and most probably, the grandfather had a hand in his youngest son inheriting it. How else could the youngest son receive preference over older sons?

There were mysteries in the family history where the solving of them would come at a later time. For now, his focus was on retrieving Harry and getting him to London to aid his wife. They needed to win the earl's favor. Harry might have forgotten about his trust fund, but Thomas knew the caveat attached to it which required their father's approval should Harry wed before he turned five and twenty

The requirement had not been an issue for Thomas since he was single when he came of age, but Harry placed himself in a predicament by marrying without notice or approval. If the earl wished he could withhold Harry's money and cause his brother a lot of trouble. He tapped his mother's letter again hoping she heeded his words.

Bolton Manor

The Countess of Belcrave; my dear mama,

Harry's wife, Rebecca, and do be sure to reference her by name when you meet, shall arrive in my crested traveling coach, with all the pomp and circumstance my title behooves. Harry and I will arrive later as we are

charged with an urgent duty. Try to remember Harry's and Rebecca's marriage is a love-match, and if you wish to remain in Harry's good graces, I suggest you treat Rebecca as if she was your own. I will also be discontented to discover if she was made to feel anything but welcome.

Rebecca will surprise you, Mother. She is quite lovely and her manners are nothing but graceful. She is a bit fearful of being presented to our lofty peerage, but be assured she will rise to the occasion. She has fortitude and remarkable compassion that will win you and your peers over. Do as you must to coach her, but do not presume she is ignorant of how a lady should behave.

I have taken the liberty to commission her ball gown with Madame Lavigne. The modiste will request a time for Rebecca's fitting. Tell Father to be on his best behavior and assure him he may trust my judgment to call Rebecca family.

Viscount Bolton, your son,
Thomas

A soft rap brought his attention from his letter to the door where the Barrington ladies stood. Arabella asked when he looked up, "May we enter, Bolton?"

"Please," he replied. Thomas rose and waved his hand to the seats before the desk. Each lady took a seat and the moment he sat, Arabella asked, "Bolton, I know you have questions, but I have a request I would like to make first, so the opportunity to do so does not pass."

"By all means," responded Thomas wearily.

"Well, you see," began Arabella. "Becca and I would like you to instruct us on some defensive moves. I would like to know the strategy you used in bringing that man at the inn who accosted me to heel. I think it might prove useful to both Becca and me."

Of all the requests, this one for defensive techniques would have never crossed Thomas' mind. He was so astounded it took him a minute to reply. "May I ask why you feel the need for such instruction? I assure you I will have your journey guarded and while in London, you may take comfort to know you will be under the earl's protection."

Arabella sighed and then said, "Bolton, I had both you and Harry for protection when we traveled, but that did not halt the indignities that man did to my person before you intervened."

Thomas's head jerked as if struck and then he retorted, "Might I remind, you refused my escort to your room. Had you allowed me to accompany you that man would never have laid a hand on you!"

Arabella's lips flattened and her nostrils flared in temper. She railed, "That is not the point!"

Rebecca intervened, seeing rising tempers and in a soft voice said, "Excuse me, Bolton. I do not think my sister meant to complain. On the contrary, she was quite praiseworthy of your actions and both of us are grateful for all you have done. May we impose upon you one more time? Please teach us some tactics to make us feel safe?"

Thomas' temper cooled immediately. Of course, they felt vulnerable having lost their father and brother. He shook his head. He could not believe how easily he let Miss Barrington rile him. He apologized and then suggested, "Let me find an instructor when I return to London who knows what to teach you. Rest assured you will be guarded throughout your stay in London."

"Why can't you teach us to bend back a man's finger?" asked Arabella. "I am sure I could do it."

Thomas sighed and explained, "Miss Barrington, I admit I did bring that cad to heel and could have easily broken the man's finger if he did not subsist. However, there were other variables that played a part in my success. For instance, I took the man by surprise. Then, my title made him consider the consequences of retaliating against a lord, as did the threat of informing his father about his ungentlemanly behavior. I also have other means available to me to ensure the man's compliance, including brute strength. None of these resources are yours to dispose. Even if you were able to get his finger into a tortuous position, what then? What happens when your strength wanes and you cannot keep him at bay? All you would have done is anger your assailant."

"Is there nothing a female can do to protect herself sans keeping a weapon?" asked Rebecca.

"You must be vigilant. Always stay in sight of your chaperone. Do not go anywhere without benefit of a family member or stout footman. Never enter a carriage that is not your own with your own servants. Never venture, even if others do, without your own guard. These are all lessons every debutante learns and are expected to adhere to protect their innocence. I know it is not what you asked. However, if you are being manhandled then strike for any central body part and run. Jam the heel of your hand at your villain's nose. Poke at his eyes. Box his ears. Punch him in the stomach. Kick him in the groin, the knees. Stomp on his foot. Do whatever it takes to break his hold of you and then run to safety. Never engage to battle your assailant, but to escape him."

There were gasps by the Barrington sisters as visions of his tutorial emerged. Thomas quickly apologized for being brutally honest, but before he could beg their forgiveness, Arabella asked, "Can you show us? Can we practice?"

"Please?" seconded Rebecca.

Thomas shook his head and then chuckled. He had thought to deter them with his graphic response and instead he rallied them. He said, "Meet me on the back lawn in one hour. Before then, I have business to conclude and a modiste to see off.

The ladies rose and left.

Thomas stared nonplussed at the door from which they made their exit. He had not asked his questions, nor gained his answers.

Chapter Fifteen

Tap, tap, tap, tap. Rebecca was in Bolton's crested carriage and as it began to slow her legs shook causing her heels to tap the floor in a rapid beat. She was frightened beyond her wits and the tapping did little to soothe her. If anything, her heartbeat increased to keep time with the tempo. She was about to meet Harry's parents and she had no idea how she would be greeted.

The pastor's wife had put all types of ideas in her head during their journey, from the whole staff waiting on the front steps to present themselves, as they did for Bolton when he returned to his manor, to her cooling her heels in a parlour waiting upon the earl's convenience. She was not even sure if the butler would let her in the front door. *Did Bolton's letter announcing my arrival precede me?*

How she wished her sister was with her, but Arabella was making her way with Bolton to retrieve Harry and to find Nathaniel. The recollection of Bolton's outrage when Arabella proclaimed neither of them would assist him in finding Nathaniel unless she could accompany him, distracted Rebecca from her mounting fear. The picture of Bolton and Arabella in battle made her grin. How they loved to engage and fight to gain the upper hand. Thomas eventually conceded Arabella could accompany him, but he refused her suggestion she dress as a gentleman to protect her reputation.

Instead, Bolton leant his elder sister's married name to her. Lady Margaret MacDougall lived in Scotland and had not returned to participate in a London Season since the year she married. No one would recall his sister's looks and he was confident since Arabella owned the same brown hair of his family they could easily pull off the ruse. Besides, he remarked after a thought, *"Who will we run into requiring an introduction?"*

The coach's abrupt stop caused Rebecca to cling to her seat dispersing her thoughts as her body jolted forward. She grabbed her straw bonnet from the seat next to her and quickly readied herself to exit by putting it on and tying the satin ribbons under her chin. She caught sight of her gloves and almost sobbed to see them saturated with perspiration. Out of sheer panic she ran them over the coach's squab and then dropped her jaw in mortification to see she had left a wet streak. She could only hope it did not leave a stain.

She came to London in Bolton's crested coach with a number of guards flanking it as if she was royalty. She even had one liveried footman, riding atop with the coachman, who was assigned specifically for her safety and comfort. His name was James and he was all consideration, having the coach make extra stops knowing her condition required her to use the privy more often than normal. Thomas had commanded his servant to stand her guard unless she was in her private room or in the company of family. He was to remain in her service until Harry returned. It seemed Thomas had heeded her concerns and took a pragmatic approach to easing her fears. The door opened and Rebecca took a deep breath, before stretching her hand out for James to help her step down from the coach.

There were no servants on the steps awaiting her arrival and for that she released a sigh of relief. The massive three story white mansion boasted of Roman pillars, and on each floor there were multiple windows with pediments. She dropped her head back to take it all in, while James hurried up the steps to drop the lion's head brass doorknocker to announce her arrival. The door opened and after James passed a few words with the butler, he beckoned her forward.

Drawing on her courage, she lifted her head, climbed up the front steps and passed James to enter the townhome as if she was used to having a servant announce her arrival. She almost gaped and stumbled at the opulence greeting her. The polished floor glistened in large checkered white and black tiles. An enormous vase filled with an assortment of flowers topped the center of an exotic amboyna and giltwood round table. The expensive furnishing made of imported wood was undoubtedly placed in the entry hall to impress arriving guests. At the front of the large table was a stack of calling cards in a silver salver with the card of their most eminent caller displayed on top. Overhead hung a large crystal chandelier and painted on the ceiling was a heavenly scene of trumpeting angels.

She forced herself not to swing her head like a pendulum for the severe butler watched her as if she might walk away with one of the silver and gilded trinkets displayed on the round table. The curios looked like snuff boxes in various shapes and designs, perhaps gifts from their guests. All of a sudden she felt gauche having not brought something for her hosts, but then she dismissed the notion since neither she nor Harry had the means to procure one. Besides, if it was necessary she was confident Bolton would have sent one with her. She removed her bonnet and handed it to the butler before inquiring to the location of his master. The butler took her hat and raised one brow at her.

Rebecca was nonplus on what to do until James cleared his throat. She looked at him and he looked at her coat which made her realize the butler waited for her to remove her redingote and her gloves. She quickly took off her gloves and thrust them into her coat's pocket before unbuttoning the garment and turning to allow the servant to pull it from her shoulders.

The butler handed her things over to an underling who stood nearby before requesting she follow him. He stopped abruptly when James also followed and raised his brow again. James waved him on and suffered an "hmmrf," for his impertinence. The butler led them to a set of egg-shell painted pinewood doors adorned with gilt-bordered panels and turned the gilded knobs to open them. Then, with a sweep of his arm, he directed Rebecca to precede him into a large drawing room.

The expansive room glittered with gilded furniture and gilt-framed paintings and mirrors on its walls. Laurel leaves and fans were sculpted in the furniture's wooden frames and carved into the arms and legs were lion's heads. All the furniture was upholstered in green brocade.

The walls were papered in cream silk and squared off with narrow gilded mouldings sculpted with laurel leaves where within their framed centers hung either a painting or mirror. There were two large pane windows draped in heavy green velveteen curtains topped with matching swag valances. The large Aubusson carpet, made of blue, green, and gold threads bearing the Belcrave crest at its center, covered the floor.

Rebecca looked up as if angels called out to her and saw another glorious heaven, painted on the high plastered ceiling and bordered with a moulding of gilded medallions. She had never seen such opulence and the sense of being out of her depth quickly overwhelmed her. She made her way to the nearest scrolled sofa before she swooned and looked to ask the butler for refreshment. To her disappointment, the servant was gone.

Her lower back hurt and her ankles were swollen. She would be sorely pressed when she arrived at Belcrave House if not for the succor given by the sister of the pastor's wife. James saw her distress and offered to seek out the housekeeper on her behalf, but she stayed him. She remembered Bolton's advice, "Begin as you mean to go on. Do not cower. The weak are preyed upon; especially among the peerage. Know your worth and behave in the manner you wish to be treated." She asked what he meant and after a long exhalation, he simplified, "If you want to be treated as a member of the peerage then act like one."

With renewed determination she asked James to pull the bell cord. She was glad she had spent days at Bolton's Manor for it introduced her to the many luxuries the aristocracy enjoyed and one was commanding the service of a tea tray and sandwiches. By the time, the butler returned, her temper was piqued. Again, she was glad to know what to expect which was speedier service than what was being offered her. Upon the servant's entry, she rose and demanded, "I am ready to retire. Take me to Harry's suite and send a tray of tea and sandwiches to me immediately. I will need a maid to assist me and I want my footman properly fed and shown to his quarters."

The supercilious butler remarked in as much hauteur as he dared, "The earl left no orders for me, madam, instructing me to do so."

Rebecca raised her chin and steeled her eyes. She chastised, "Do you dare to refuse the order of Mrs. Harry Bolton? Say so, and I will retire myself to Bolton's townhome, but rest assured the earl and countess will hear of this impudence and learn I will only be appeased by your dismissal!"

The butler's eyes widened and his face paled, but before he could determine what to do, a voice called from behind him. "Do as she says, Dawson."

Dawson turned and said to the earl's daughter, "As you wish, my lady."

"No," Charlotte replied, "It is as she wishes and I suggest you take heed the next time you question a family member."

Dawson said to Rebecca, "This way if you please, madam."

Charlotte instructed, "Have her bags placed in the Garden Suite instead of Harry's. It is larger and has the better view. Tell Mary the First she will be her personal maid, and be sure to order her some food and see to her footman's comfort. I will escort Harry's wife myself after we have introduced ourselves to one another."

The butler gave his nod, asked James his name and then instructed him to follow. James replied, "I will see my mistress settled first."

Angered, the butler chided, "I command the servants here and you will do as I say or I shall have you turned out."

James replied without hesitation, "I answer only to the viscount and the lady if her directives do not conflict with my master. Turn me out and you turn out my mistress."

Amused, Charlotte asked of Rebecca, "Is this so?"

Blushing, Rebecca confirmed, "Indeed, Bolton is a most protective brother and has sent me here with all the pomp and circumstance deserving of an earl's daughter-by-marriage."

Charlotte laughed as she addressed the butler, "Well then, see to your other duties, Dawson, while James sees to his own. I will send him to the kitchen once Harry's wife is settled." Turning to Rebecca she said, "How shall I address you? I cringe to call you Mrs. Bolton and I cannot keep referring to you as Harry's wife!"

"I am Rebecca," she replied with a smile, "though my family calls me Becca. You must be Charlotte or Charly as Harry calls you."

Charlotte, like her brother Harry, had brown hair and hazel eyes, but where Harry's features were very masculine, Charlotte's features were feminine and pretty. She had high cheekbones, a straight narrow nose and heart shaped lips. Her round eyes reminded Rebecca of Harry for they sparkled with laughter and were beautifully framed with thick lashes and arching brows. Charlotte was of average height, slender in form and held herself as one who did not care what other's thought.

"Do not let the earl or countess hear you address me so," laughed Charlotte. "They will turn beet red hearing the misnomer my brothers laid at my feet for always wanting to play in their games when I was a youngster. They always told me, 'act like a boy and we will call you one.'"

Rebecca chuckled and asked, "Are the earl and countess at home?"

Charlotte frowned and replied, "No. I hope you did not believe they would not greet you. Papa is doing his duty in Parliament and mama is no doubt making the rounds to pave the way for your introduction. I do not believe she expected your arrival until tomorrow, or else Dawson would have been apprised this morning to expect you. I was in the process of dressing or else I would have welcomed you sooner. You must forgive Dawson," she added soberly. "He takes his duties as gatekeeper quite seriously."

Rebecca frowned so Charlotte added, "Do not judge him or us harshly, but you would be surprised how many people with nothing to recommend them wish to impose themselves on my mama and papa."

Rebecca responded wearily, "Forgive me, Charlotte, for appearing judgmental. I am truly tired and only seek a bed."

"Oh, my goodness," replied Charlotte. "You must find me a poor host, indeed. Let me show you to your room. I am sure Mary the First awaits you in your chamber."

Charlotte eagerly took Rebecca's hand and pulled her out of the drawing room to lead her to the prominent horseshoe stairs in the entry hall. James watched out for her as she climbed the stairs, ready to catch her if she fell. As they ascended, Rebecca asked Charlotte, "Why Mary the First? Is that her name?"

"Oh, no!" Charlotte exclaimed, "She is simply Mary, but we have more than one, so whenever we summon one, we differentiate them by attaching a number. Mary the First was our first Mary. She is also our most skilled at being a lady's maid. You will share her with mama and like her for she seems to know what you need before you even know it."

Rebecca nodded. She feared she was about to fall asleep before she even reached her bed. By the time she was in her room Charlotte's voice was unintelligible. She never heard her sister-by-marriage or James take their leave, nor the door close. Her dress fell to her feet when without instruction Mary the First took charge. The last thing she remembered was taking a deep sigh when her head hit her pillow.

Rebecca woke, having slept through the evening and opened her eyes to a sunlit room. She paid close attention to her body. She hated the surge of nausea that hit her every time she woke in the morning. The queasiness never occurred after an afternoon nap and she could not understand why there was a difference. *Would I suffer in the morning if I never slept during the night? How nice it would be to have my mama around to tell me what to expect?*

She grinned at the notion of asking Harry's mama and then another thought made her mortified. *Heavens be! I missed last night's dinner to meet Harry's parents. Fine impression my absence made.*

Rebecca almost jumped out of bed in order to extend her apologies to the countess, but her better sense took command and she reassessed her body. To her amazement, she was hungry, not queasy. She placed her hand on her stomach to settle the rumblings and her eyes widened in surprise. There was a bulge or more specific, a baby. Until this morning, there had been no visible sign of her pregnancy, aside from morning sickness. Oh, how she wished Harry was here to witness the miracle of this moment and then it hit her how she was truly alone for neither was Arabella nearby to share in her revelation.

She sat up slowly and took inventory of her surroundings and delight marked her expression. *What a beautiful room!* The suite was large with multiple windows dressed in heavy green damask drapes pulled to the side with tiebacks and topped with a boxed valance. The upper part of the walls were silk papered with mint green stripes, while the bottom half was paneled with rich wood.

There was a tall boy, a dresser, a full-length cheval mirror, a toilette table, a desk with chair, a chaise lounge and the four poster bed from where she took stock of her room. She brushed the satiny bed cover made of the same material used for the curtains and upholstery. Every piece of furniture was beautifully appointed with carvings, inlaid woods, and ornate brass fixtures.

Rebecca saw other furnishings through the door's opening giving evidence her room was part of a suite. She liked how she and Harry could indulge in an intimate dinner or meet company in the privacy of their own room

if they wished. She sighed, longing for the company of her husband. How she missed him and his touch. She missed the way he made her smile with his teasing manner and the way he eased her burdens with his assurances.

Sadness began to overcome her, so she pushed the covers aside and swung her legs off the bed to rise. She would not dwell on missing Harry, but would endeavor to nurture a happy household for him to enter and not one divided because she failed to win his parents over. She would begin by offering an apology for missing last night's dinner.

She wore an old dress that did not necessitate the aid of a maid to button her up for she did not want to reveal her *enceinte* state before Harry arrived. At a time when she preferred comfort to fashion, she was glad she thought to bring the well-used garment. Bolton, no doubt, believed the Barringtons' old wardrobe was discarded, but Rebecca had hid one away for comfort's sake.

Once dressed, she felt foolish for not ringing for Mary the First to attend her since the maid had undressed her the night before. Hopefully, the servant took no note of her abdomen's small bulge and would credit her new mistress with only being plump. Now, she worried the maid would take offense for not being called to service.

Bolton's staff had been prickly whenever she or her sister did for themselves. She decided her best plan to keep from offending her maid was to search out her own meal so Mary did not discover she had dressed herself. She headed for the main staircase and upon spying a footman

inquired where she might go to break her fast. The servant looked at her as if she was joking, but when she prodded, he led her to the dining parlour where a number of silver sterling covered trays were on a side console. The footman suggested he pass on her preferences to the cook for surely everything on the table was cold, but Rebecca waved him off and said, "Perhaps, tomorrow I will send forth my order, but for now all I require is some bread and whatever else I might find under a cover."

Rebecca was sure she just committed her first error, but she was too hungry to give it much consideration. She saw the footman take his leave and then turned to inspect her offerings. She quickly put a slice of ham between two slices of bread made fashionable by the Earl of Sandwich when he refused to leave his card playing to take a meal.

She took a healthy bite, and feeling it settle in her stomach, made herself another and wrapped it in a serviette. She pushed the linen wrapped food into her skirt pocket and took another bite from the sandwich she held. Knowing no one was about, she walked on to explore the first floor and learn the layout of the mansion. There was no better time to take her inspection than when her hosts were out. She remembered the earl spent his days in Parliament and the countess made her rounds visiting friends.

She was passing the gilded doors of the drawing room where she was made to cool her heels the day before when she heard voices. *Did I err? Is the countess home?*

She quickly stuffed the last bite of her bread and ham sandwich into her mouth and wiped her hands on her skirt. She chewed in earnest to swallow the huge morsel. Her cheeks bulged with food as she readied to greet the countess whose voice she heard nearing the drawing room doors, but before they opened, she was pulled and shut into a nearby closet. Frightened, she began to push on the door. A clear "Shush!" kept her still. She pressed her ear to the door and recognized the voice of Harry's sister.

"What am I doing?" Charlotte echoed in response to the question put to her by her mother. Rebecca waited anxiously for Harry's sister to answer.

Chapter Sixteen

Rebecca pressed her ear further into the closet door to hear the exchange between Charlotte and the countess. The leaning caused her feet to slowly slide out from under her and bring her bum to the ground. She placed her hand on the door to aid her rise, but before she could stand, the door opened and she tumbled forward as if she had been stuffed into the closet and was now released.

Charlotte caught and steadied her; then pulled Rebecca's arm to drag her away as if the house was on fire and she was leading her to safety. Rebecca tripped after Charlotte, not having the breath to ask where they were going.

She barreled into Charlotte's back when Charlotte abruptly stopped to open a hidden hallway door. Before she could ask where the door led, Charlotte pulled her into the dark passage and up a wooden staircase, holding onto her as if Charlotte thought Rebecca would flee.

Charlotte towed Rebecca until they were inside Rebecca's private suite and then she railed, "I cannot believe Mary the First dressed you this morning! Nor can I believe the other option where Mary did not answer your call to help you dress. What were you thinking to wander the first floor looking as if you had just rolled out of bed with clothes from the rag bin?"

Charlotte did not wait for Rebecca to answer and went to the wall to pull the bell cord to ring for the maid. Without a by-your-leave, she returned to remove Rebecca's dress. Rebecca was used to Arabella helping her undress, so Charlotte's maneuverings did not confound or embarrass her. Even her reference of her dress being a rag did not disconcert her. What had her wide-eyed and fretting was the notion the sandwich stored in her pocket was about to be squashed and crumbled. Her stomach grumbled as if in concurrence with her worry and she quickly thrust her hand into her pocket to retrieve her morning meal. To Charlotte's amazement, Rebecca jammed the sandwich into her mouth and took a huge bite. Her cheeks bulged and her eyes rolled up in gratitude.

"For heaven's sake," scolded Charlotte. "You cannot possibly be that hungry."

Rebecca took another mouthful and shook her head up and down to argue the point. She chewed until the sandwich was gone, making little mewling sounds of enjoyment. Charlotte watched in amazement and then her eyes widened at the revelation of why Rebecca was downstairs, she shouted, "Good heavens! Is that why you went downstairs dishabille?"

"I was perfectly dressed," Rebecca replied after her last swallow.

"I shall not argue with you," rebutted Charlotte as she tugged Rebecca's dress down over her shoulders to pool at her feet. "However, you will not earn mama's favor if you go about in such a fashion. Consider the first floor open for public inspection. You never know who mama or papa may be entertaining or who may stop by without warning; especially when it is mama's at-home day."

Rebecca asked, "What is an 'at-home' day?"

"It is the day mama stays home to receive visitors and return the hospitality she received when she called on others during the week. You should always dress as if you are going out if you wish to wander downstairs. Otherwise, there is a small parlour at the end of this floor where you may dress informally." After a pause, Charlotte asked, "Why do you even own a dress that looks like it was pulled from a rag bin?"

Rebecca frowned and answered, "It is still quite serviceable. Besides, it is soft and comfortable, unlike my new dresses which are fitted to my figure. I thought I was adequately dressed for staying indoors."

"You will have to rethink your notions," remarked Charlotte. The door opened and Mary the First entered. Charlotte ordered, "Mary, help me dress Rebecca and style her hair. Mama is anxious to meet her and present her to her friends who are beating a path to our door. Someone has let the cat out of the bag and it seems Rebecca's presence is widely known."

"Oh dear!" cried Rebecca. "How could that be? I only arrived yesterday?"

"No doubt one of the servants remarked to another household's servant," replied Charlotte.

Rebecca's face paled and Charlotte scolded her to be calm and not swoon. Then, she turned her attention to Mary and asked, "What dress does she have to wear, Mary? Is there anything to not put mama into an apoplexy?"

Mary pulled a floral pink muslin dress from the dresser and showed it to Charlotte who said, "Oh, indeed! That will do nicely." Charlotte took a seat using the time Mary dressed Rebecca to offer some sage advice. "Sleeping away the morning is quite *de riguer* among the *ton*, but sleeping through the afternoon is suspect. Mama insisted I smell your breath. She is under the misimpression you overly imbibe. I tried to assure her you were simply wearied from your travels, but mama's imagination can be easily sparked, especially when Mary the Second reported she could not wake you this morning. 'Out like the drunks,' she said.'"

Rebecca laughed and then her shoulders were pulled back as Mary struggled to close some of her back buttons as her bosom was fuller since her last fitting. She flattened her lips together considering what she should do and settled with offering the easiest and direct solution, "I suggest you loosen the tapes on the sides." Her remark captured Charlotte's attention and Harry' sister rose from her seat to come and inspect the tapes Rebecca referenced.

"How clever!" exclaimed Charlotte. "I have never seen anything of the sort. Does your weight fluctuate often?" Alarmed, she asked, "Heavens be! Do not tell me you subscribe to those purging toxins to reduce your weight?"

Rebecca was sure Mary the First was familiar with the use of tapes to expand the girth of a dress for her stoic expression did not alter when Charlotte voiced her outrageous query. Rebecca did not want to lie or prevaricate with Charlotte. Harry's sister had been nothing but kind to her and she did not want to break the burgeoning trust between them; especially when the truth was soon to be revealed. She confessed, "You are to be an aunt, Charlotte. I hoped to keep it a secret until Harry arrived, so please keep my confidence until he speaks with your parents."

Charlotte jumped up and down in excitement clapping her hands as if she was applauding the end of a performance. "Oh! Of course, I will keep your confidence," she exclaimed and then went and hugged Rebecca, remarking, "How perfectly marvelous. Of course my elder sister has a bevy of unruly imps living in the savages of Scotland, but I rarely get to see them. It will be nice to hover around Harry's little one. You will buy property close to Belcrave, won't you?"

"Buy?" asked Rebecca.

"Once Harry gets his trust money," Charlotte explained. "I will get great satisfaction watching all those debs who shunned Harry in order to cast their lures at Tommy."

Rebecca smiled and asked, "You call Bolton, Tommy, too?" Then, the rest of what Charlotte revealed resonated and she frowned learning her husband had been rejected as an eligible suitor. "There were ladies who shunned my husband? Were they cruel to Harry?"

Rebecca's face had turned ferocious and Charlotte laughed. "Oh! How I adore you! I am glad Harry found someone who recognizes his noble and wonderful traits."

"I do not understand," asked Rebecca. "How could anyone be cruel to Harry? He is amazingly kind and handsome and a myriad of other traits I love about him."

"Oh, it is not him exactly," explained Charlotte. "It is just the way of the *ton* to aspire for title and wealth in a marriage. Harry is a second son with nothing to recommend him in terms of title and property. I doubt they knew of his trust and may not have forgotten his ridiculous attempt at dandyism when he first made his debut. Even you would have been appalled at the outlandish clothes and affected speech he used."

"Oh," Rebecca laughed. "He told me about it himself. You should see him cringe every time he recalls his salad days. I wish he would have kept one of his tailcoats. I would have liked to have seen him dressed in puce."

Charlotte laughed and Rebecca joined in. They were in a state of near hysterics when the countess walked in.

"What in the world is going on?!" exclaimed the Countess of Belcrave.

Charlotte scolded, "Oh, mama! Do not look so fierce for you will surely scare Rebecca!"

Emily Bolton, the Countess of Belcrave waved off her daughter's exclamation as nothing but theatrics. She was an elegant lady, still owning the beauty and figure that beguiled and brought up to scratch the then Viscount Bolton. Both Harry and Charlotte favored her in their features. Like them, she had brown hair, hazel eyes, high cheekbones and a straight narrow nose.

She walked forward and inspected her new daughter-by-marriage. It was obvious she was wary of the woman who had captured her son's heart; so much so, he had not bothered to seek his parents' approval or even inform them of his marriage until months after the so called "happy event."

The secretive nature of their marriage was enough to concern her, but in addition there was the scandal attached to the Barrington name. Emily did not know what to think, but she had no choice other than to take the chit in hand to make sure scandal and gossip did not tarnish the Belcrave dynasty. In a tone demanding obedience, she chastised her daughter, "Your manners, Charlotte. I have not yet had the pleasure of an introduction."

"I beg your pardon, mama," Charlotte apologized. "May I present Mrs. Harry Bolton, previously known as Miss Rebecca Barrington and whom her family addresses as Becca." Turning to Rebecca she continued, "Rebecca, my mama, Lady Emily Bolton, The Countess of Belcrave."

Rebecca curtsied and replied, "My lady."

Emily sighed. She did not have the time to ask the myriad of questions she wished of Harry's wife. Her son Thomas supported the marriage and the viscount was no fool. Harry, on the other hand, was known to act foolishly and it would not surprise her to learn he rushed into marriage to save the girl from some unknown circumstance as he had a habit of befriending and caring for those in need.

Thomas said Rebecca would surprise her and she hoped it was in a good way. At least, Rebecca knew how to address her betters. The rest would surface as needs be and she would deal with it as she must. She only hoped a son's broken heart was not in the mix. She sighed again at the enormity of what was being asked of her and scolded herself for conjecturing problems.

She had too much to do to worry over things out of her control. Shaking off her troubling thoughts, she said to Rebecca, "Unfortunately, there is no time for civilities. It is the social hour and we must make an appearance at the park." To her daughter she ordered, "Fetch your new poke bonnet, Charlotte. The one with the pink ribbons and bring your pink satin slippers and a pair of your new gloves."

Charlotte asked, "But, why mama?"

"We must make do with what we have for Harry's wife until we can purchase all that is needed to launch her."

"But mama," countered Charlotte. "I do not even know if my shoes will fit her."

"It does not matter; she will manage as many before her have done."

Rebecca interjected, "I have a bonnet, gloves, and shoes, my lady."

"As I have seen and fear must not be seen by others," retorted the countess with a frown. To her daughter, she added to her list of collectables, "Bring my pink fringed India silk shawl from my room, too."

By the time Charlotte returned, Mary the First finished styling Rebecca's hair and the items retrieved by Charlotte were put on her. Her spectators complimented her good looks and a glimpse in her cheval mirror confirmed they spoke truthfully.

"Come along, Charlotte," ordered her mother. "I will need you to run interference if anyone dares to seek answers to which I do not yet know."

"But mama, I am not out," she reminded.

"There is no lack in propriety for a daughter to ride with her mama through the park. I will inform every gentleman we meet how you will not make your debut until next Season which will check their behavior. However, I am counting on you to talk of the weather and any other dull subject to interrupt any line of questioning delving into Harry's wife's background."

"Mama," chastised Charlotte. "Her name is Rebecca.'

"Indeed," offered Rebecca looking mildly piqued.

"Good," Lady Belcrave remarked with a smile. "Thomas said you would surprise me. I am glad you have steel in your spine, Rebecca. You will need it whenever anyone attempts to cast you out from our sphere. Remember you have Belcrave's protection. Never forget you are a member of this family and are entitled to the respect due the earl's rank. Never let anyone suggest otherwise, if they do, turn up your nose and walk away. They are not worthy of your attention and you are permitted to tell them so."

Rebecca and Charlotte smiled at the countess' sudden rage; and much like a lioness protecting her cubs, Emily Bolton would not tolerate any threat to one of her own.

Lady Belcrave commanded, "Come along. I have ordered the barouche to be made ready for us."

Rebecca followed the countess into the open carriage where the driver sat perched on a box seat high above the high-sprung carriage. The large barouche was made to accommodate multiple passengers with two plush red leather seats facing each other. The countess directed Rebecca to sit beside her while Charlotte took the back-facing seat. Harry's sister showed her excitement by bouncing on her seat which prodded Rebecca to remark to no one in particular, "Where are we going?"

The countess looked at Rebecca and inquired, "Have you never been to London during the Season?"

Rebecca replied she had not and then her brows furrowed in concern. The countess saw the worry and said, "Forgive me, Rebecca. Thomas wrote me how the peerage frightens you, but I am afraid there is no way around being in their company, since the purpose of the Season is to gather all the nobles together to marry off their children.

"The Season is known as the Marriage Mart and most debutantes come for the singular purpose of bringing an eligible bachelor up to scratch. Now, granted you are already married, but for Harry's sake you need to be accepted. He will argue it is of no significance, but his tender heart will suffer if you are not welcomed into the sphere he was born.

"Now to answer your question, we are on our way to Hyde Park because it is the social hour when the peerage drive along Rotten Row to see who is in Town and for others to see them in all their finery. Many will be curious about you and so will seek an introduction which I will manage selectively.

"I will instruct our driver to move on if I do not want to acknowledge the toadeaters, those who look to glorify themselves by pretending they have a connection with us. Unfortunately, the crush of traffic will keep us at a crawl. Do not be alarmed if I turn my head to those I do not want to acknowledge.

"You will think me rude, but it is the way of the *ton* to keep those unworthy from infringing upon us. You must aid me by looking away as I do. Charlotte will also help with mindless chatter when anyone I do wish you to meet tries to delve into your background."

Rebecca looked at Charlotte who gave a hearty laugh and then confirmed, "I am well-versed in mindless chatter, Becca. You should hear my extensive dissertation on bonnets or my wealth of information on flowers. A rose is simply not a rose, but a species of various traits. Did you know Sir Joseph Banks, our esteemed royal botanist, named one type of rose he discovered after his wife when on expedition with Captain Cook to the South Seas? We have the Lady Banks Rose in our garden, do we not, mama?"

"Yes," Lady Belcrave affirmed. "Our gardeners work hard to keep it in check. The flower, like ivy, is a climbing evergreen and can take over a garden if not pruned regularly."

"Charlotte," asked Rebecca, "if you are not out, does that mean you will not be keeping me company when I attend *ton* events?"

"Exactly," Charlotte replied. "I am but seven and ten and while some girls make their debut at the early age, mama wants me to wait until next year. I am only in Town and not in Scotland with my siblings visiting my elder sister for mama feared a barbaric Scotland would sweep me away as one did my sister."

The countess scolded her daughter, "Shush, Charlotte! Stop spouting nonsense. You are here to see the Season in its glory before entering it. Plus, may I remind, you asked to come."

"Indeed I did," replied Charlotte. "There is nothing to do in Scotland's mountains except to watch over my siblings. I preferred to find amusement in Town."

"Not too much amusement," cautioned her mother, "only those entertainments of which I approve."

Rebecca said to Charlotte, "Harry promised to take me to a multitude of sights when he arrives. Perhaps, you will join us."

"I would very much like to accompany you," she replied.

"That reminds me, Rebecca," remarked Lady Belcrave. "I requested vouchers to the Almack's Assemblies for you, but have yet to receive them. If we come across one of the Patronesses just sit and be demure. Let me manage the conversation, for aside from Lady Sefton, the Patronesses can be very high in the instep, especially Lady Jersey who is a stickler for rules. We would not want her to take you in dislike."

Seeing Rebecca pale, Charlotte soothed, "Do not worry, Becca. My papa has political power and too many peers hound Tommy for investments. No one in their right mind would wish to displease them, so do not let them worry you."

"Charlotte," scolded her mother again, "you speak too freely. A lady should not speak of politics or of business affairs in mixed company."

"But mama, I am not in mixed company."

"True," she agreed, "but you must set a proper example for Rebecca so she knows how to go about in society."

"Do not be concerned, my lady," Rebecca consoled. "My mama tutored both me and my sister on what behooves a lady's conduct. I may not know what to expect in the gaieties of a London Season, but I do know how to behave."

"Indeed, my mind is eased, Rebecca," Lady Belcrave replied. "The idea of my family being the center of gossip among a bunch of vicious matrons with nothing better to do than spread tales, has had my pulse racing in anger ever since I learned Harry married a girl deep in scandal. Thomas' letter only made me more concerned when he said you feared the *ton*, but now I have met you, I believe you will do quite well, even though you are being thrust into the *ton* with little preparation."

"Mama, this conversation is turning gothic," scolded Charlotte. "I for one believe Rebecca will be dubbed one of this Season's diamonds. She has beauty, grace, and an intellect every man will admire upon meeting her. Let us return to the topic of amusements. Tell me Rebecca, where does Harry want to take you when he comes to Town?"

Rebecca laughed at Charlotte's boldness and replied, "He named too many places for me to remember, aside from Gunter's. My mouth waters at the idea of eating a flavored ice."

The countess offered, "That delicacy is easy to obtain, Rebecca. We can stop by Gunter's on the way home."

"If you please, my lady," informed Rebecca, "I would wait for Harry to take me as not to disappoint him."

"Very well," replied Lady Belcrave with a grin. "It pleases me to know his happiness is important to you."

"Of course," responded Rebecca. "I love him."

Charlotte clapped her hands together and exclaimed, "I knew it! I could tell you loved him when I told you how badly he was treated during his Season's debut and your temper rose."

Lady Belcrave remarked sagely, "Well, I fault his attire and not him. He, as you know, is quite remarkable. Now Rebecca, there will be no sleeping in tomorrow. We have appointments with Madame Lavigne in the morning and other shops to visit. Then, you shall nap when we return and be ready to attend a musicale in the evening. Do you play the pianoforte, by chance?"

Rebecca grinned, shaking her head side to side. She revealed, "My sister has the magical fingers. I play no instrument, my lady."

"Oh, well," sighed the countess. "You will just have to suffer the taunts regarding your negligent upbringing and allow the other debs to outshine you with their talents. Can you dance or do I need to hire an instructor?"

"I am adequate, my lady," replied Rebecca, "but I will only dance with Harry. I am not comfortable to do so with anyone but him."

Lady Belcrave's jaw dropped in astonishment.

Chapter Seventeen

The Earl of Belcrave stood at the marble-faced fireplace in the drawing room for Rebecca to be introduced to him. His brows drew into a severe frown as he watched her approach. He inspected her from head to feet and back to her head with such an unwelcoming expression she instinctively sought to protect her unborn child as if they were under attack. She had to remember to stop her hand from shielding the small mound under her clothes, lest she bring attention to her impending motherhood. She had no wish to reveal to Harry's parents they were to become grandparents until Harry was by her side.

Belcrave owned a formidable presence and Rebecca wondered how Harry managed to be so tenderhearted. There was no doubt Bolton was the earl's son for they had the same color of hair, eyes, and features. They both stood tall and they were both haughty and proud. Bolton did not suffer fools gladly and neither did the earl by the look of him. The earl took his time looking Rebecca over and she might have given into the vapors if his expression had not softened upon her curtsy.

She started to offer him a smile, but his gruff order for her to sit on the sofa stopped her. He instructed his wife to take a nearby seat and then, the moment they were both seated, he began to pepper Rebecca with questions. He kept a diligent pace in front of her, back and forth with his hands clasped behind him. He fired his queries rapidly, timing them so they were asked at each turn of his stride. Rebecca barely had time to answer one question before another one was thrust at her. She was saved from further interrogation when Charlotte entered, followed by the butler announcing dinner was served.

The earl and countess preceded Rebecca and Charlotte into the dining parlour to sit at a large mahogany table. Twenty chairs were tucked in around its perimeter with extra chairs placed against the walls to suggest the table could expand even further to seat more guests.

This morning Rebecca had not taken in the enormous table or room. Her mind was on her hunger and what was to be found under the silver covers on the marble-topped side tables where the servant led her, but now entering the room glistening in candlelight, she stood in awe of its opulence.

It was as elegant as the drawing room, but instead of cream silk, the walls were papered in a sky blue sprigged pattern. The furniture and drapes were richly matched in blue brocades. Where the drawing room glistened in gilt-furniture and mouldings, the dining parlour glowed in rich mahogany and glossy marble.

White, crisp linen, set with fine china, crystal, and silver services covered the massive mahogany dining table. A large silver epergne was prominently displayed in the center. There were two overhead chandeliers, multiple table candelabras and wall sconces brightly lighting up the room and making the crystal and silver twinkle.

The earl sat at the head of the dining table after seating his wife to his right and telling his daughter and Rebecca to sit as they wished. Charlotte directed Rebecca to take the chair to the left of the earl and then sat next to her. Belcrave nodded to his wife, granting her permission to ring the bell to start the meal's service.

They ate their first course in silence and after their plates were removed Belcrave shook his head at Rebecca and questioned her as if his earlier interrogation had not been interrupted by the call to dinner "How can you not know your mother's maiden name?"

Rebecca crimsoned. The earl was not happy to learn her father came from a family of fisherman and he soon moved his line of questioning to her mother's family connections. Her temper rose at being pressed to answer the same question. *Does he think my faculties are diminished?* She heard, understood his query and already answered him succinctly. Patience expired; she raised her chin and with steely eyes retaliated by asking him, "What is my middle name, my lord?"

Her random question made the earl scowl and respond crossly, "How the deuce would I know girl? I have never met you, nor questioned my son regarding it!"

"Exactly!" exclaimed Rebecca in a roar. "My mama never informed me or my sister about her family. The need never arose and at this late date we can only surmise she severed the connection or they disinherited her. Arabella and I know nothing, though I cannot speak for my brother and since he is not here I cannot ask him!"

The earl looked at his wife and remarked in a surprisingly and almost cheery voice, "She has a temper."

Astonished and embarrassed, Rebecca countered in a softer voice, "I do not."

"She has backbone, Richard," interjected his wife, "and she used it wisely today. You will be proud to know she handled Sarah Villiers admirably." Emily smiled as she recounted for her husband what had transpired.

They had just turned into the drive known as Rotten Row in Hyde Park when their carriage came to a halt due to someone in the line of carriages stopping to greet a passerby. The multitude of vehicles on parade slowed to a crawl as stops and starts rippled to cause jams and delays. Aside from the coachmen, no one seemed to mind the pace for it gave them the opportunity to preen among their peers and scan the crowd for the newest arrivals to Town. They barely traveled the span of a carriage when the countess found her barouche next to Lady

Jersey's. The Almack's Patroness looked smug and haughty wearing a high plumed hat and redingote trimmed in mink. Sarah Villiers sat erect in her open carriage with her chin lifted so she looked down her nose on anyone who dared to approach her without her permission. Her cold manner cowered or at least made a person pause before they greeted her, but Lady Belcrave owned as much consequence as Sarah and she did not think twice to offer her salutation. Maybe it was because she understood the power of Belcrave's political influence or maybe because she was confident in her own lineage that she could easily greet the Countess of Jersey.

Regardless, Sarah Villiers took exception to not being esteemed in a manner she felt befitted her position as an Almack's Patroness or countess of prominent lineage and retaliated by saying to Emily, "I expect you want to know if we have approved your vouchers for Harry's wife. We have not had the time to consider the matter." Pointing to Rebecca, she asked, "Is this the chit?"

Lady Belcrave took umbrage to Lady Jersey's pointed finger and to her use of cant. She returned the insult by introducing the countess to Rebecca rather than adhering to protocol which demanded a person of lower rank or age to be introduced first. The hit was noticeable and Sarah Villiers, the condescending Countess of Jersey, steeled her eyes.

Rebecca was alarmed by the battle of wits about to convene between two countesses on her behalf and quickly intervened, "My lady," she said to Lady Jersey, "it is an honor to make your acquaintance. Your name and all your good deeds precede you."

Taken by surprise, Lady Jersey inquired, "Good deeds?"

"Of course," replied Rebecca. "For what other reason could motivate you to dedicate yourself to overseeing the fulfillment of matrimony between lords and ladies. I understand why you hesitate to send me a voucher, since I am already married and have no need to attend Almack's."

"A voucher to attend Almack's Assemblies means The Patronesses recommend you as good *ton*," rebutted Sarah Villiers in a huffy tone.

"But you forget, my lady," retorted Rebecca with uncommon steel in her voice, "I am Mrs. Harry Bolton, and therefore, need no more than his good name to recommend me."

Lady Belcrave was horrified Rebecca took on a battle with Sarah which was hers to engage and watched wide-eyed as her daughter-by-marriage and the Countess of Jersey crossed words. Never, had she witnessed a conflict reminiscent of David and Goliath where courage and faith overcame the impossible. To her knowledge, no commoner ever dared to rebut the influential Lady Jersey. Even Sarah's peers would never attempt to risk Sarah's good opinion for she had the social influence to ruin a family's good name.

Their volleying and heated discourse drew a crowd among the passersby for nothing amused the *ton* more than witnessing the birth of a scandal. The crowd waited in anticipation for the Countess of Jersey to spew her acrimony at the unknown girl who had the audacity to engage the countess as an equal. Emily, caught up in the discourse, finally came to her senses and opened her mouth to redirect Sarah's anger.

The last thing she needed was for more speculation about Harry's wife; a battle of wits between Rebecca and Sarah would do just that if she did not put a stop it. No sooner did she decide her course than a loud and resounding bellow burst from Sarah's mouth. The laughter hushed the riveted crowd. Mouths gaped and then shut into frowns when they realized there would be no brouhaha.

They were further astonished to hear Lady Jersey exclaim, "Somewhere in that girl's lineage is noble blood. She has consequence and I should know. You may expect your vouchers tomorrow, Emily."

Emily had not a moment to close her mouth or to voice her gratitude before Sarah's carriage rolled forward. Drivers clucked at their cattle to step in line and the disappointed crowd deprived of their scene was left to disperse. Charlotte, sitting on the edge of her seat without an audience to witness her, let loose her laughter and unwittingly fell back against her seat. Her feet came off the ground, much like a puppy wanting its stomach scratched. Mortified, she quickly righted herself and kept her eyes on smoothing her skirt, praying no one had seen her faux pas.

Lady Belcrave shook her head unable to comprehend what had just transpired, but before she could utter a word, her carriage was overwhelmed by a number of lords who had spied the scene. She was not the only one surprised by Lady Jersey's approbation. Sarah's outburst and laugh had the gentlemen beelining on their horses to be introduced to the girl who received Lady Jersey's good opinion, while ladies who witnessed the same scene glared at Rebecca for drawing away their beaus. The assault on both fronts overwhelmed and turned Rebecca into a timid specimen which further intrigued her gentlemen admirers and enraged her foes.

Belcrave listened intently to his wife's recollection of Rebecca's exchange with Sarah Villiers and nodded his approval at Rebecca for winning Lady Jersey's favor where others had failed. He repeated what Sarah had opined, "So, you have consequence. Well," he laughed, "I suppose you do."

Dinner ended on a high note and Rebecca asked to be excused claiming exhaustion. The earl bid her good evening and thereby reprieved her from further inter-rogation. Mary the First undressed her and put her to bed. Rebecca fell soundly asleep and woke when a bright light pierced her eyelids after Mary pulled back the window drapes to let in the early morning sun. Groggily, she opened her eyes, stretched out her limbs, and in a panic felt for her baby. She relaxed once her baby stirred assur-ing her all was well.

Rebecca watched as Mary the First went about her duties. She was getting used to being served, of having someone set up her toiletries and assist in dressing her, and sighed knowing the indulgence would not continue once she returned home. Of course, she would not be changing her clothes as often as Town life dictated.

She was glad to learn Charlotte was to accompany her on the multiple errands the countess planned for the day. Lady Belcrave was a conundrum bouncing between haughtiness and remarkable affection. Rebecca was not sure whether Harry's mother approved of her or not, but she knew Charlotte did and that was a beginning.

Their first stop was to Madame Lavigne's shop. Rebecca was surprised at the number of gowns finished and upon her inquiry for how it was possible she learned Bolton had again paid for the employ of additional seamstresses to finish the work. Camille confessed she had hired women to sew around-the-clock to complete the commission. The modiste looked exhausted, but Camille assured Rebecca she had no regrets. Bolton was paying her handsomely and she found herself even more in demand when her other clients learned she was not accepting new commissions. Her customers, she gloated, were waiting impatiently for her to reopen her shop to them.

From the modiste, the countess ordered their coachman to take them to Bond Street first, then to the streets of Oxford and Picadilly. Boots, slippers, gloves, hats, shawls, and a number of other accessories were all ordered and purchased as they visited one shop after another. The day passed in a blur and Rebecca was exhausted; especially knowing she still had a musicale to attend in the evening. She quickly excused herself from taking tea when she entered Belcrave's townhome and went directly to her room for a lengthy nap. Mary the First woke her when it was time to get dressed for the evening's event and she begrudgingly stirred herself to wake.

Chapter Eighteen

The musicale was Rebecca's first event to attend without the support of Charlotte. She trembled, unsure how she would react when in the company of aristocratic gentlemen. Charlotte warned her how these events were not considered successful unless the hostess filled her home beyond capacity. A *crush* it was called, referring to how people were crushed into a home with little room to move. Rebecca's pulse raced as she envisioned being pressed among a crowd of gentlemen. Mary the First sat her down and pushed her head down between her legs at the first sign of her distress. Mary held her in the position and asked, "When are you going to tell milady you are with child?"

She continued her ministrations and placed a cool rag on Rebecca's neck and when no answer came, Mary asked her question again. Rebecca raised her head and answered, "I am waiting for Harry to make our announcement."

Mary prodded in anger, "Master Harry would have informed his parents the moment he learned he was to be a father. Why hasn't he?"

When Rebecca gave no answer, the maid angrily asked, "Is the babe Master Harry's?"

Rebecca paled and Mary scolded, incensed on her mistress' behalf, "Don't be swooning. I want an answer and I want it now."

Rebecca pulled back her shoulders and defiantly responded, "Harry says it is."

"That is no answer, madam," rebutted Mary. "My loyalties are to milady and the earl. There has been much talk about this marriage and it will come to no one's surprise Master Harry came to your rescue. You will inform milady or I will do it."

"I do not know if Harry is the father, but he may very well be," confessed Rebecca.

"How can that be?" asked Mary. "Master Harry would never bed a lady."

"Harry and I married for love," informed Rebecca, "but before our marriage I was attacked and beaten. I have no memory of what happened while I was unconscious. Only my brother knows the extent of my injuries. Harry has never doubted he was the father. Only I have questioned the parentage for I do not know what happened."

Mary's outrage diminished and her face softened with compassion. She sat next to Rebecca and wrapped Rebecca up in her arms. Rebecca cried; she was exhausted, tormented and afraid.

"Now, now, madam," said Mary. "I see we have a kettle of fish here. My lips are sealed until Master Harry arrives, but if he is not here within a week, you must speak with milady. She will discover for herself you are with child. Milady would have recognized the signs as I have done if not for all this business with your debut. Now let's get you dressed."

"What signs," sniveled Rebecca, her cries reduced to an indiscriminate sob. "I have not been sick in the morning since I arrived."

"Well, that is good news," replied Mary, "but there are other signs. Your growing figure, your fatigue, your swollen ankles, your voracious appetite and your missing courses. The laundry maids will inform milady when that happens."

"I see your point," Rebecca acknowledged.

"Good," said Mary. "Now, let me put a cold compress on your eyes to reduce the swelling and then get you dressed."

The evening gown designed by Camille was beautiful. Married, Rebecca had no need to subscribe to the white and pastel colors of debutantes and Camille knew Mrs. Harry Bolton had no wish to draw attention with bold colors, so a bolt of Georgian cloth in cerulean blue was used to make her dress. The high-waist dress was ornamented in horizontal waves of silver and white trimmings across the bodice. Full puckered sleeves with bows placed at her shoulders were made of the same trim. The hem's border was also decorated with the same silver and white ornaments. The classically styled dress drew attention to her bosom and not her stomach. Her condition was not yet visible to which she was relieved.

Around her neck hung a three strand pearl necklace with a sapphire pendant at its center and on her ears she wore matching ear-rings of pearl and sapphire. The earl had sent the jewels to her as a bridal gift for her to wear to the musicale, but Rebecca discerned the jewelry was more a testament to the earl's wealth than evidence of her being accepted as Harry's wife.

Rebecca descended the staircase and saw the earl and countess at the bottom landing. They were waiting for her to arrive and when the earl saw her, he gave an approving nod. Whether his approbation was for her looks or because he saw her wearing the jewels he gave her she did not know. Lord Belcrave was dressed in a dark blue tailcoat with a silver and blue embroidered waistcoat over a white pristine shirt and grey trousers. A diamond stick pin set in gold stood out among the folds of his white cravat.

The countess stood next to him dressed in a deep blue gown trimmed with gray Belgian lace to match him in color. A diamond necklace with matching ear bobs glittered from her neck and ears. Ostrich feathers rose from the back of her elegantly styled coif. Together, they made a handsome pair, complimenting each other as if the earl allowed his wife to dress him. Rebecca in her own blue dress matched Harry's parents and the notion Harry's mother had a hand in selecting her ensemble this evening made her smile.

A thick line of people crowded the steps into the highly illuminated townhome of the Earl of Southwaite. He had a daughter making her debut and his wife wanted to display the girl's skill at the piano by hosting a musicale. A number of other single ladies would also perform, but according to Harry's mother, those debutantes were selected for their less than stellar talents in comparison to the earl's daughter Lady Caroline.

As they waited to enter the Southwaite townhome, the countess informed Rebecca that Belcrave would escort them to all affairs until Harry or Bolton returned to do the service. The earl escorted them, one on each of his arms. As the line pressed forward, he moved Rebecca between him and his countess to shield her from unwanted attention. The earl's actions reminded Rebecca of Harry's protective and caring nature. Perhaps, Harry took after his father, after all.

They progressed slowly, taking small steps as the crowd pressed forward to enter the townhome, the stench of heavily perfumed bodies was thick in the air. Once they crossed the entryway, the press of bodies broke and the crowd dispersed into other rooms.

Rebecca had to fight the urge to drop her chin and close her eyes to hide from the mass of people overwhelming her, but she rallied herself by thinking of Harry and how she was determined not to shame him. She forced herself to meet the eyes of the gentlemen and ladies around her and was surprised when she found nothing in their gaze to frighten her. The men did not leer, but simply gave a nod in greeting as behooved a gentleman who had not yet been introduced to a lady.

Some men did not acknowledge her at all, but there were some ladies who made their contempt of her obvious, loudly chatting amongst themselves about the scandal attached to her name or as the lady who received Lady Jersey's approval in Hyde Park. Their expressions reminded her of the year leading into her womanhood when her bosom blossomed before other young girls her age and the unkind remarks they made about her. She saw the same discontent in these debutantes and found amusement in the notion the young ladies envied her.

Absorbed in her thoughts, she was caught unaware and stumbled when the earl moved forward. Concerned, he asked, "Are you well, Rebecca?"

"Yes," she replied surprising herself.

Satisfied with her answer he informed, "I will find you and the countess seats to watch the performances. Emily told me you were out all day and are no doubt exhausted from today's excursion."

He led them to the large drawing room where the furniture was moved to accommodate a piano and chairs for an audience. Belcrave told his wife he would be in the room set up for the gentlemen to play cards and she need only send a servant to retrieve him if he was needed. Emily thanked him and reminded him how they would leave at the end of the performances. Rebecca gave a sigh of relief in knowing she would not be expected to mingle. She need only sit, watch the performance, and present a genteel image of polite decorum. She could do that.

Lady Caroline was to exhibit her skills last as not to diminish the inexperienced pianists who played before her, but also to be remembered above all other performers. Many of the participants were in good cheer, regardless of the level of their talent and Rebecca discovered she was enjoying the show. The recitals began with Lady Margaret who played adequately on the piano. Lady Deborah followed on the harp, which Rebecca had not noticed was in the room. Two more piano sonatas were played before Lady Caroline took her seat on the piano bench.

Rebecca recognized Caroline as one of the ladies from Hyde Park who gave her the evil eye, most likely for drawing away the attention of her suitors. Rebecca thought the glare unbecoming from the lady noted as this Season's diamond of the first water. Her auburn hair framed a narrow forehead, high cheekbones, a tapered chin, with big slate blue eyes that bespoke arrogance.

Unlike her predecessors, Caroline gave no cheeky grin to her audience before her performance. She smugly fanned out her dress skirt while lowering herself onto the piano bench. Her fingers danced along the ivory keys until they settled where she wanted them. She raised her chin, pointing her nose to the ceiling and waited for the room to quiet. She glared at the culprit who dared to cough and waited until the room silenced again. Satisfied there would be no further interruptions, she began to play.

Caroline's fingers pressed the ivory keys softly, and then after a few bars, she began to attack the piece with gusto. Rebecca listened and then turned her head to observe the audience, wondering if she was the only one who found the music lacking. Caroline was indeed proficient and never missed a note. In fact, Rebecca was hard-pressed to explain why she was unmoved. She was familiar with the sonata for it was one Arabella played and to her discerning ear, her sister played the piece much better. *Am I being biased?* The resounding applause halted her musings and gave evidence she was not in concert with the audience's opinion. She belatedly clapped her hands, but not before her hesitation was witnessed by Caroline.

The lady stood and shushed the audience with her hands. She said with mischievous amusement, "Thank you for your praise. I am truly unworthy and while I planned an encore performance I see there is someone in our company that was not granted the opportunity to perform. She is new to our Society and I do mean "new." Shall we coax Mrs. Harry Bolton to perform for us?"

All heads seemed to turn at once to Rebecca and she would have swooned if not for the fact Caroline was gloating. Harry's mother touched her arm and whispered, "I have sent for Richard. We may leave. There is no need to be disconcerted."

"Perhaps, the lady needs encouragement," prompted a smug Caroline who put her hands together and clapped.

The audience added their own applause as motivation and Rebecca found herself being raised by the hand of the person sitting to the other side of her. Emily rose in tandem believing they were to make their exit, but Caroline's next taunt not only stopped Rebecca but rallied her.

"You look unwell, Mrs. Bolton," remarked Caroline. "Perhaps, you are not used to being in our esteemed Society and prefer to take your leave."

The room hushed at the insult and Rebecca froze. She looked at her mother-by-marriage when Emily's fingers tightened around her arm. Lady Belcrave was angry and Rebecca knew the next moment would forever define her as either a coward if she let Harry's mother speak for her or a Bolton who demanded respect. She remembered Harry and why she was here. She remembered Bolton's and Lady Belcrave's advice on how to handle the *ton*. The Earl of Belcrave stood haughty and proud in her sight, awaiting her decision.

She turned her attention to Caroline as she gave Emily's hand a pat to release her and said in a clear, loud and haughty voice, "I shall be magnanimous and forgive your impertinence, Lady Caroline, for surely you meant no insult to a guest in your parent's home, and definitely not to a Bolton. Such behavior does not behoove a lady, nor reflect a wise person."

Among the hushed crowd rose the Countess of Southwaite from her seat looking fearful of what might be her daughter's ruination. The countess thought Caroline's affront to Mrs. Bolton was a stellar hit until Rebecca turned the table on her daughter. Caroline looked ready to lose control of her rage, so the countess rushed to her daughter's side before the scene became the talk of tomorrow's parlours.

Using a cavalier manner, she said to her guests, "Caroline meant no offense. She was only offering Mrs. Bolton an opportunity to shine." However, her loyalty to her daughter and her own outrage of having her daughter's musical debut spoiled made her add spitefully, "Of course, if Harry's wife has no talent, we apologize for bringing it to light."

Heads turned to see which of the Bolton's would address the verbal attack, but before Harry's parents could open their mouths, Rebecca stepped forward and said, "I do not play the piano, my lady, but if your guests permit I would be happy to sing. Perhaps, Caroline would like to accompany me?"

The audience roared with applause and one piercing whistle. Comments of "Jolly good sport" and "Harry would be proud!" were heard.

Rebecca met Caroline at the piano and asked so the audience could hear, "Can you play *Beethoven's To the Distant Beloved?*" Rebecca knew Caroline could not by her pallor. The popular song was fairly new to the general public even though it was published a few years ago. Most debutantes would not have it in their repertoire, but Arabella loved Beethoven's music and she was quick to acquire and learn all his new pieces.

It was the one indulgence their papa did not forbid and since the piece was singularly composed for the pianist and singer to participate equally in its performance, she and her sister had learned it proficiently. The song, made up of six parts, relates to the loneliness and inner pain of missing a loved one. It was said Beethoven made notations in a sketchbook of the musical ideas that came to him as he walked the lanes around the country villages near Vienna, and that he later used those notations to compose his work.

Before Caroline could ask Rebecca to pick another song, Lady Belcrave walked forward informing the mass at large she knew the piece and would accompany Rebecca. Caroline was forced to sit down and move out of the spotlight. Rebecca faced her audience once Harry's mother was seated and gave a nod she was ready to begin.

There was a bit of chatter among the doubtful, but Rebecca gave it no mind. She opened her mouth and once the beauty of her voice penetrated the room, silence reigned. Rebecca lost herself in the poetry of the words evoking the longing for a lover far away. Lyrics speaking of nature's wonder describing mountains and valleys, clouds and birds, the rebirth of spring with babbling brooks and meadows blooming, imparted a poignancy that touched every soul in the room. Lady Belcrave's fingers danced across the keyboard creating rustic rhythms with light triplets and trills bringing the sounds of water flowing and birds in song to the score.

Rebecca sang out the final stanza.

Receive these songs, my love, the outpourings of a full heart, and sing them at sunset behind the mountain peaks; for a loving heart will overcome the barriers that divide and reach that which it has sanctified.

She was greeted with silence and wide-eyed wonder at the end of her song and blushed when the audience did not applaud. To hide her embarrassment she turned and thanked the countess for her accompaniment. She did not doubt her voice, but the absence of applause confirmed to her how blood took precedence over character. Every debutante who performed earlier in the evening received some degree of approbation and when none was given to her she knew it was because the *ton* did not accept her, even with Belcrave's patronage.

Emily rose from the piano bench and embraced Rebecca. Harry's mother laughed upon seeing Rebecca's astonished expression and whispered, "Oh my! You do surprise one!"

And then before Rebecca could process the meaning behind Emily's words a hearty applause erupted. The audience stood and shouted, "Brava!" And before Rebecca could prepare herself she was flanked on all sides by lords and ladies wanting to congratulate her. Belcrave pushed his way to her side when she looked like she might faint.

He wrapped his arm around her shoulder to shield her from those pressing into her, and quickly walked her out of the room resounding with effusive praise.

Chapter Nineteen

The memory of last night's triumph over Lady Caroline gave Rebecca the confidence she needed to make her evening debut at Almack's. Surprisingly, the anxiety she owned ever since coming to London diminished with the proof of Belcrave's protection. He rescued her last night from the pressing crowd and he was not the only one who watched over her. The countess was ready to defend her against the Ladies Jersey and Southwaite, and Charlotte was always quick to rally to her side. She did not fool herself to believe she was accepted or approved by Harry's parents, but she trusted as Harry's wife she would come to no harm under their care. That was enough for now.

Mary the First entered to help her dress in a high-waist evening gown made of a mint green silk slip and overdress of matching net. The dress sported short puffed sleeves. Ribbons and rosettes of various sizes were beautifully appointed on her shoulders, under her bodice and in two glorious rows on her hemline. She looked like a woodland nymph; especially with her hair cascading in curls around her face like a flowering vine.

She entered the drawing room and saw the complimenting shades of green between the countess' dress and her own, and knew Emily had a hand in coordinating the dressing of her party again. Emily wore her hair loosely twisted and pinned into a simple coif that bared her neck and ears to display the emerald necklace and ear bobs worn to match her bottleneck green high-waist dress.

Rebecca wore the earl's bridal gift of pearls and sapphires and though the earl was constricted to wearing the black formal tailcoat and breeches required to enter Almack's, he matched his countess by wearing a substantial glittering emerald stick pin in the folds of his white cravat. They presented a united front and Rebecca embraced the idea as a good sign.

The main ballroom in Almack's was forty feet wide by one hundred feet long and was filled to capacity. The band played in an overhead balcony. Crystal chandeliers glistened and illuminated the floor where lords and ladies of the realm danced. On the sidelines, near the white Roman columns stood groups of men talking indifferent to the ladies fluttering around them; other men seeking courtship or mild dalliance maneuvered to position themselves in their lady's circle.

Young debutantes preened and waved their fans as they were tutored to do until an eligible gentleman requested an introduction or dance. The room was full of gallantry. Some gentlemen made sweeping bows, others rushed to acquire the insipid watered down lemonade provided for their ladies to drink. A few responded to a lady's dropped square of laced linen with a knowing grin.

An initiate, like Rebecca was to the Season, marveled at what she saw, but to those gracing the assembly room for weeks on end, the scene was both scripted and boring. These idle malcontents were the ones with ears perked and eyes ready for any action or remark for which they could expand upon in tomorrow's drawing rooms.

Talk of Rebecca's singing debut had spread like wildfire and monopolized the conversations in Mayfair's drawing rooms and dining parlours. Her arrival drew immediate attention as the peerage tried to reconcile the gossip surrounding her. Curiosity prompted questions. *Who is Mrs. Harry Bolton?*

The scandal about her father's death was dismissed. The *ton* wanted to know of Rebecca's lineage for surely no commoner was bred with the grace, nor tutored in voice as was Harry's wife. Besides, most agreed, the Earl and Countess of Belcrave would never sanction a marriage with one of their own among the common...or would they?

And if they did, wasn't that a morsel to entertain the *ton* during the rest of the Season? For then, the question became, why? What other scandal could be attached to the lady's name? The temptation to learn more of Harry's wife riveted the *ton* and so, as the Belcrave party entered the assembly hall, whispers escalated into a vociferous chatter.

"Stay near, Richard," Emily whispered to her husband who was ready to head to the smaller room designated for card playing. He raised his eyebrows, which prompted her to elaborate. "I have a funny feeling in the pit of my stomach and need you at hand in case something runs afoul."

He looked down at his arm being tightly clutched by his wife and placed his other hand, made free when Rebecca released his arm, on hers to assure her. He soothed, "I will stay here, Emily, but I would not worry. Rebecca proved she is more than capable of handling any offense and none would dare to impugn your good name or I would have their head."

"And you would not do the same for Harry's wife?" Emily asked.

The earl's expression clearly showed he was deliberating his wife's question. After a moment's thought, he smiled and replied, "I do believe I would, Emily. Do you suppose in such a short acquaintance I have come to like the chit?"

Lady Belcrave looked up with sparkling eyes at her husband and grinned as she placed her other hand on top of his before saying, "I believe Harry, by letting his heart guide him, chose better for himself than we ever could have done."

The earl grinned at his wife with an affection he rarely displayed publicly that made her blush. His grin turned to a full out smile knowing she misread his expression for something more heated. He briskly checked his smile, before he gave the gossipmongers something to remark upon, and escorted his ladies over to greet the patronesses who oversaw the balls. After a minimal exchange of greetings to satisfy decorum, he walked them over to a row of chairs settled against the wall.

A number of gentlemen quickly rose upon spying them to make their seats available to Emily and Rebecca, which necessitated the earl to make their introduction. Polite discourse was entertained, *"Are you enjoying the Season, Mrs. Bolton? The weather has been most fair. Do you find it so, or perhaps the air was too chilly today?"*

Lady Belcrave asked after the health of the men's family when inquiries after her son Harry were made. The earl tried to waylay further inquiries about Harry by asking Rebecca to dance. He was nonplussed when she demurred.

"Oh, my lord," she exclaimed after seeing his astonishment, "I meant no offense. I just choose to wait for Harry to partner me in my first dance."

"By jove!" exclaimed Lord Glassmere, one of the gentlemen paying her court. "Harry is one lucky gentleman. I, like a bunch of other hopefuls here wished to dance with you, but I admire your devotion to your husband. I can only hope once Harry arrives I may secure the next available set on your dance card."

Rebecca blushed. The gentlemen responded with admiration in their eyes and then took their leave explaining they were engaged to dance and must seek their partners. Rebecca's devotion to Harry became Glassmere's topic of conversation to all he met. Before long, ladies tired of hearing their gentlemen speak of Rebecca's virtues, began speculating about her flaws, for surely, they tittered, she must have some.

There were many who believed Rebecca had aimed too high and was being accepted by their peers too easily. Many would like to see her taken down a notch, if for no other reason than to have something new to talk about in their drawing rooms. They were alert for any indiscretion, so when Lady Jersey beelined her way with an unknown to the Earl of Belcrave and his party, everyone paid attention.

Eyes darted from the Belcrave party to Lady Jersey and her smug smile. The countess looked as if she knew something no one else did. Watchers wetted their lips in anticipation of a possible scandal.

After all, one cutting word from the Patroness would ruin Rebecca's newly acquired cachet and wasn't that a splendid morsel to talk about. The gentleman was handsome, of average height with the figure of a man still in his prime. Ladies looked at him with admiration and wondered over his eligibility. *Is he a man of title, fortune?* There were as many ladies looking at him as there were gentlemen looking at Rebecca for recognition of the man blatantly staring at her. *Does he know her or something of her background that will bring shame to Harry and his family?* The room quieted as more and more peers hushed in anticipation to better hear the upcoming discourse.

"Lord Belcrave," called Lady Jersey, bubbling with excitement as she brought a gentleman with dark brown hair and eyes across the dance floor to greet the earl.

"Belcrave," Sarah explained once she reached him, "Viscount Ketterling requests an introduction. You will permit?"

The earl nodded and Lady Jersey continued, "Allow me to present William Keane, the new Viscount Ketterling to you."

Turning to William, Sarah introduced, "Lord Ketterling, I present Richard and Emily Bolton, the Earl and Countess of Belcrave and their daughter-by-marriage Rebecca Bolton, Mrs. Harry Bolton."

William made his bow. He greeted the earl by his title, and offered his salutation, "your servant," to the ladies.

The ladies made their curtsies and then Belcrave proffered, "My condolences on the loss of your father, Ketterling. He died last year?"

"Yes," replied William. "Thank you. I have just come out of mourning to honor his final request of me to find a bride, although I sorely feel I am not up to the task."

"If you seek a wife," retorted Richard, "you will not find one among my ladies. They are already taken."

William laughed. "I beg your pardon. I did sound impertinent, but the purpose for my introduction while personal is in no way to secure a wife."

Richard raised his brows and waited, as did the rest of the *ton* within hearing distance.

"You will think me ill-mannered, Belcrave," he informed, "but may I ask Mrs. Bolton her name before she married?"

The earl took affront. *Is the viscount probing into the scandal surrounding Barrington and Damburten and if so, for what purpose?* He replied, "Your curiosity is indeed impertinent and suggests you are motivated by mischief."

William's eyes widened in alarm and he quickly responded, "Indeed not, Belcrave. Truly, I only wish to learn if there is a family connection between Mrs. Bolton and myself."

"How so," frowned Belcrave.

William looked at Rebecca soberly and asked, "Your name, Mrs. Bolton, before you married?"

"Rebecca Barrington," she answered.

William asked, "Rebecca Jean Barrington?"

Astonished, Rebecca asked, "Yes, how did you know?"

"It was my mother's name, Mrs. Bolton. You are my niece and aside from your name to confirm our connection, you look just like my sister as I remember her. I was not sure if you were of this world when I first caught sight of you." He grinned and added, "I thought my sister had come to aid me in my quest to find a wife."

Gasps resounded through the ballroom in peaks and valleys as the news of Harry's wife being the granddaughter of a viscount undulated among the peerage like a cresting wave.

The growing exclamations prompted the earl to say, "This is a private matter, Ketterling. I suggest if you are free tomorrow you come to my home at eleven in the morning where we can further discuss this revelation."

William replied, "I will be there." He bowed and took his leave.

The Countess of Jersey having been forgotten, beamed with the pride of one victorious and reminded Emily, "I told you she had consequence." She bid the Belcrave party a good evening and smugly took her leave.

Richard and Emily looked at Rebecca in astonishment and before the observers brazened themselves to approach them, the earl and countess helped a dumbfounded Rebecca to rise from her chair. Deep in her thoughts, Rebecca was easily led from the ballroom where she left the gossipmongers behind to chew on what they just learned.

Rebecca did not sleep well worrying over Harry and her predicament. The countess had brought her to bed immediately after arriving home from Almack's and had called for Mary the First to assist her. Once alone in Mary's care, the maid expressed her disapproval with a "tsk," and then scolded her for not eating and resting properly before putting her to bed. The maid also shook her head in a silent rebuke that reminded Rebecca she had yet to keep her promise to confess her concerns about her baby to the earl and countess.

She was running out of time. She smoothed her hand over her rounding stomach and knew someone would remark upon her blossoming figure soon. *Where is Harry?* She needed his support desperately and was regretting sending him to search for her brother. *Am I to confess on my own? Is it what Harry would want? Will the earl and countess repudiate me? Should I return home without Harry?*

The questions whirled in her mind like a windstorm and on top of everything else, she had to come to terms she had a viscount for an uncle. The reality of it seemed preposterous and wonderful all at the same time. There was something marvelous about a living connection to her mother and she wanted to share the news with Harry. It astonished her to know her grandfather had been a viscount and her mother, the Honorable Abigail Jean Keane, had been a debutante. Her mother had curtsied to the Queen and attended the Season's balls where she could have met and married a titled gentleman. Instead, she had humbled herself to marry her papa. The idea boggled her mind.

Chapter Twenty

Rebecca entered the drawing room wearily after breaking her fast in her room with some dried toast and tea. She had not suffered morning sickness for almost a week, but her nerves were playing havoc with her indigestion. Mary said she looked worn to the bone and she was feeling the fatigue. She had not indulged in a long nap since she arrived and the constant activities and anxiety over Harry were taking a toll not only physically, but emotionally on her.

The earl stood by the window deep in thought and the countess sat on one of the gilded scrolled sofas upholstered in green brocade, beckoning Rebecca to join her. Emily's expression revealed concern as she appraised her daughter-by-marriage and once Rebecca sat, she asked, "Are you ill, Rebecca?"

Rebecca offered a weak grin and then replied, "I am just a bit overwhelmed and fatigued."

The butler entered before Emily could press further to announce Viscount Ketterling's arrival. The viscount walked in, made his greetings, and sat across from the ladies in a matching upholstered gilded chair. Belcrave walked over and took a protective stance behind them.

In the light of day and with her wits about her, it was easy for Rebecca to see the features marking William a relative. The viscount, like her mother and herself had rich dark brown hair, though his was sprinkled with grey. His lips were thinner; but his almond-shaped dark brown eyes and patrician nose mirrored her classical features. There was no mistaking the family connection between them.

Looking at Rebecca's drawn expression, William asked with concern, "I hope my revelation of being your uncle has not distressed you, Mrs. Bolton?"

Before Rebecca could answer, Belcrave intervened, "Of course, she is distressed, Ketterling. The news is alarming; especially announced publicly at Almack's. Perhaps, you would be kind enough to explain why Harry's wife did not know she was your niece?"

Rebecca would have laughed at the earl's bold rebuke if she had not seen her uncle's astonished face. The poor man looked as if someone just threw a bucket of water on him. He practically blubbered, before regaining his composure and apologized, "I beg your pardon, Mrs. Bolton. I was not thinking last night. The vision of my sister alive disconcerted me into acting precipitously. You see, I was very fond of my sister Abby and felt her loss greatly. It was hard enough losing her when she married your father."

"I do not understand why you lost my mama when she married my papa, Viscount Ketterling?"

"Oh, please call me Uncle and if that is too much to expect, then at least call me William."

Rebecca looked to the earl for direction and when he gave a nod of approval she asked, "Well then, Uncle, perhaps you can explain why I do not know you."

"The simplest explanation is my father disinherited my sister when she chose to elope with your father instead of marrying the duke with whom he wished an alliance. The duke was in need of an heir and was very interested in marrying my sister. Abby caught his eye at an assembly before her come-out and his grace thought to claim her once she was of age. The duke was older than my own father, so I never blamed Abby for running away. Unfortunately, my father was too blinded by the duke's status and wealth to believe anything other than he was settling his only daughter exceptionally."

Rebecca asked, "Your mama approved of the marriage for her only daughter?"

"I was away at school when this all transpired, so I am not sure of the details or of what my mother approved. I do know my father suffered ridicule when my sister refused the duke's offer. I am sure the duke aided the gossip with quips about my father's inability to manage his family, so as to manipulate my father into forcing the marriage. In a way, the duke succeeded because my father's anger over being derided led him to demand my sister wed the duke or be disinherited. My sister responded by running away to my aunt in Truro where she met your father and eloped with him shortly after. My father took the marriage as an insult to his station and Abby's name was never mentioned again.

"After my father's death, I came across a bundle of my sister's letters she wrote to my mother. Through reading them I learned my mother never disowned my sister, nor failed to come to her in need. She attended the births of your siblings and it was in her race to be at your own arrival that she died. Her driver was pushing the cattle to excess speeds on her command when one of the wheels hit a deep rut causing the carriage to tilt. The unbalanced weight made the axle crack and the carriage broke from the horses and tumbled. Both the driver and my mother were thrown. She died from a head injury."

Rebecca rasped out in sorrow her condolences and then asked through a sob, "Why have you never come to visit us?"

"I was first constrained from visiting by filial duty," William replied. "My father never recovered after my mother's passing and I had no wish to grieve him further by disregarding his feelings. I believe he carried guilt for her death. He once confessed to me how she had delayed her departure to speak with Cook and the housekeeper to ensure he was well-cared for while she was gone. He always turned medieval and helpless whenever she went away. I think he feared she would not come back if she thought him capable. I attempted to find your family after my father died, but was unsuccessful."

"But why do my siblings have no memory of my grandmama visiting. If you say she came to each of our births, should not there be a recollection by one of them."

"Perhaps if my mother had come to your birth, for by then your sister would have been four years old and your brother older. No doubt, your brother was taken from the house and distracted when your older sister was born and has no memory of the event aside from acquiring a baby sister. I don't think my mother stayed longer than to see my sister and her child were well."

"No one ever mentioned our grandmamma, nor did Bella and I ever think to ask about her."

"Well, we are reunited now and I have every intention of presenting myself to your father and siblings once you give me their address."

Rebecca's lips trembled before a sob burst from her mouth. She dropped her face into her hands to muffle her crying.

Alarmed, William jumped to his feet and looked to Belcrave for help, but it was Emily who scooted over on the sofa to wrap Rebecca up in her arms and whisper words of comfort. She helped her daughter-by-marriage to stand and then walked her out of the drawing room.

Belcrave apologized to the viscount for Rebecca's outburst and suggested they retire to his study for further discussion, "My countess will care for Rebecca while I explain what brought her to tears."

"Was it the circumstances of my mother's death? Should I have refrained from revealing it?"

"No, Rebecca has the right to know. It was the mention of her father that caused her to lose her composure. You see, Mr. Barrington died earlier this year in a duel."

William dropped his mouth in astonishment and then quickly shut it. He followed Belcrave into his study and looked at the stiff-backed chair in front of the earl's desk. He waited for the earl to take his seat before complaining, "What an abomination of a chair, Belcrave. Do you subject all your guests to this discourtesy or just me?"

The earl laughed and replied, "You are the first to remark upon it, but yes, that chair has served me well from suffering intolerable and obsequious discourses from those seeking my wealth and support. The chairs also rile my boys which brings me much pleasure. We should have gone to my library for a more comfortable discourse, but my study provides privacy and this is a private affair.

"I trust my personal staff, but human nature compels us to chat and oftentimes than not, information I prefer kept among family is discussed and then before you know, it is a topic of conversation in another household. While servants might remain invisible to their masters, they hear and see everything, and without consideration share those morsels we want kept private to earn themselves a bit of admiration or if they are disloyal, a bit of coin." He waved his hand to the corner of the room and said, "There is a more comfortable chair in the corner you may pull forward, or I can ring for my butler to do it."

"I am not in my dotage, Belcrave," retorted the viscount who proceeded to stand and exchange his archaic oak chair for a plush wing leather chair. Once settled, he asked, "How was my brother-by-marriage ever engaged in a duel? What nobleman seeks satisfaction with a commoner?"

"It was Barrington who sought satisfaction with Damburten. Barrington was a man of property and since Damburten was his neighbor, the baron could not easily refuse him without being marked a coward by his tenants and villagers."

"What offense did Damburten inflict to compel my brother-by-marriage to risk his life and or exile?"

"It is believed he assaulted Rebecca, but the degree of the attack is unknown."

Stunned, William rasped out, "Rebecca was violated?"

"I do not know the particulars and Rebecca has revealed nothing. The rumor mill was rampant for months with not what caused the duel but what happened after it."

"What do you mean?"

"It is said Damburten turned before making his final step and shot Barrington dead before the man had a chance to turn and set. Your nephew bore witness and picked up his father's gun from where he dropped it. He fired at Damburten and ran. There are various stories of what transpired. Regardless, the combatants are dead and other than gossip there is no report to explain precisely what happened."

"My nephew is in Newgate?"

"I have not heard of any arrest. If he is at Newgate I have no knowledge of it, nor do his sisters."

William's expression was marked with worry and anger. He stood and announced, "Well, I shall learn soon enough if my nephew was imprisoned and if so, why his family was not informed. You will forgive me for taking my leave, Belcrave?"

"Of course," the earl replied.

"If you permit, I shall return later this afternoon to check how my niece is feeling and if she is better I would like to take her for a drive during the fashionable hour in Hyde Park."

"Being seen in your company after last night's revelation will do her well, Ketterling," replied Belcrave. "It is good of you to think of it. I will apprise my countess and Rebecca."

Ketterling nodded and left.

Chapter Twenty-One

Charlotte was enthusiastically expounding on the various exhibitions she had just returned from seeing when her mother entered Rebecca's room and admonished, "Charlotte, cannot you see Rebecca is worn to the bone? What are you about exhausting her with your recitation?" To Rebecca, she scolded, "Why are you not resting?"

"The fault is mine, mama," interjected Charlotte. "I sent Mary the First for tea and in my distraction to converse with Rebecca I failed to see her fatigue."

At that moment, Mary entered with the tea tray and quickly sobered when she saw her mistress' angry expression. She continued with her task, placing the tray on the table, before turning to the countess.

Emily scolded, "Mary, why in the world did you allow my daughter to supersede my instructions. Did I not tell you I wanted Rebecca to rest?"

"Yes, milady," Mary answered without expression, keeping her eyes fixed beyond the countess, so as not to rile her further.

"I think I must send for our family doctor," announced Emily. "Harry would never forgive me if I neglected his wife's care."

Mary jerked her head towards Rebecca and gave a pointed look which did not go unnoticed by Emily. After a moment's thought Emily brusquely sent her daughter out of the room and then inquired to no one in particular, "What is it I do not know?"

Rebecca's eyes widened and she instinctively placed her hand on her baby. The behavior was a recent reflex whenever she was frightened. Emily's eyebrows rose in awareness and her nostrils flared in rage. Harry's wife was with child and the baby could not possibly be his if Rebecca was keeping it a secret. She steeled her eyes and railed, "You are with child?!"

Before Rebecca could answer, Charlotte rushed back into the room to divert her mother's anger. "Oh how wonderful!" she exclaimed with honesty. "Harry is to be a papa!"

All eyes turned to Charlotte. Emily scolded, "How often must I remind you ladies do not eavesdrop!"

"Mama," Charlotte murmured. "Do not be mad. It is unlike you to show me such discourtesy and I was worried something is afoot, but I am relieved to know there is only good news. What does it matter if Harry rushed his vows? He is a man, after all."

The countess' face crimsoned to hear her daughter speak vulgarly and rebuked, "Do not speak of things you should have no knowledge. Now retire to your room and do not let me find you on the other side of this door when I leave!"

Charlotte turned quickly, left, and proclaimed her displeasure by slamming the door behind her.

Emily shook her head and then returned her focus to Rebecca. She asked, "Did Harry marry you to save your reputation?"

"No," simmered Rebecca her face warming at the accusation.

Surprised, Emily enthusiastically asked, "The child is Harry's?"

Rebecca burst out in tears and Mary having been a retainer for more years than she wished to admit, suggested the countess allow Mrs. Bolton to regain her composure.

Emily left Rebecca to Mary's care and went to inform her husband of the new development and more specifically, to ask him what they were to do about the ball they were hosting to formally introduce Rebecca to the *ton*. Should they cancel? Harry would never forgive them if they did; especially if what Thomas wrote about Harry and Rebecca being a love-match was true.

She found the earl in his study and the moment she entered he stood and asked, "What has happened? Is it Rebecca?"

"Yes," she said.

Frowning, he inquired, "Is she ill? Have you sent for Reynolds?"

"No," Emily took the winged chair recently vacated by Ketterling and replied, "She is with child."

At first, the news made the earl beam, but upon further consideration and seeing his wife's distress, understanding settled. He asked, "It is not Harry's. This is why he married her. She is but another one of his rescues."

The countess recalled what Rebecca said and informed, "She says Harry did not marry her to save her reputation."

The earl took his seat looking nonplussed at his wife. He asked, "Did she explain herself?"

"She cried, Richard," informed Emily. "Mary the First had the presence of mind to advise me to leave her to compose herself. She will come to us soon and then we will have our answers."

"You allowed a servant to advise you?" scolded the earl.

"It was Mary the First, Richard," she countered. "I would never give any other servant such lenience, but how could I argue with sound reasoning. Nothing would be achieved by haranguing Rebecca and I had no wish to add to her distress when it could harm the baby. Surely you remember how emotional I became each time I carried."

The earl stared at his desk, expressing his unfiltered thoughts, "A baby that might not be Harry's. A baby without Bolton blood who would be in line to inherit." He fisted his hand and slammed it onto his desk, shouting, "I will not allow it!"

A soft knock on the door broke the taut tension. The earl, through force of habit, barked "enter" giving no mind to who entered his study. Emily's gasp turned Belcrave's attention to the door and to the intruder who stood at the threshold. His face crimsoned in anger. He did not care one whit if she heard his outburst. Better for her to learn he would not be as generous as his son was to her predicament.

Rebecca apologized for her intrusion, her cheeks pink from hearing the earl's rant. "Forgive me, my lord, but Mary the First said it was best I seek an audience with you sooner than later."

He turned his head to glare at his wife and silently rebuked her for once again allowing Mary the First to advise her betters. His temper unchecked, he stood and ordered Rebecca through his clenched teeth, "You will leave my house immediately."

"Richard," cried Emily in distress. "Do not act rashly. Let us hear what she has to say."

"I am to trust in her word when the whole time under our roof she lied to us," he argued.

"Not true, my lord," retorted Rebecca, "but I will not stay where I am not wanted."

"Well, you are not wanted," he rebuked. "I cannot believe I gave hospitality and the protection of my name to a conniving chit who took advantage of my son. Harry will repudiate the marriage once he learns you have misled him."

"How so, my lord?" asked Rebecca. "Harry sought me out. He proposed to me. Even my journey here to London to be introduced to the *ton* was for his sake and yours. Do not paint me the villain who married to elevate her position or to bring legitimacy to her child. I am not of such ilk, or have you forgotten how my mother, the daughter of a viscount, married a commoner."

"Do not think your mother's misalliance lends you any credit," Belcrave argued.

The countess anxiously rose from her seat and begged her husband, "Let her explain, Richard." She directed Rebecca to take her vacated seat prompting Richard to tell her to also sit down. Gentlemanly manners required him to stand until the ladies were seated and even in a pique of anger, he adhered to protocol. When his wife demurred, he ordered gruffly, "Sit down Emily!"

Begrudgingly, the countess sat on the reviled stiff-backed chair. Then, the earl sat, scowled at Rebecca and commanded, "Explain."

Rebecca looked directly at Belcrave with unwavering eyes and began, "Damburten hated my family, my lord. He wanted the property my papa inherited and named the Barrington Farm because he had promised his father on his deathbed he would return the land to their holdings. He and his father believed they had been bamboozled out of the land and hated my papa's cousin for it. That hatred festered and was directed at us when we became the new owners. Damburten tried to make us sell by turning the villagers against us. He sullied our reputations and when his efforts failed, he fixated his anger solely on me.

"He made it look as if he was smitten with me by performing gentlemanly acts, but the man had always frightened me. I saw the hatred in his eyes, and each time I refused or ignored his overtures he became more lewd in his remarks and propositions. At first, they were meant only for my ears and then he began to speak boldly in public calling me a tease and later *haymarket ware*.

"Looking back, he probably saw me as the easiest target among my family. I do not think he ever considered how I would simply isolate myself. My papa sought the vicar's help to settle the matter; especially when my reputation began to suffer. He considered sending me away to a safe haven, but I did not want to go. I had no desire to live with strangers or tax the family coffers. I was content to isolate myself at home.

"I had my family to keep me company and chores to occupy my time. I like to read and our evenings were filled with banter, party games and music. Bella is my best friend, so I never felt lonely or deprived. However, my self-imposed retreat angered Damburten and his slander became rampant. I don't know what set him off the day he attacked me, but the rage I saw stole my voice and paralyzed me. Sheer instinct drove me to fight for my life."

Rebecca continued her story, recalling every detail from the moment Damburten found her alone in the orchard to the aftermath of the duel. Her body shook and her eyes teared as she recalled the terror, assault, and grief she experienced, capturing every one of Damburten's vicious slaps, bruising grasps, suffocating chokes, brutal drags, and her own determined fight to escape his hands and vile intentions to her person.

Her voice cracked. Tears ran earnestly down her cheeks as she described the assault and the final blow that rendered her unconscious. Emily pushed her square of linen into Rebecca's hands and then watched as Rebecca smothered her uncontrollable sobs with it. Lost in her grief, Rebecca confessed her sorrow over the death of her papa and the loss of her brother. It was heart-wrenching to watch; especially when there were no adequate words of consolation to offer.

It was not until her story came to the point when Harry entered her life that she calmed and stopped crying. Her desolation diminished as quickly as striking a match and in her features was joy. Her cheeks blushed prettily and her eyes sparkled when she recounted how she met Harry, the number of times he came to her aid, and his poignant marriage proposal.

Grinning, she pointed out his cheerful manner, his compassion, and his witty repartee. She shared some anecdotes in case her listeners did not recognize his wonderful traits. Her affection for her husband was evident in the way she spoke of him and their time together. She explained how Harry won her over with his kind heart and generous spirit, how she felt safe around him which after her attack, she had never thought possible. Her body and spirit healed under his patient devotion.

She spoke how each day offered them joy and hope for a happy future. They were building dreams which were turning into expectations as they planned their life together. She did not even know she was with child until months into their marriage and only after her sister inquired. She and Harry are happy about their baby, and if not for her residual guilt over Damburten's attack, she never would have questioned the baby's paternity. Her guilt plagued her to the point she was making herself ill.

She explained how Harry noted her worry and demanded she place her burden upon him. Revealing a truth that could hurt him had made her hesitate, but in the end her conscious demanded she confess. The truth is she does not know if Damburten violated her and until her confession to Harry, neither had he considered it. Her husband left to find Nathaniel; the only living person who knows exactly what happened to her, not to verify paternity, but to allay her fears. Harry never once doubted the child was his own.

The silence was deafening. Both the earl and countess stared at Rebecca, but said nothing. What could they say after hearing her tragic and horrendous tale? Their stunned expressions turned to bewilderment when Rebecca stood remarkably composed and announced, "I shall take my leave by the end of day. If you cannot provide a coach for me, then I ask you to send a runner for Bolton's coach. I am authorized to use it. I will also do my best to reconcile Harry to your actions. Family is important. It is a sad thing to not have a mama and papa at hand to share in your joys and sorrows. I offer no apology for I have done nothing wrong. I do not harbor you or the countess any ill will for I truly understand the earldom is yours to protect."

She started to turn around to take her leave, but changed her mind and stepped back instead to express her gratitude. "Thank you for treating me like a daughter for the short time I was here."

The earl frowned then curiosity prompted him to ask, "You expect Harry to keep his vows?"

The smile Rebecca returned the earl was blinding when she said, "Of course, my lord, we love each other. Nothing else is important." She stepped back again, this time catching her heel on the wing chair's leg and tripped. Her fall might have come to naught if her head had not struck the back of the second sturdy oak chair set back earlier to make room for the winged chair.

Rebecca's eyes immediately rolled back and her body collapsed onto the floor. Emily screamed and the earl rushed to Rebecca's side pushing the sturdy oak chair out of his way. He did not like Rebecca's pallor, but relaxed when he discovered her pulse. Belcrave quickly chastised his wife for her hysterics, "This is not the time for the vapors, Emily. Send someone for Doctor Reynolds." He then lifted Rebecca up into his arms and rushed her to her room while Emily sent a footman to retrieve the doctor.

Emily and Richard were in the drawing room, awaiting the doctor's report of Rebecca, having left Mary the First to stand witness to Rebecca's examination. Thankfully, Rebecca regained consciousness when the earl placed her in bed, though her eyes were dazed and her words slurred.

The doctor arrived and Belcrave's questions forced Reynolds to ask him and the countess to leave while he assessed his patient. They begrudgingly left and made their way to the drawing room to wait. Emily sat on the gilded and green brocade upholstered sofa fiddling with her hands while Richard paced the floor before her.

Emily asked sadly, "Are you set to have her leave, Richard? I doubt she is well-enough to travel and Harry will not think kindly of us if we eject her from where he believes her to be safe. Are we to cancel the ball? Who knows if Harry will even arrive in time to attend?"

"He will be here, Emily," the earl replied. "After all, it was the sole purpose of sending Rebecca early to us so you could do what was needed to ensure her success. He would not shame her or you by being absent."

"You have changed your mind, then? You will accept Rebecca as Harry's wife?"

"Tarnation woman!" he exclaimed. "She IS Harry's wife and by all that she said, will continue to be. I will not suffer this farce again, so yes, the ball will continue. Any other course would lead to scandal and I will not be the cause of it." After a slight deliberation, he remarked, "Can you believe she had the audacity to say she would offer no apology for she did nothing wrong?"

"Do you think she did, Richard?"

Richard frowned and begrudgingly admitted, "No, I do not. She did nothing to deserve the assault. No young lady deserves to be hurt in that manner. If anyone dared to batter any of our daughters I would have demanded satisfaction just like Barrington. Her brother Nathaniel should be applauded for eliminating society of Damburten instead of being sought for murder."

Emily opined, "It is frightening to think a gentleman of title, property and means could behave so dishonorably."

"You are being kind, Emily," Belcrave retorted. "Damburten was no gentleman. Most likely, he was mad."

"What about the baby?" Emily asked anxiously.

"The baby is fine," interrupted Doctor Reynolds as he entered the drawing room misunderstanding the countess' inquiry. "I detected a strong and rapid heartbeat and since there were no other injuries I could ascertain, aside from the head injury, I see no cause for alarm."

Emily rose and exclaimed clasping her hands together, "Oh that is good news!"

Belcrave argued, "She passed out, Reynolds. Are you sure there are no other injuries or possible complications?"

"She hit her head, my lord. The knot on her head was significant, but her skull is not cracked, nor are there any lesions on her skin to warrant bandaging. She should be up and about by tomorrow."

"Tomorrow!" exclaimed Emily. "Is that wise?"

"Indeed, but I recommend lots of rest and nourishment. She looks exhausted. I dare say she was doing too much and if you want her ready for her debut ball, then no more strenuous outings or late nights. Keep her walking to a minimum. She may venture out on a short drive or entertain a visitor as she likes. She can also have willow bark tea if she experiences any head pain. If anything changes, send for me; otherwise, I will return tomorrow in the afternoon to check on her."

Chapter Twenty-Two

Rebecca woke in her cozy feather bed, pulled her arms out from under her green satin cover and pointed her toes in a full body stretch. She practically purred like a well-rested cat until she recalled her fall. Fear for her child had her frantically placing her hand on her rounded stomach and she was awestruck when her baby pushed back. Oh, how she wished Harry was with her to share in the moment. She was anxious to see him and tell him all that had passed.

She was not sure how Harry would feel over her confession to the earl and countess, but she had no regret. Withholding the information regarding her assault was a secret she could no longer harbor and she was glad the truth was out, until she remembered the earl had ordered her to leave his house. His command would disappoint Harry, and then he would take offense on her behalf and possibly do something he might regret.

She would not let that happen. She would not allow the earl to taint the love she had with her husband, nor would she be the reason behind an estrangement.

She rose from her bed and pulled on the bell cord to await Mary the First to help her dress and then to help her pack. She came with little, but she had acquired a lot of dresses and accessories since the short time of her stay. She would not quibble to whether her new attire belonged to her. The items were purchased for her use and she needed her new wardrobe with her burgeoning waistline. If the earl felt differently, then it was upon him to make issue of it.

Mary entered bearing a tray piled high with an assortment of meats, cheeses, breads, fruits, a silver dome covered plate and a pot of steaming tea. She placed her heavy laden on one of the many mahogany pedestal tables and then looked at Rebecca with assessing eyes. She remarked, "You look well-rested and ready to eat having missed last night's dinner and this morning's meal." She lifted the silver dome to show Rebecca what was under it and said, "I did not know if you wanted eggs or being the time of day preferred more of a luncheon. I can order anything else if none of it looks appetizing. The countess said to be sure the food was to your liking."

Rebecca's eyes widened in astonishment at hearing the countess' command and then silently chastised herself for thinking unkindly of Harry's mother who had been nothing but kind since her arrival. Rebecca remarked, "Thank you, Mary. There is plenty here to satisfy me though I don't know how much rest I will have since I must make ready to leave. Can you acquire a trunk and help me to pack?"

"My instructions are to inform you to eat and then for you to seek out the earl and countess. Her ladyship awaits you in the drawing room."

"I have too much to do," exclaimed Rebecca with marked irritation. "Surely, there is nothing more to be said." Rebecca looked at Mary's stoic face and knew the loyal servant would not discuss the earl and countess. She restrained her anger and said as calmly as she could, "Please inform the countess I will see her once I break my fast and dress."

"Very good, madam," replied Mary.

A half hour later, Rebecca came down the staircase and stopped at the landing when a middle-aged matron upon seeing her briskly turned from leaving. The lady wore finery marking a woman of means, and most likely title, and looked at Rebecca as if she was her favorite dessert. Rebecca stepped back when the lady reached for her hands to offer her vociferous felicitations.

"Congratulations Mrs. Bolton! I understand you are with child and I wanted to express my good wishes to you and Harry. He should be here but I daresay I will see him at your ball."

The lady turned away without waiting for a response and delivered a backwards wave to Emily who watched the exchange with wide-eyed astonishment.

Dawson without the hint of an expression opened the door for the lady to make her exit and closed it the moment her foot crossed the threshold. He stood stoically, as if nothing remarkable happened, while the countess fumed.

She had suffered through an onslaught of well-wishers exclaiming how they were "simply thrilled" with the news of Rebecca being with child, while making insinuations the baby was the reason behind Harry's abrupt marriage. The moment the door shut, Emily instructed her butler to tell future callers she was "not at home."

The countess released a curse few rarely heard and then blasphemed Reynolds for her insufferable number of callers because the doctor did not know how to keep his mouth closed. She might have expanded on her diatribe if the sight of Rebecca's pallor did not stop her. She quickly lowered her voice and relaxed her irate features, urging Rebecca to join her in the drawing room before ordering her now amused butler to ask the earl to join them.

Rebecca walked straight to the gilded and green brocade upholstered sofa the countess favored. Her comfort in so doing made her smile for she remembered how she once stood in awe of the room's gilded and rich furnishings. She was now quite comfortable in her surroundings; at least she was until last night, when the earl ordered her to leave his home. She warily sat next to Emily and turned her body to face the countess who blatantly inspected her and asked, "You are feeling better?"

"Indeed," Rebecca replied, adding, "and well-rested. Thank you for accommodating me last night and letting me sleep late."

Emily blushed at the reminder of her husband's outburst demanding Rebecca to immediately leave his house, but before she could apologize the earl entered the room. He strode forward, a frown creasing his forehead and assessed Rebecca. He looked at his wife for her own conclusion and asked, "She is well?"

Rebecca interjected heatedly, "I am perfectly capable of answering for myself, my lord. I am not a child who requires an adult to speak for me."

The earl looked at Rebecca as if she had just blasphemed him and retorted, "Indeed, but I was not sure you would answer honestly."

"Richard!" scolded Emily.

Richard raised his brows at the notion he insulted Rebecca again and quickly explained to his daughter-by-marriage, "Do not get your dander up, girl, I did not mean the remark disparagingly, but you are proud and stubborn. I could easily see you say you are well, regardless of how you feel."

Rebecca took umbrage at the earl's remark and pressed her lips together not wanting to rant like a banshee at him. She breathed in deeply to calm her anger and the sight of her flaring nostrils made the earl laugh. Her temper rose again at the added insult. She was no jester for court amusement and was about to tell him so, except he preempted her by telling her to smooth her hackles.

"Let us cry peace, Rebecca," Belcrave suggested. "It was wrong of me to order you from this house; especially after Harry left you in my care. I am honor-bound to keep you safe and that includes protected from scandal. We will proceed with the ball and I will not speak of the baby's paternity for now."

Rebecca sat speechless. She did not know what to say. She knew she should acknowledge the proverbial olive branch and apology the earl offered, but she had no wish to stay where she was not welcomed. However, she did not want to cause Harry's family injury which would happen if she left the earl's home. Her departure would force the earl to cancel the ball. Everyone would want to know why and if there was no immediate answer, then a tale would be construed by the gossipmongers to satisfy the curious. She had little choice but to stay.

The earl sadly confessed when Rebecca did not respond, "You have placed a great burden on me, Rebecca. Do not think I dislike you, if anything I admire how you fought off a man like Damburten. You not only battled him, but survived the atrocity with spirit intact. However, the notion of a child not of Bolton blood in line to inherit the title is anathema to me. I cannot allow the possibility."

"Can you not trust in Harry to nurture our baby to be honorable, steadfast, and compassionate? Would he or she be anything else with Harry as parent?"

The lines between the earl's brows furrowed in thought. He asked, "And what would the child receive from you?"

Rebecca chuckled and replied, "No doubt, my stubbornness, temper, and determination, but also my unwavering trust in those I love."

"And you love Harry?" the earl asked, surprising himself with the question.

"Yes. A love so profound I cannot describe it with words."

"Try," he ordered.

Rebecca smiled and said, "Well, love can be a conundrum in that regardless of what temperament you might be feeling, it never wavers, nor does it create doubt. Love strengthens and endures. Love forgives, prospers and bears fruit. I love Harry for a number of reasons for which it would take me a lifetime to list, but the most important reason is because Harry loves me."

Belcrave shook his head as though he had just ended up in the same place he had begun and wondered how it had happened. He rolled his eyes and remarked, "You are spouting poetry."

"Richard!" scolded Emily again. "I found Rebecca's description of love endearing. Do not be critical!"

"Hmf," grunted the earl, before he voiced what was a high concern among the peerage when negotiating marriage contracts, "We have gotten off track, Rebecca. Damburten was insane. Your child's blood could be tainted."

Rebecca's anger rose and she rebutted, "Damburten was not insane! He grew wicked from living a life unchecked and believing he was entitled to do whatever he wished without consequences. He might have been mad, but of temper where like a child he acted out when he could not get what he wanted. My child is a blessing and over time you will discover he or she is worthy of being a Bolton. Besides, Harry might indeed be the father. Had it not been for the guilt I festered over keeping the assault a secret from Harry, I doubt if I would have ever questioned our baby's paternity. Harry never did."

Looking crestfallen at possibly repudiating a true grandchild, the earl said, "Let us hope Harry brings good news. Until then, we will proceed as before, aside from your exerting yourself. You must rest and eat."

Rebecca conceded with a nod and then to divert from the uncomfortable discussion she asked the countess, "Did you inform the lady visiting I was with child?"

"No, that impudent doctor of ours spoke indiscreetly," replied Emily. "He might as well have placed an advertisement for all the well-wishers plaguing me today. No doubt the parlours are speculating on whether to expect a seven month wonder. That is absurd considering your figure."

"My clothes hide my baby well. Madame Lavigne made my dresses to expand," Rebecca replied.

Emily looked at the high-waist of Rebecca's dress and saw the tapes that could be loosened to increase its girth. She said, "I have been too occupied or else I would have noticed."

"Enough," shouted the earl. "Am I expected to listen to women's chatter? Desist until I take my leave."

With that announcement, the earl left and took his exit through the door the butler opened upon entering to announce Viscount Ketterling wished an audience. "I know, my lady," Dawson explained, "I am directed to refuse callers, but I thought I should ask anyway since the viscount is a relative of Mrs. Bolton. He seemed highly distressed and wished to inquire on Mrs. Bolton's health. I thought it unwise to send him on his way. However, I shall do so if you wish me…"

The countess raised her hand to halt her butler's soliloquy and chastised, "For heaven's sake Dawson. If I wanted a Bambury tale I would have gone to Drury Lane. Cease your speech. You did right to inquire since the caller is for Rebecca and not me."

Emily turned to Rebecca and asked, "Do you wish to see the viscount?"

"Oh, yes," replied Rebecca.

The countess remarked to her butler, "Well, you have your marching orders, Dawson. See the viscount in."

William rushed in moments later offering his salutations before inquiring to Rebecca's health. Lines creased his forehead as he inspected his niece. His voice was marred with anxiousness as he explained, "I was at my club when I heard of your fall. I rushed over immediately. Are you well?"

"Sit down, Ketterling," demanded the countess. "I shall get a kink in my neck if you continue to hover over us."

"I beg your pardon," he apologized contritely before taking the matching gilded wing chair across from the sofa where the countess and Rebecca sat. He looked beseechingly at his niece for the answer to his question.

Rebecca responded with a sympathetic smile and said, "I am well, uncle. Do not distress yourself."

"I was told your injury was grave." he countered.

"Not in the least," Rebecca replied, her lips turning up in a true grin from her uncle's sincere concern. "I tripped, hit my head and suffer from a small bump, but nothing more. Be at ease."

"Thank goodness," he sighed and finally sat back against his seat and relaxed.

"I am sorry to have missed our ride yesterday afternoon," she remarked to distract him from his worries.

The reminder made William realize he had been gulled. "They informed me you were asleep and not taking visitors. I thought you were tired. It never occurred to me I was being told a bouncer. You must think me an ill relation to not have called upon you."

Rebecca laughed at hearing her uncle's cant and replied in earnest, "But uncle, you did call on me."

William's features softened as his lips turned up in response to his niece's cheerful retort and offered, "Shall I take you up in my curricle now. Is it permitted? I do not wish to contradict your doctor's instructions, but it is a beautiful day for a ride as the sky is clear of overcast. You can actually see the sun."

"That sounds lovely, uncle" answered Rebecca with delight. "The doctor suggested fresh air would do me good."

The countess interjected, "Ring for your gloves, bonnet, and coat, Rebecca. The sun may be shining, but our English weather is much like a book that starts out good but ends deplorably."

Rebecca grinned and did as bid. Her uncle helped her put on her coat, then escorted and helped her onto the perch of his two-seater curricle. He explained, "It is no fancy phaeton, but has served me well. I will have to look to purchase something more elegant if I wish to court any ladies, otherwise they may think me without means." He smiled and Rebecca laughed.

"Your beautifully matched pair of bay horses will put to rest any ideas you have pockets to let," remarked a mischievous Rebecca.

The viscount laughed as heartily as if his feet were being tickled. "Where did you learn such vulgar cant?"

Rebecca blushed and replied, "Oh, say it is not so. I thought to prove myself fashionable. As to where I learned it, must I remind you I have a brother and recently acquired a husband and brother-by-marriage, all of whom fail to curb their tongues within my hearing?"

Sobering his features, her uncle said, "I will have to rebuke them for behaving indiscreetly, or at least I shall chastise your brother. I do not think Bolton or your husband will take kindly to being reprimanded by me."

"Indeed not," laughed Rebecca.

"I am glad to see you smiling and perhaps the news I bring will lift your spirits even more."

Rebecca sat straighter and turned in her seat to watch her uncle. The man could hardly take his eyes off the road, but she did not want to miss one bit of his good news. She waited in anticipation and saw him smile before he began his announcement.

"I spent yesterday at Newgate and sent a number of solicitors to the prison hulks to do a thorough search. There is no record of your brother, nor a warrant for his arrest. I spoke to the London magistrate directly and no one has made any claims against your brother for murder. Are you sure Damburten is dead?"

Rebecca's face went pale and she started shaking. Her uncle felt her tremors reverberate through the seat and took a cursory look at her. Alarmed at what he saw, he instinctively pulled up on his horse's reins and turned his cattle about to return Rebecca to Belcrave House.

Chapter Twenty-Three

William jumped from his curricle hating to leave Rebecca on her seat alone, but had no other choice without a servant to whom he could hand off his reins. He quickly tied the leather ribbons to a post, hoping his horses would calm down without a walk after pushing them hard to return to Belcrave's townhome. With his horses secured, he raced back to Rebecca's side of his curricle and gathered her into his arms.

Her trembling form concerned him, as did her unfocused eyes and silence. He expected her to disabuse him for carrying her and when she did not, he ran up the front steps and kicked the door with his foot. The attending footman dropped his jaw when he opened the door and saw the viscount carrying Rebecca. He gave no argument when William pushed his way in.

William commanded in a voice worthy of a military officer ordering his troops, "Close your gaping mouth and send for your mistress. Then, see the doctor is summoned!" He headed for the stairs and upon spying the butler asked abruptly, "Which room is hers?"

Dawson snapped his fingers to the wide-eyed footman whose feet seemed glued to their spot and woke the servant to action. He then hurried up the steps to lead the viscount to Rebecca's room. William was beyond worry. His niece had not uttered a word to explain her shivering, nor had she come to her senses. Her eyes were open, but she was not cognizant.

Dawson opened the door and stepped aside to allow William to enter first. He followed quickly behind the viscount and then stepped forward to pull back the bedcover so William could lay Harry's wife down. Rebecca shivered uncontrollably as if she was in a winter storm without benefit of a coat.

William pulled the brocade cover over her body and tucked it around her sides. He stood up from his bent position to assess his administrations and saw his niece still wore her bonnet and gloves. He looked at where her feet should be and remembered she wore shoes. The notion of undressing her made him craven. He looked to Dawson who looked as nonplussed as he and ordered, "Get a maid."

Harry was in the drawing room when the commotion of doors slamming and voices raised broke the discussion he was having with his parents. His arrival was met with animated welcome, and a confession that soon left him confused and worried. He deduced from his mother's apologies and his father's brusque explanation, that Rebecca was injured during an interview with them where the baby's paternity was brought into question. The idea Rebecca suffered alone under his father's imperious questioning made him angry, but his concern for his wife took precedence over chastising his parents.

The earl quickly informed him as he turned to leave that Rebecca was out on a drive with an uncle of whom he had no knowledge. He was deliberating his next course of action when the parlour doors slammed open and an anxious footman hurried forward to inform what had transpired.

Harry did not wait to hear more. He raced out of the drawing room and up the staircase to find his wife. His parents followed him and when he turned down the corridor to his room his mother yelled, "She's in the Garden Suite."

Harry made a quick turnaround and raced past his mother until he reached the guest suite. He found Mary the First making his wife comfortable in her bed and hurried to her side. He called out her name and when she did not respond, his chest tightened and his inquiry to no one in particular escaped in a gasp, "What happened?"

Mary the First answered, "I do not know, Master Harry. The viscount brought her in this state."

Rage overcame Harry and he turned towards the sitting room connected to the sleeping quarters. He strode forward and searched for an unknown face. By now, his father and mother were among the group awaiting news of Rebecca and there, striding to and fro, was a man unknown to him. He stalked over and grabbed William by his lapels. The earl intervened and commanded, "Desist, Harry. Ketterling is Rebecca's uncle. You have no quarrel with him!"

Harry released William and ran his hands through his hair. He asked Rebecca's uncle, "What happened? I understood she was under your protection. What ails my wife?"

The sorrow in William's eyes forced Harry to sympathize with the man and temper his voice. He apologized for his hostility and said more gently, "Can you tell me what you know?"

William took a seat and mirrored Harry's earlier frustration by running his hands through his hair. He dropped his head and replied, "It happened so fast. One moment, I was informing Rebecca what I learned of Nathaniel and the next she was shivering as if she saw a ghost." William's head shot up. "By jove!" he exclaimed remembering the precise moment when Rebecca began to shake, "I asked if she was sure Damburten was dead."

The doctor arrived and went straight into the bed quarters, shutting the connecting door behind him. Harry rose to follow him, but his father stopped him remembering his own interference the day before. "Let him examine her first, Harry. You will only keep him from doing his job."

Harry conceded and sat back down. No one spoke, as if fearing to break the silent vigil. Moments, minutes, or maybe an hour passed. Time stood still as worry froze everyone into silent prayer. Finally, the doctor emerged shaking his head. Harry jumped up and met the doctor as he exited the bedroom. He waited for the man to speak.

"Your wife is in deep shock, Mr. Bolton. I do not know what caused it, but she is fraught with worry. None of my tests brought her round. She is physically sound. Her reflexes are good. Her heart beats strong and there is no tenderness anywhere I could find."

"The baby?" asked Harry.

"Fine, as far as I can tell. The baby's heartbeat is good and your wife is not bleeding. No, I think your wife ails mentally and there is little I can do for that, aside from the draught of laudanum I gave her to sleep. Perhaps, after a sound slumber she will come to her senses."

"You will speak of this to no one," chastised the earl. "You were indiscreet after your last visit and if I hear you blab of my affairs again, Reynolds, I will see you ruined."

"Pull in your claws, Belcrave!" retorted the affronted doctor who had cared for the family for years. "I had no reason to believe your good news was not meant for announcement. Heavens be! Why wouldn't you want me to speak of it?"

"Because it is not your affair, Reynolds, do not test me. Rebecca's condition is not for the gossipmongers to chew on. I'll have your word as a gentleman on it."

"Of course," replied a frowning Reynolds offended by the slur to his character. "Do you wish for me to return tomorrow?"

"You already said there is nothing you can do, so no," responded Harry. "I will see to my wife's care."

Dawson escorted the doctor out of the room. Once Reynolds left, Harry said to Rebecca's uncle, "Will you wait, Ketterling, until after I see Rebecca so I may have further speech with you."

"Of course," replied William.

William left with the earl and countess while Harry turned to enter the bedroom to see his wife.

Rebecca lay in a deep sleep and her pallor drove Harry to place his finger under her nose to ensure she was breathing. It was easy to understand Rebecca's reaction to the news Damburten might be alive. It had taken him months after her assault to ease her fright and part of her comfort came from knowing the baron could no longer harm her. The notion of him alive must have recalled her worst fears. He closed his eyes, feeling overwhelming remorse for not being there when she needed him most.

He bent over and kissed her forehead. Then, he placed his hand under her head to feel for the lump he was told she received from hitting a chair. He moved his hand to her neck's pulse point and was relieved to find a steady heartbeat. He continued with his assessment, gently running his hands over her limbs for his own peace of mind to ensure her body was whole and then he rested his hand on her stomach.

He was surprised how much her belly was rounded and firm since he last saw her; and almost jumped when his baby moved. It was so fleeting he was not sure of what he felt until his baby moved again and then he smiled at the wonder of it all. He wished Rebecca was awake to share the moment with her and then wondered if she had already felt their baby stir. There was so much for them to celebrate and discuss.

She would not see Damburten's emergence as a celebration, even though it meant Nathaniel was free to come home. Her brother could no longer be held responsible for murdering Damburten if the baron was alive, nor could he be held accountable for shooting him without accusation which Damburten could not do without admitting to his own misdeed. It mattered not if the duel was or was not engaged honorably for dueling was illegal.

More than one justified gentleman seeking satisfaction through death had to flee England to escape transportation or hanging. It served the challenger no good to leave all they owned to kill a villain. For that reason, most gentlemen deloped, shooting their weapons into the air to satisfy honor, unless one of the gentlemen was a renowned shooter or swordsman. Then, that person might seek blood instead of death, but be it pistols or swords no one ever knew what might transpire in the heat of the moment, and that was the reason duels were a deadly venture to engage.

Harry whispered in Rebecca's ear, "Do not worry, love. I am here. You are safe."

Rebecca whispered Harry's name in a sigh. The sound of her saying his name made him confident she would recover. He beckoned Mary the First from the adjacent room and told her to sit by Rebecca's side until he returned and then he kissed his wife again before he took his leave. There was work to be done to ensure his wife's peace of mind and safety. He would begin by speaking with Ketterling.

He found the viscount with the earl in the drawing room. His mother, he was informed, retired to her room. The viscount began to stand the moment Harry entered and Harry waved him back to his seat.

"Take your seat, Ketterling," commanded Harry. "I will join you and then you may enlighten me to why I have no knowledge of your connection to my wife and how you have come to be in her company."

William jerked his head back as though he took a punch to his jaw. Of all the questions to be asked, his connection to his niece was the least of them. He quickly collected himself and answered, "I can only surmise why I am not known to my nieces and nephew, though through my mother's correspondence with my sister, I knew of them. Needless to say, my father and sister had a falling out after her marriage to Mr. Barrington. I had no idea where Rebecca or her siblings lived. I did not have the liberty to search for them until my father died and I inherited his title."

Harry asked, "You have been looking for them since then?"

"I hired a detective but with little to go on aside from the Barrington name his effort was futile and to my discredit, between settling my father's affairs and managing my newly inherited estate, I was distracted from pursuing the investigation."

"Were you close to Rebecca's mother?"

"We were as close as any two siblings with a vast age difference between them could be. I remember her fondly and see her likeness in my niece. I was sent away to Eton at a young age, so I did not see her often, but recall her beauty and tender heart. She always made time for me and leant an ear to all my troubles."

Harry smiled, knowing his wife would like to know her mother was fondly remembered.

"Now," began the viscount with a stern voice, "tell me why my niece has not been under your protection?"

Harry's smile flattened and his face grew rigid in anger from being assessed by Rebecca's uncle. He began to rise until his father scolded, "Sit Harry. You cannot interrogate the man without expecting the man to retaliate. He has every right as the head of his house to ask his questions."

Harry sat and glared at the viscount. To his surprise, William chuckled and confessed, "I have heeled and held my tongue more than once as is a son's duty. I apologize for speaking thoughtlessly, but my concern made me speak precipitously because you did not inform us if Rebecca woke?"

"I beg your pardon. No, she is sleeping, but I have every expectation she will wake fit," Harry answered. "As to my absence, I was searching for Nathaniel. I left my brother's men to continue the search for I did not want

Becca to fret upon my arrival. Our debut ball is but two days away."

"You know Nathaniel's location?" asked the viscount anxiously.

"No," replied Harry. "We looked in the most likely places he would have sought shelter and when we came up empty, I headed for London. My brother's men will report to Thomas and then search for Nathaniel's grandfather."

William queried, "And what of Arabella?"

Surprised, Harry asked, "She is not here?"

"No," exclaimed William in alarm.

"Do not fret, Ketterling," responded Harry. "I left both sisters in my brother's care. If Arabella is not here, then she is with him."

The viscount's eyebrows rose in clear disapproval.

Harry added before Ketterling became enraged, "You can trust my brother to ensure her safety."

"What of her reputation? How does Bolton guard it while traveling alone with her?"

"My brother would have taken every precaution, Ketterling," replied Harry.

William huffed and opened his mouth to voice what he thought of Harry's assurances, but the earl immediately interrupted him.

Belcrave was not about to have Ketterling demand the banns be read for his heir to marry Arabella. The idea was insufferable and so he loftily informed, "Ketterling, my son is diligent in these respects and I can assure you Bolton would insist upon all forms of protocol to protect

Miss Barrington's reputation. Stop baiting Harry. He has enough on his mind."

Duly chastised, William responded, "I shall demand reparation if you are incorrect in your knowledge, Belcrave. I will desist for now and wait to see what comes to pass."

"Indeed," replied the earl brusquely.

William stood ignoring the earl's retort and said to Harry. "I shall take my leave and call on Rebecca tomorrow."

"Water," rasped Rebecca into the blackness of the room. She was not sure if anyone was at hand to hear her, but her throat was parched. The stirrings of a chair being pushed back comforted her and when she saw it was Harry who tended her, a flood of tears fell from her eyes.

"Do not cry, Becca," soothed Harry placing a glass of water to her lips. "I am here and will carry all your burdens. You have no reason to be afraid or to worry of what is to be done. I will handle everything. Rest and take comfort in knowing I am here."

"Oh, Harry!" she exclaimed after taking a sip of water. "Damburten is not dead!"

"Possibly, but do not let it alarm you. He can no longer hurt you. Take comfort in knowing Nathaniel may come home. Soon your family will be reunited."

"Nathaniel may come home?"

"Yes, Becca, now sleep. I shall join you in bed if you like and tomorrow we shall spend the day together. What say you?"

"Oh, yes Harry. Come to bed and hold me. May we spend not just tomorrow, but all our days together?"

Harry grinned, wrapped his wife up in his arms and said, "It is my greatest wish."

Chapter Twenty-Four

Harry pulled Rebecca back into bed as she tried to escape. His maneuver landed her on top of him, giggling at his shenanigans. She tried to pull free and scolded him for not releasing her.

"You are too cruel, Becca," he replied. "We have been apart for over a week and yet you are ready to take your leave of me at the slightest provocation."

"My growling stomach is not slight, Harry," she retorted. "I need food. Our baby needs nourishment. Besides, I am sure your parents are worried we have yet to make an appearance. For heaven's sake, it is midday!"

"And your point?"

Rebecca laughed and Harry moved her to the side of his body so he could see her smiling face. He was glad the terror she suffered during the night was banished. He hugged her close and placed his chin on top of her head. He had joined Rebecca in bed after she first woke from her shock and immediately wrapped her up in his arms. He held her and lulled her weary spirit into a slumber that also put him to sleep. Unfortunately, their respite did not last long.

Rebecca woke up quaking and her screams catapulted him awake. The knowledge the baron might be alive manifested into a nightmare where Rebecca was once again in Damburten's clutches. She lashed out, fighting the baron in her mind until Harry's embrace and soft spoken assurances pulled her from her fright.

She blinked her eyes open and recognized him immediately. The sight of him released the emotions she had kept at bay during his absence. She trembled and cried until Harry convinced her Damburten could no longer hurt her. He explained there were probably witnesses to testify the baron shot her father in cold blood; and while these gentlemen might not speak up for a commoner, they would stand witness for his father.

Belcrave was a powerful and influential lord who took umbrage with any person doing his family harm. Harry informed her Thomas was already investigating Damburten and if he found the baron alive, she could rest assured the baron would be transported or hung for his crimes.

Harry tried to soothe Rebecca by reminding her how Nathaniel was no longer a fugitive and could now come home and take care of Arabella. He spoke of their own bright future, adding amorous kisses into his narrative.

He kissed her tear-filled eyes and then progressed to other points that soon had her returning his affection with abandon. Their long separation fueled their ardor and Rebecca's nightmare was forgotten. They woke in the early morning replete and smiling at one another.

Harry wrapped up his wife in his arms and upon seeing her forehead crease asked what was wrong. Her face immediately relaxed and she grinned at her husband for knowing her so well. She confessed her troubles. What if the earl does not accept our baby? What if the ton does not accept me? After all, there are those who think me an encroaching mushroom who hoodwinked you into marriage. Oh, Harry, what of the scandal attached to my name?

Fretfully, she admitted she was reluctant to make her debut. What if I do something to shame you and your family? She expected Harry to offer sympathy for her plight, so when he smiled, she swatted his arm resting across her stomach. Harry laughed and hugged her tighter, so he would not suffer another attack.

"Becca," he informed. "Every debutante is reluctant to make her debut. They fear no one will attend their ball, or they will trip, or do any number of embarrassing things to reduce their chances of making an eligible match. You have nothing to fear. Our ball will be a crush and it matters not if you trip or say something untoward. You are my wife. You have already secured me and have no need to impress a suitor."

"They will think I am putting on airs, behaving above my station," she replied.

Harry chastised, "Bella, the ball is in honor of our marriage. You are not trespassing into a sphere you do not belong. The sooner you accept your station has changed, the sooner you can enjoy the benefits of it. You think you are undeserving, but you forget you are the granddaughter and niece of a viscount. Our marriage did not raise your consequence. You were simply unaware you had any. What does it matter what others think? I love you. My family loves you. That is all that matters."

Rebecca gaped at the idea of Harry's family loving her. She reminded him, "Your father does not love me, Harry. He ordered me out of his home just days ago. He might not accept our child. Then, what will we do?" Her voice rose as she exclaimed, "I will not have our baby hurt and rejected!"

Harry grinned at his wife defending their unborn babe. "The earl is more bark than bite when it comes to his family," he soothed. "I wish you would trust me when I say I am our baby's father, but the truth will be revealed by either Nathaniel or when our baby is born. Bolton blood runs true and our baby will have my features. You just wait and see."

Rebecca harrumphed and remarked, "Maybe our baby will look like me."

Harry laughed and said, "It matters not who our baby favors. He or she is a Bolton and no one rejects a Bolton."

"Harry," laughed Rebecca. "I never knew you could be so lofty."

"Becca," he replied, "When I am with you I feel like a king. Why shouldn't I think 'the world is mine oyster'?"

"Are you not worried regarding the scandal attached to my name?"

"That on dit is passé. Every drawing room is re-marking about Lady Berkshomp taking a whip to her husband's mistress after the lady bird had the audacity to greet him while in her company. Rowlandson has already illustrated the scene characterizing the indomitable Lady Berkshomp perched in her open curricle holding a whip directed at the doxy's back. The print is being displayed in all the shops. The duel is old news, Becca."

Harry regretted bringing up the duel when Rebecca's lips trembled. He tightened his embrace of her and soothed, "It is all right, Becca. Nothing can harm us anymore."

It was another hour before Harry left Rebecca in Mary the First's hands to help her dress. He made his way to the drawing room to find his parents and await his wife. Mary was dressing Rebecca in a new walking dress and full-length redingote trimmed with white ermine on the front collar and lapels. The white fur trim contrasted brightly against the finely woven cobalt blue of the coat. She and Harry were going to take a stroll through the park before the social hour began and then procure an ice from Gunter's. It was one of the promises he made to her before he left to find Nathaniel.

Rebecca practically skipped into the drawing room, anxious to show Harry her new finery. She was so excited she saw no one but him. His fretful face made her stop and be wary. She had no idea what was afoot, but after yesterday's revelation about Damburten, she was not sure she wanted to know. She might have turned tail and run except Harry stepped forward and took her hand.

He walked her over to stand by his parents who also looked troubled. It was then she realized another person was in the room. His height and features were remarkable and worthy of wearing the impressive red and heavily gold trimmed royal livery. The footman stepped forward and inquired to Rebecca's identity. Once assured she was Mrs. Harry Bolton he proffered an envelope sealed with a dab of wax bearing the royal crest.

All eyes were upon her as she opened the envelope and read the enclosed card. Her arms dropped in astonishment with the card barely held between the tips of her thumb and forefinger. Her stunned expression propelled Harry to take the card from her fingers and read its content. He turned to his parents and informed, "She is being summoned to the Queen's House for a royal audience."

"She must change her attire," exclaimed his mother.

The royal servant announced, "The queen awaits her, my lady. I am commanded to bring her post haste. I have the royal carriage waiting to transport her to Buckingham Palace."

Panicked, Rebecca looked at Harry and pleaded, "You will come with me."

Harry looked to the queen's footman. He could not enter the queen's home without permission so he was glad the royal servant informed, "My Queen welcomes Mr. Harry Bolton to accompany his wife."

Without another word the footman made his exit. The countess was the first to come to her senses and push her son and Rebecca forward, urging them to make haste.

Rebecca stood next to Harry in the receiving line, waiting to greet the guests who would soon arrive for their ball. She was still dazed from yesterday's warm and effusive welcome from Queen Charlotte. The queen confessed she had been waiting decades to repay the debt she owed her grandfather for offering aid to her favorite godson who found himself stranded while traveling abroad. The queen's accent and quick speech made it difficult for Rebecca to understand all the details, but it was clear Queen Charlotte held her grandfather in high regards for bringing her godson safely home.

She deduced it was her mother's father who aided the queen's godson, even though she had trouble reconciling the generous act with the man who disinherited her mama, but who else had the means to travel abroad? She knew her paternal grandfather had little means and stature.

Before she could press for more details, the queen remarked Rebecca looked just like her mama. The observation made Rebecca forget her questions. Hearing the queen recollect her mother's presentation drew her singular attention. "A diamond of the first water," the queen exclaimed, "owning a gracious curtsey and manner to outshine every other debutante of the Season."

Rebecca saw the grin made pointedly at her and smiled. Be it truth or fiction, Rebecca enjoyed the queen's compliment to her mother, but not for long, for the queen frowned abruptly and then proceeded to scold her.

She was displeased, she announced, that Rebecca and her siblings were not presented when they came of age, and then in the next breath, the queen congratulated Rebecca on her exceptional marriage to Harry. There were other words expressed, and orders for Rebecca and her siblings to return for a formal presentation in the drawing room at St. James Palace.

Rebecca was too stunned to truly take note of any of it, until the queen grabbed both her hands and looked her straight in the eyes. "No one," she declared slowly and succinctly, "will dare impugn your good name now I have acknowledged you. Trust me; heads will roll if I hear otherwise." Rebecca was not sure it was said in jest.

Chapter Twenty-Five

Rebecca suffered the appraisal of the first guest introduced to her at her ball and then gathered all her courage to tolerate the rest. She might have stumbled from the occasional sneer or lofty remark if her gallant husband had not cheered her on with his solid strength, cheery repartee, and unwavering support.

He brought her arm through his own to keep her safe by his side and retorted to every smirk with a query, *"Are you ill, by chance? Are you suffering an apoplexy? Perhaps you should seek your physician. Your lips are grotesquely twisted."*

Rebecca had to bite her tongue to keep from laughing. The earl soon excused them from their duty saying their ballroom would be empty if they kept telling guests to seek out a doctor. Of course, that was a bouncer.

The ball was a crush. Rebecca doubted anyone sent their regrets. All the guests stood in their finery, the ladies hoping to outshine every other titled lady with all their ribbons, lace, furbelows and gemstones on their person. Ostrich feathers, diamond stick pins, satin bandeaus topped their heads and strands of diamonds and gemstones hung from their neck and ears. Some touted the family heirlooms, while others showed off their newest baubles.

The debutantes came in their white netted or laced gowns. Their hair was ornamented with strands of pearls or fresh flowers. Pearls graced their necks and ears. Every man was attired in formal black tailcoats, black pantaloons, a white waistcoat, a crisp white shirt and white cravat. Some gentlemen displayed their sense of style with an embroidered waistcoat.

The floors glistened from being waxed and polished. The chandelier crystals sparkled from being thoroughly cleaned, and now with hundreds of candles in their holders lit, the ballroom radiated glittering light. There were white Roman urns filled with white gladiolas, carnations, roses and greenery placed on top of white Roman pillars situated around the perimeter of the room.

Swaths of white tulle hung in swags on the walls tied in bows at their peaks. There was enthusiasm and gaiety among the guests for the first dance to open the ball. Rebecca's nerves overwhelmed her and she wished Harry was her partner instead of the earl. However, the ball was designed to proclaim Belcrave's support of Harry's marriage, and so she was to dance with the earl first, and then her uncle to show her own connections to nobility.

Rebecca managed not to stumble or fall during the opening set and received the earl's approbation for her effort when the dance ended. Looking haughty, he walked her over to her uncle who greeted her with affection. No sooner did she make her curtsey than her uncle escorted her back onto the dance floor.

She still trembled from being the center of everyone's attention, but unlike Belcrave who was cognizant of the high sticklers, and therefore danced with a sober decorum, her uncle's expressively warm and cheery nature immediately calmed her nerves. He made her forget she was on display. She was flushed, smiling, and anxious to find Harry by the time the set finally ended.

She was to waltz with Harry and since the dance preceded supper, he would not only be her partner for her meal, but she would get a reprieve from being on stage. She eagerly placed her hand on her uncle's arm to let him lead her to Harry.

The musicians paused to let the dance floor empty and for the gentlemen and ladies to locate their next dancing partners. The violinist would play a few bars to warn the dancers to take their places before the set was to begin. William maneuvered Rebecca through the dancers and having spied Harry, teased her about Harry's obvious impatience to dance with her. Laughing, she stopped and playfully chastised him. Sheer happiness radiated from her, making her look even more beautiful.

She wore a high-waist net dress of sheer white over a pink satin slip. The bottom half of her skirt was ornamented with three falls of white lace confined at the edge by a narrow pink satin rouleau. Her narrow heart-shaped bodice was trimmed in white lace and pink satin as were her pretty short puffed sleeves. She wore long white satin gloves, white satin slippers, and pearls around her neck and threaded through her elaborate Grecian-styled hair. She outshone every debutante in style and grace; even those marked a diamond of the first water.

A grating chuckle made her frown and drew her attention away from her uncle. She searched the crowd for the culprit who made the offensive sound and her eyes landed among a group of young debutantes and their escorts. Her temper piqued upon seeing she was the brunt of their mirth.

Rebecca might have stepped forward to confront her ill-mannered guests, if her uncle had not placed his free hand on top of the one she had on his arm. She looked at him and saw he was angry on her behalf. He took a step to escort her back to Harry, but she refused to budge; especially when the group chuckled as if they had just witnessed a victory. She scoped out the group of young peers again, taking each person's measure and was not surprised to find the one person she knew wished her harm.

Lady Caroline locked eyes with Rebecca and the lady's obvious scorn had Rebecca pulling back her shoulders in defense. In a clear voice Caroline informed, "He married her because she is with child." Caroline did not use Rebecca's name but all knew she was the one whom the lady spoke.

Rebecca tried to take a step forward to confront her adversary, but her uncle's grip held firm. She looked up at him and he said, "Are you sure, Becca?" Rebecca smiled, patted his hand and returned her focus to Lady Caroline. Her look must have been fierce for the crowd surrounding Lady Caroline gasped.

Rebecca walked up to Caroline who had the effrontery to give her the cut-direct, an insult, used by members of the peerage to someone not worth acknowledging. Surprisingly, the peers who were engaging in gossip with Caroline stepped away the moment she turned her back on Rebecca. They might enjoy observing the birth of a scandal, but they had no wish to be a part of it. They cleared the space around Caroline, but stayed close enough to hear what was said. Their interest drew the attention of nearby guests and the whisper of an explanation built into a crescendo of chatter until it broke and only silence remained.

"I see you are as rude and vulgar as the last time we met, Lady Caroline," stated Rebecca in a clear and steady voice to the lady's back. Caroline's spine stiffened so Rebecca knew the lady was listening. Even if she was not, every guest would pass the details on in tomorrow's drawing rooms. Rebecca continued, "I gave you the courtesy of turning a blind eye to your ill manner the last time I was in your company, but I will not tolerate your viciousness towards my family in my home. You are no longer welcome. I suggest you return to the nursery to relearn the manners that behoove a lady for you have forgotten how to behave as one."

A number of gasps, snorts, and chuckles echoed through the ballroom. Caroline turned to face Rebecca with rage clearly expressed in her features and shouted, "Who are you to question my manners or demand I leave? I am an earl's daughter recognized by the queen herself. I have more right than you to be here. If not for that babe you carry, Lord Harry would never have married you!"

The ballroom erupted with exclamations and queries to whether Caroline spoke the truth. Rebecca raised her hand for silence and felt a hand press against her back. She turned to see who stood by her and grinned when she saw her husband. Her uncle and Harry's parents were also there. They must have come the moment they saw the confrontation.

She almost laughed when Harry tried to push himself forward to slay her dragon and she had to grab his wrist to stop him. This was her battle and by the grin he gave her he knew it as well. She returned his grin and then lifted her chin to confront Caroline.

In a clear voice for all to hear, she proclaimed, "I am Mrs. Harry Bolton, Lady Caroline, and this is my home and my ball. You are not welcome. You may leave of your own accord or Belcrave's footmen shall remove you. Take your pick and remember the next time you want to spout lies, I do not take kindly to anyone who disparages me or my family."

By now, the Earl and Countess of Southwaite had made their way to their daughter's side. They took offense at hearing their child was to be physically removed and the earl shouted his outrage at Belcrave.

Belcrave countered angrily, "Southwaite, I cannot believe I welcomed your family into my home. My daughter asked you to leave. I suggest you do so immediately before I call my footmen forward to assist you. Do not sully my door again for you will not be received. Consider our relationship null and void."

"B-but," Southwaite stuttered, "We are to be in business."

"Not anymore. I only allow those I trust to invest with me. You are not one." Belcrave snapped his fingers beckoning his footmen forward to escort the Southwaite party out.

"Well, I never," exclaimed the Countess of Southwaite who refused to budge until her husband yanked on her arm.

"What's this?" exclaimed the Prince of Wales as he entered the ballroom, his stays creaking with each step he made. "Where is the music and gaiety Belcrave? I was assured by the marquis your ball would be the success of the Season."

The crowd opened a path for the Prince Regent and his entourage to make his way to Belcrave. Prinny, as he was known to his friends, was once a handsome and charming man in his youth, but decades of dissolute living, gluttonous eating and heavy drinking turned him into the realm's most disliked royal, often characterized with a bulging belly and florid face by cartoonists in their illustrations. Regardless, Prinny was an intelligent man of style and when sober could charm and amuse the best of men, so his attendance assured Rebecca's entrée into society.

The Marquis du Benoît walked by the Prince Regent's side and was the prince's opposite in both stature and size. The French aristocrat was tall, fit, and handsome for his age. Aside from his weathered skin and the gray mixed among his dark brown hair tied with a ribbon at his nape, he owned a straight patrician nose, firm chin, and dark brown eyes that were gleaming in amusement.

He wore the court dress from the reign of Louis XVI, *a habit á la française*, which consisted of a brocaded coat that fell to his knees and was heavily embroidered, a silk waistcoat embellished with exotic Oriental patterns, tight breeches worn with silk stockings, and a lace jabot that surrounded the neck of his shirt. The ensemble was made of richly embroidered French silk, adorned with the Lyons lace that went out of fashion when Napoleon came into power. The marquis' dress spoke of a time long gone in France and outshone the portly prince who strutted unaware of the comparisons being made between the two of them.

Belcrave signaled the musicians to play, but everyone stood frozen watching the royal scene unfold. Rebecca and Harry turned to look at each other and then back at Prinny and the marquis who looked amused. Rebecca could not hold her tongue and queried, "Grandpapa is that you?"

She had never seen him with his hair in a queue or in such a stately dress. She had a handful of memories as a young girl when he and her uncles visited her family in Truro, but that recollection was of a common man wearing the box cut of a woolen coat, pants, cap and muffler. She might not have recognized him except she saw her father's features in him; especially when he smiled.

The marquis opened his arms and Rebecca stepped forward to be quickly wrapped in his embrace. Her grandfather whispered for her ears only and said, "Bolton suggested I wear my ceremonial dress which I haven't worn since my visits to Versailles."

Clarity came immediately to Rebecca as she said to her grandfather, "It was you the queen spoke of regarding a debt of gratitude she owed when we met with her yesterday."

"*Tres certainement,*" replied her grinning grandfather.

Rebecca had a slew of questions she wanted to ask him, but when the Prince Regent muttered, "What's this?" she quickly made her deep curtsey, blushing at how she completely forgot to greet him. Prinny laughed off her embarrassment and apology, then, relayed his mother's message, "Your Queen was quite happy to make your acquaintance yesterday and looks forward for you and your siblings to make your official curtsey to her at St. James Palace."

He spoke in a voice that carried to the watchers and even if all did not hear, then his words would be passed on assuring Rebecca's acceptance into the *ton*. No one would dare shun her, for doing so insulted the crown. The prince turned to the marquis and said, "I leave you here, Louis. My duty to my mama is done and now I am off."

Louis made his bow and watched the prince make his royal exit. News that Rebecca was to make her curtsey to the queen at St. James Palace and the marquis was her grandfather made its way around the room as the musicians began to play. The ball resumed with dancing and chatter over the recent disclosures. Many confessed they knew all along Harry's wife was blue-blooded, while others exclaimed their shock over the vulgar behavior of Lady Caroline. The information would fuel gossip for weeks as each matron put their own twist to the story.

Once the astonishment of her grandfather's title wore off, Rebecca asked her grandfather, "Is there news of Nathaniel?"

Louis smiled and pulled from his inner pocket a letter. Harry and Rebecca's uncle closed ranks with Louis to shield Rebecca from prying eyes. Her grandfather explained, "A courier found me just as I was making my way here. I did not open the letter. I believe it carries the news you await."

Rebecca looked at Harry with fright in her eyes. He responded, "It matters not what is written, Becca. The babe is mine."

Rebecca began to open the letter, but Harry stilled her hands by placing his own on top of them. He said, "You do not have to do this now. It will wait."

"I have waited long enough Harry," she replied.

Harry released his hold of her and watched as she opened the letter and read its contents. The letter was not long and within seconds she handed it to Harry. He read it cautiously and then passed it on to her grandfather to read, who then gave it to Ketterling. Harry took possession of the letter once Ketterling finished and turned to hand it to his father. Then, he pulled Rebecca onto the dance floor where other couples were getting into position for the next set.

"This dance is mine, Rebecca," he announced as he positioned her to waltz with him.

Rebecca laughed and responded, "As is this babe."

Emily watched Harry and Rebecca giggle and twirl around the dance floor like two love birds in flight. She asked her husband what the letter said and Belcrave gave her the missive to read.

Becca,
The babe is Harry's.
Damburten never had his way.
I could not protect you from his fists, but I did save you from his ill intent.

Your loving brother,
Nathaniel

"Well," sobbed Emily. "She has Harry to watch and protect over her now."

The earl added, "She has us, Emily."

The marquis hearing their declarations, informed, "She has all her family to watch and protect over her."

Ketterling who had drawn near to hear what was being said, added, "Indeed." Then, he took his leave with Louis who exclaimed he was much interested in making the acquaintance of his granddaughter's uncle.

Emily grinned and brought her hand through her husband's arm to draw him near. She looked up into his eyes and the earl smiled down upon her. No words were necessary to express the joy they felt in seeing their son happy. They turned their gazes upon the dance floor to watch Harry and Rebecca.

Belcrave informed, "I will announce Rebecca's happy circumstances at supper."

Emily looked up at her husband and grinned. "You will please your son and Rebecca with the announcement acknowledging your acceptance of the babe."

"The child is a Bolton, Emily."

"Yes," she replied and then was astounded to see him frown. "What is it?" she asked.

"I am glad to see Harry happy, but it is Thomas who should be breeding and securing the line. Where the deuce is he?"

Emily rolled her eyes and returned her focus to the ballroom floor where Harry and Rebecca danced. No one looking at the giddy couple could ever doubt theirs was a love-match for their love shown brilliantly for all to see.

Acknowledgements

It's amazing how a great photography director can make a photo shoot a wonderful experience and lots of fun. I want to thank Christina Brusaca for managing all those elements covering equipment, lighting, scenery, props, and a host of other things. Normally, Christina works behind the camera lens, but for this book cover she stepped in front of it. She still managed to direct the shoot to ensure its perfection and smiled while she did it.

A fun "behind the scenes" fact is I designed and made this cover's Regency era dress. Other covers also showcase my work. It's another creative outlet for me in addition to my writing and I am most appreciative to all my models for their patience as I design and then, measure, pin and sew their Regency outfits.

It is easy to write romance when your life is full of it, so I want to thank my amazing husband for loving, cherishing, and supporting me. I also want to thank my wonderful and ever-inspiring children, grandchildren, my mom, and all my readers for their continued feedback and support. I couldn't do it without you.

About the Author

Teresa Sweeney is a Golden Leaf Award winner for her novel *Only A Captain Will Do* and Golden Quill finalist for her novel *The Reluctant Viscount*. She takes great pleasure penning historical romance novels focusing on the charm, wit, and banter of courtship.

She is a wife and mother of four adult children. She dotes on her seven grandchildren. She loves to read, write, and a myriad of other pursuits where she can use her creativity and imagination. Visit her website www.teresa-sweeney.com for the latest information on her novels.